Praise for Michele Mit{ }

"Sassy, smart, sexy, and savvy . . . Comically insightful about the nastiness that occurs in the hallways, hideaways, and bars of the nation's capital."
—*USA Today*

"You find yourself rooting for Kate as she reveals herself to be a hard-boiled gal classy enough to wear ridiculous Italian footwear but sly enough to gauge its effect . . . An unflagging, consistently entertaining Washington caper delivered with considerable assurance and flair."
—*Newsday*

"Reads as smart and savvy as its heroine . . . With sparkling prose and a smartly ironic flair, Mitchell crafts a tidy little tale. Neat and sharp, it's political beach reading one won't have to hide."
—*The Baltimore Sun*

"Intriguing . . . Savvy, gleeful take on the ins and outs of Washington politicking, which will have the *Primary Colors* crowd rapt."
—*Publishers Weekly*

"Michele Mitchell has obviously absorbed more than her share of Beltway insider info. Normally this would spell doom for a story set mostly within that same, self-obsessed region, but in her first fiction, Mitchell manages to stitch the politicking into her story so seamlessly that you're never able to confuse the book with a lengthy, fictionalized op-ed piece . . . Beats Joe Klein at his own political insider game."
—*Kirkus Reviews*

"Insightful and hilarious, *The Latest Bombshell* is a novel that is About Something: politics, honor, charm, loyalty, and human nature. Denizens of Washington, DC, and small towns everywhere will recognize this cast of characters, from the feisty heroine to the friends and fiends that surround her. A terrific read!"
—Laura Zigman, author of *Animal Husbandry*

"Michele Mitchell's *j'accuse* not only wonderfully captures the various blood sports of Washington, but gives us Kate Boothe—a bright, funny, and spirited heroine with a literary future."
—Jeffrey Frank, author of *The Columnist*

ALSO BY MICHELE MITCHELL

The Latest Bombshell

OUR GIRL
IN WASHINGTON

A Kate Boothe Novel

Michele Mitchell

A PLUME BOOK

PLUME
Published by Penguin Group
Penguin Group (USA) Inc., 375 Hudson Street, New York, New York 10014, U.S.A.
Penguin Group (Canada), 90 Eglinton Avenue East, Suite 700, Toronto, Ontario,
Canada M4P 2Y3 (a division of Pearson Penguin Group Canada Inc.)
Penguin Books Ltd., 80 Strand, London WC2R 0RL, England
Penguin Ireland, 25 St. Stephen's Green, Dublin 2, Ireland (a divison of Penguin Books Ltd.)
Penguin Group (Australia), 250 Camberwell Road, Camberwell, Victoria 3124,
Australia (a division of Pearson Australia Group Pty. Ltd.)
Penguin Books India Pvt. Ltd., 11 Community Centre,
Panchsheel Park, New Delhi–110 017, India
Penguin Books (NZ), cnr Airborne and Rosedale Roads, Albany, Auckland 1310,
New Zealand (a division of Pearson New Zealand Ltd.)
Penguin Books (South Africa) (Pty.) Ltd., 24 Sturdee Avenue, Rosebank,
Johannesburg 2196, South Africa

Penguin Books Ltd., Registered Offices: 80 Strand, London WC2R 0RL, England
First published by Plume, a member of Penguin Group (USA) Inc.

First Printing, March 2006
10 9 8 7 6 5 4 3 2 1

 REGISTERED TRADEMARK—MARCA REGISTRADA

LIBRARY OF CONGRESS CATALOGING-IN-PUBLICATION DATA
Mitchell, Michele
  Our girl in Washington : a Kate Boothe novel / Michele Mitchell.
    p. cm.
  ISBN 0-452-28607-7 (trade pbk.)
  1. Women political consultants—Fiction.   2. Washington (D.C.)—Fiction.   I. Title.
  PS3613.I86095 2006
  813' .6—dc22

                                                                    2005020888

Printed in the United States of America
Set in Century Expanded

PUBLISHER'S NOTE
This is a work of fiction. Names, characters, places, and incidents are either the product of
the author's imagination or are used fictitiously, and any resemblance to actual persons,
living or dead, business establishments, events, or locales is entirely coincidental.

For Erica Cantley,
who told me to get over myself

OUR GIRL
IN WASHINGTON

1

The Fault, Dear Brutus

I t was the best line I ever heard in my life: "Come to Beirut. And don't worry about a visa. My soldiers will meet you at the airport." Not many guys could come up with *that* one, and it was quickly followed by another winner: "And please bring a bottle of good tequila."

"What is this—nail the Christian girl at the airport with a bottle of Petron?" Jack asked me when I mentioned it to him. Because, after all, this wasn't about seduction, this was about politics, which I suppose *can* be (and often is) the same thing. Still, neither Jack nor I had ever heard the likes of it before, which was why he fiercely sucked a cigarette while I packed (because, of course, I was going—we didn't have a lot of other options at this point). My partner, by the way, wasn't a smoker, unless the occasional cigar was involved.

Jack coughed and pursed his lips, glowering from the velvet chair in the corner of my bedroom as I threw jeans and a couple of tweed jackets into my suitcase and observed, "Beirut is supposed to be a lot more chic than that."

"So what do I bring, Jack?" I asked, exasperated because I

was so tired. "The little black dress or track shoes to dodge the bombs?"

He thought a moment. "Both."

I rolled my eyes. This was, simply, where we were at, the crossroads of the capital of international intrigue, far, far off our usual beat. After all, how often did political consultants consort with men whom they were reasonably sure were arms dealers? I clicked the suitcase shut, and Jack and I headed grimly to his car.

This wasn't what our line of work was supposed to include. Political consultants live a notoriously dull existence. The cocktail party circuit to troll for potential clients, that is, candidates; Saturday night dates cut short so we could be fresh for the Sunday morning television shows, even just to watch, let alone appear on; the slavish months on the campaign trail, with an occasional and invaluable Post-it note on your hotel bathroom mirror—*You are in [INSERT CITY] to run [INSERT NAME]'s campaign*; the stupid lines that passed for wit in our town, like, "I have no idea what to order for an appetizer—let's CR it." As in, pass a continuing resolution. Ha ha ha. That would never work in more cosmopolitan towns like, say, Atlanta. It only made you sound like the kid who got the crap kicked out of him in grade school. Which is, of course, what most of the people in Washington had been.

I was *not* that kid. I could console myself with that fact, during that first long leg of the flight to Lebanon, a place I had always regarded as being in a perpetual state of war. I asked the flight attendant for a second scotch, which reminded me of my father, and from the comfort of that refill it was easy to remember his advice: Break down a situation methodically, and without emotion. That, he always said, was power.

Even through an alcoholic haze, it was pretty hard not to see the situation any other way: Jack and I had screwed up spectacularly. We had been friends a long time, partners for a bit less time, but still, I had to call it like it was. We, undeniably, were in way over our heads. I was on a plane to *Beirut*, for God's sake.

It hadn't always been this way. Once, one of the rags that covered Capitol Hill called us "the little firm that could, run by the dynamic duo of Jack Vanzetti and Kate Boothe" (Jack always got top billing). And on one occasion, just last year, there was a presidential election that was supposed to have been ours. Everyone said so. Our former boss, the one whose lousy, mousy paycheck had driven us into business in the first place, even stopped us on the street. "You two have your pick, eh?" he grunted. We offered up what all consultants did: media strategy, campaign logistics, polling results. And like all the other firms that clustered along the K Street canyon, we had worked hard, paid our dues—whatever cliché you wanted to apply. But no one could deny that during the Gold affair we had basically resurrected a dead body. We made the impossible possible. And that made us undeniably attractive to that most desperate of species, the presidential hopeful.

To be *wanted* was a mad, thrilling rush, all right. We would walk into Le Sénateur, the swank downtown restaurant that my best friend, Lili, ran, and when people looked at us, they knew who we were. I would push my straight hair, which was longer than usual, across my forehead and behind the blue topaz chunks sparkling from my ears. I had bought the earrings for myself to add some dash to my black suit, cut to fit me when I was literally in marathon shape—which I was, having convinced Jack to run one with me. (He hated every mile of it, but he did it, nearly vomiting on the shoes of the marine who hung a finisher's medal around his neck in the shadow of the Iwo Jima memorial.) And Jack, whose dark brown hair was salted now, would flash his broad grin at Lili, who trilled "hello, dahlings!" with exaggerated affection and led us past the alert politicos to our table by the palm tree in the corner. We were the talk, and I would be lying if I didn't admit that we enjoyed every minute of it.

"We've got the tiger by the tail," Jack whispered in my ear one evening there. His dark blue eyes shone with excitement. He had always been a good-looking guy, but now, with immense success at hand, he was irresistible to the women of Washington, who trooped by our table, leaning in at him and cooing, "Hel*lo*, Jack. Are you going to yoga class tomorrow morning?" I sucked back a groan, because the only reason Jack even went to yoga was to meet girls—the odds were excellent when you were the only straight man in the room, breathing deeply on a squishy mat. He beamed at me, and raised his glass. We were, without a doubt, about to have the time of our lives.

And then, suddenly, it all disappeared. Because of me, I suppose, as I found a fault with every single presidential candidate who passed through our rose-colored conference room; too eager, too dumb, too brittle, too . . . too spongy. Jack stomped around the office, shouting, "If we had to *like* the people we represent, we'd starve!" Then again, Jack dithered, too, because he wanted a specific amount of money. "We're worth more," he would say, hanging up the phone after yet another discussion with a pol who lamented our terms. "If we don't set a certain rate now, when we've got momentum, what kind of message will that send?"

The kind of message that suggested to presidential candidates that they seek support elsewhere. Which they did. And then we were forced to scrape up clients where we could. In an inordinate amount of local races in New Jersey ("the armpit of the world," grumbled Jack on his umpteenth trip to Trenton), among a few of our old standbys in Congress, in the gubernatorial race in Vermont.

I took stock of things on election night. My eyes ached with fatigue and my hair had gone unwashed for days, and I found myself standing in a dingy campaign office in Burlington with my hand around a cold cup of watery coffee, realizing that not only was my candidate going to lose but that there wouldn't be enough money to pay our fee.

So. Our newfound confidence was shattered into a thousand unpaid invoices. A miserable, cold, flat January had set in. We didn't even attend any of the inaugural balls—and we always tried, as a matter of good business, to go to all the major soirees. We couldn't afford the tickets, and no party bigwig tossed any comps our way. We did not discuss the yawning possibility that we could be washed up. And then, one grainy day, Jack leaned against the doorway to my office and flashed his old smile, the one that made him look like a kid hiding a swell present, and declared, "*This* is our year."

Well, why the hell not? We'd lost more than half the races. Lili had moved away; Le Sénateur had closed. We weren't sure we could afford to pay our assistant. Barring the existence of a pool of champagne that I could snorkel through until the entire twelve months evaporated from my memory, *something* had to happen to deliver us.

And now, it had.

"The Essex Group called," Jack told me. Despite what I proudly thought of as my inability to be shocked, I stared at my partner.

"Why?" I asked, almost in a whisper.

"It ain't because they want to buy us out," Jack said with a wink.

"Well." I finally remembered how to breathe. "Let's take the meeting."

As if we had any other choice. No one would turn down an opportunity like this, and we had bills to pay. The Essex Group! I sat at my desk and stared at my flickering computer screen, the flashy flat kind that Jack insisted on stocking our office with. They were the charter members of the Old Boys' Club themselves. Technically, the company labeled itself an "investment group," but it was so much more than that. For one thing, Essex didn't hire Wall Street gurus. Essex hired everyone who was anyone in worldwide politics—lawyers, diplomats, former politicians—the collection was quite extensive. And Essex leveraged the value of this crew against global deals. This was one reason why, for example, out of all the world's drilling companies, the one controlled by Essex got the rights to explore for oil off the coast of Japan: One of the group's partners used to be the prime minister of Japan. Now *that* is clout.

And they wanted to meet with us!

I knew that Jack was a bit nervous—he checked his silver cuff links several times as we pulled up to the Ritz-Carlton for lunch. ("Just want to make sure they're still there," he muttered.) The Ritz was slightly off the path for us in Washington; most of our clients are politicians, so we usually spent lunch meetings suffering through cloying cream sauces on Capitol

Hill. But our new potential rainmaker had its annual investor conference at the posh hotel (when not holding meetings on yachts). Jack and I walked into the hotel, across the thick oriental carpeting toward the parlor, not knowing who our new client had sent forth as an emissary. We knew we were meeting with a managing partner, but that was it.

Nevertheless, I had an idea of what to expect. A cut far above everyone else in town, no khakis-and-blue-blazer Capitol Hill combination for Essex, not even a straight-up suit. No, you adopt a certain uniform when you're attached to a company that rakes in hundreds of millions every year, when your chairman worked previously for a Republican president, when most of your partners had done time with Democratic presidents (and one had actually *been* a Democratic president), when your advisors include a former chairman of the Federal Reserve Bank and a one-time British prime minister. That's when you switch to hand-tailored suits, clipped and buffed fingernails, and perhaps a monogrammed gold ring to pass off as a family heirloom. And indeed, the gentleman we saw waiting for us in a high-backed leather chair was all that, and more.

He smiled tightly as we approached. He had a long, angular, conventionally attractive face, with prominent cheekbones and just enough lines to suggest what my mother would call "seasoning." His tie was salmon pink and dotted with golden horseshoes—expensive, and what passed for daring in this town—and his suit, probably custom-made on Savile Row— was chocolate brown. The man was resplendent in the confidence that he was in control of the world. I couldn't stop staring at him. What, I wondered, must his house look like?

The man stood, and said with icy reserve, "You must be

Kate Boothe. Very pleased to meet you." He gently took my right hand and lifted it to his lips. A courtly gesture, one not often seen in the political trenches. He smiled. "And Mr. Vanzetti." He turned and seized Jack's hand. "I am Philip Cross."

He said this like, "I am Jesus Christ." He might as well have been, from how enthusiastically Jack pumped his hand. Philip Cross practically had to pry it away. "Martini?" he asked us. Cross already had one in front of him, so strong and raw I could smell the gin.

"Not for me," I said, never having been a fan of the drink, but Jack was eager.

"Love one," my partner said. "A double." He took the chair closest to Cross. "How did your team do in the bowl game?"

This was Jack's favorite way to kick off a conversation with a new client. In Washington, D.C., with the highest concentration of advanced-degree holders in the country, chances were pretty good that someone attended a university whose football team played in one of the fifty or so bowl games at the end of the year. And, indeed, Cross smiled, this time more genuinely; he revealed a fine line of teeth.

"Not bad," he said. "We beat Ohio State."

Jack's face clouded. "I went to Ohio State."

"Sorry, fella," Cross laughed. "Well, we'll see if I can make you feel a little better about the new year." He took a sip of his drink. "So," he said, turning to me, "I saw your work during the Gold affair. Quite impressive."

"Thank you," I replied. The Gold affair was our dead body, of course. A journalist, Lyle Gold, had been falsely accused of committing treason in a case that had split the country. A lot of people made their names off of flogging him, and Vanzetti/Boothe,

Inc., had been the only consulting firm willing to spin his case in the court of public opinion. It wasn't very tidy—a murder on the subway tracks of New York City, a suicide, and the real traitor got away (although, I note with some satisfaction, he is presently fat and broke)—and many people wished to forget how they behaved at the time. But Gold was now vindicated and free, and our media skills were generally credited for righting him.

"Your time is coming," Cross said to me. "That was just the beginning for you. You've become someone to watch."

I didn't quite know how to react, but obviously if I was *someone to watch*, I needed to maintain some modicum of poise. I kept my hands folded in my lap and tried to muster a serious expression.

"Someone who can anticipate a cycle, someone who knows how to control certain elements of it," Cross went on. His voice was warming up, and I felt the delight that comes from flattery. "As I know both of you are well aware, it is a different world now than it was two years ago. Times are static. Values are stable. The enemy is identified."

He listed these with the casual self-importance of those in the know. I tried to appear bright enough to understand what the hell he was talking about. Jack drank deeply from his martini.

"Mr. Cross," I began, "I appreciate that sentiment. I do. But why us?"

Jack shot me a glare, but I did not care. I wanted to know—we were coming off a rotten year, and Cross had to be aware of that. A second drink was set before Cross, who paid no attention to it. He kept his focus on me and Jack.

"We are an investment firm. The bulk of our business is in the field of national security, energy, areas like that. We have a high-profile staff and high-profile clients. This has made us . . . interesting . . . to the press. Understand me, we don't mind what the press writes or says. If some sod pulling seventy-K a year wants to take a few shots, that's fine with us." He shrugged. "We don't lose sleep. It's all inside-the-town coverage. The average American doesn't grasp what we do, and they're happy as long as we keep the oil prices down."

We keep the oil prices down? Well, it could be true. Or, Cross could just be like the rest in Washington, where an overweening ego was not rare. Jack, however, nodded. Maybe he knew something I did not.

"What we are concerned with," Cross said with almost courtly mien, "is perception. Our clients want us to make them money; our clients would like to keep those matters private. They do not take kindly to being deemed part of the 'evil empire'."

So, Essex was calling us in to do media strategy. Give Vanzetti and Boothe a crisis of bad press, and we'll manage you out of it.

"It is not a good time to be a gadfly," Cross said, his eyes suddenly cold, "but that does not mean there aren't those irresponsible enough to give it a try." He smiled at me, warmly. "The firm is in agreement. You are the best at what you do."

"You bet," Jack said. He firmly believed in the benefits of post-cocktail palaver. He tapped his foot on mine. My cue.

"And you," I returned brightly to Cross, "are the best at what you do, so it only makes sense that we work together."

"Indeed." Cross rose. His pants fell perfect and unwrinkled. He took my hand in the time-honored Southern tradition of clasping a woman's fingers. I read the signal. Our audience was over.

"We'll be in touch," he said, and quickly shaking Jack's out-

stretched hand, Philip Cross strode through the softly lit hallway as if he could buy the place several times over. Which he
probably could.

The Essex Group promptly faxed over to our office their
proposal for a monthly retainer fee of sixty thousand dollars,
six months guaranteed.

Jack, the lapsed Catholic, found religion again at that very
moment. "It's nearly four hundred thousand dollars—for *one*
client. I have climbed the mighty mountain. I see the valley below, and it is a valley of peace!"

I shook my head—he was imitating a particular and unap-
pealing faux-Calvinist politician—but I did laugh as he fairly
danced out of my office, hopping on our assistant's desk and
planting a kiss on her cheek before jigging into his, probably to
call his father and tell him the good news. We were swimming
through that champagne pool, all right.

In fact, we had been brought into the proverbial bubble. I
noticed the difference straight away, trotting from appoint-
ment to conference to meeting that week. "Sweet Kate!" exclaimed a porcelain doll-like aide at the White House, the one
who had never before deigned to speak to me even as we
wended our way through the same cocktail circuit. I once heard
that she regarded me as "inappropriate," because we had been
mentioned in the same *Washington Post* article about single
women in the District (she was upset because she professed to
be a born-again Christian and I was, well, not). "Kate, we *must*
have a coffee," she was now saying insistently.

"Katie! Baby! Whaddya think about taking on the boss's
campaign?" asked a congressional communications director, a

stocky man with small eyes, who I could imagine kicking up his alligator boots (he never wore anything else with his beige suits) while he tossed out what would have been a major race for us. His boss was in line to chair an important committee. He never would have considered us before.

Yes, Essex was the stamp on our credentials that made us safe for other players in town. And for my mother, which was a *much* tougher task. She called me at the office, which was unusual—she worked long days at the family law firm in Chicago, and she never took kindly to personal phone calls during office hours.

"*Katherine*," she said in her scratchy vowels, "I had the most interesting discussion with Jack's father."

My mother adored Jack. She probably would have preferred a son, anyway. Her father had run a baseball camp in Montana, and Jack had been a pretty good shortstop in high school, so they had something to bond over. And when Jack's mother passed away five years ago from ovarian cancer, my mother, the same woman who missed all my high school track meets ("Work, darling, how do you think we pay for tuition?") and fiddled with my "scraggly" hair every Christmas, saw it as her duty to step into the maternal role—Jack, at least, pointed out the humor in this ("Does this make me the brother you never had?"), which probably saved me a few grand in therapy bills.

"He told me that you two have signed a deal with the Essex Group. Why didn't *you* tell me?" She sounded irritated. As usual.

"I wasn't—I wasn't sure about it," I said lamely.

"Wasn't sure about it! Katherine, this is very important! Do you realize what is happening to you?"

I braced myself.

"I haven't been too sure about some of your choices. I still don't understand why you had to leave Chicago and move to Washington—"

At this, I audibly sighed.

"—but at least you haven't ended up like those silly girls writing on the Internet about their sex lives with congressmen, or those gold diggers drinking martinis in Georgetown."

"Thanks," I said dryly.

"You've broken through! This is *it*."

I nearly dropped the phone. Some people go their whole lives wishing to hear such words. I was thirty-four—not old, but not young, either—and for once my mother didn't bother to hide the pride in her voice. The earth must be spinning backward, or else I had come a long way since being rejected by every law school I had applied to.

"Imagine everything you can do," she continued, "if you're part of the Essex Group. You'll have all the financial security and access you want."

"I suppose I will," I murmured.

"Well, I'm going to call your aunt Hester right now," my mother said briskly. Hester was married to my father's older brother, and she and my mother had always competed over whose child was doing better. For a long while, Hester's three daughters, all lawyers, had won. But now my mother had ammunition. I was her only child, but I sure had zoomed to the top of the pile all of a sudden.

It was going to be a great gig. I knew this, because the first duty I was asked to fulfill was to visit the Paris office for Essex. "You need to become acquainted with our major branches,"

Cross told me over the phone. He wanted Jack to visit the offices in the Far East, and I got Europe.

"That's hardly fair," Jack grumbled. "I don't even like rice."

"But my best friend lives in Paris," I reminded him.

Lili was translating menus for the Paris Bristol from her cozy alcove in the Marais (which was, like Washington, formerly a swamp). Lili knew everything about fine food and people management, because that had been her job when she presided over Le Sénateur. That restaurant had not survived the fickle American economy, but Lili had—she packed up her fishnet stockings and moved to the city in which she had always wanted to live. I myself did not have such warm memories of the place; my expectations inevitably fell short there. (How, for instance, did a city that hosted one of the bloodiest revolutions ever get a reputation for romance?) But I would take a free trip: a quick seventy-two hours, hi-hi-hi, yes-yes-yes, and then back to the grindstone on K Street.

Lili knew I was coming—Jack had called her—but I was mildly surprised to see her waiting for me at the airport. Her blond hair was clipped back in its usual unruly twist, and her fingers danced up and down a silvery cell phone, into which she jabbered in (presumably) fluent French. When she spotted me, she winked and clapped shut the folding phone. "*Bienvenue!*" she exclaimed, sing-song, kissing me on both cheeks. "Welcome to a magic land, where you can eat anything you want and you won't get fat, and drink as much as you want and not get a hangover."

"How does that work, exactly?" I asked, shifting my battered leather satchel onto my other shoulder. The campaign trail was never kind to luggage.

"Antioxidants in the wine, I think." Lili smiled and put a hand on my arm as we walked to the taxi stand. A barrel-bellied driver stabbed out his reeking Gauloise and threw my bag into the trunk.

I leaned back against the scratchy upholstery. No matter how many times I flew (and I was platinum grade on four different airlines), I always felt mottled and queasy once I landed. I didn't need to check myself in a mirror to know that my skin looked more green than olive, that my lips were chapped, and my hazel eyes shot with red. Not exactly the picture of a power player on the rise.

"How's Jack?" Lili asked after rattling off directions to the driver.

"Pouting," I said.

Lili laughed. "Of course!" She paused a moment, and then said, "So. I met a boy."

"Really?" I squeezed her arm.

"A wine merchant from Beaune," she said. "We met during a wine expo at the Bristol. Kate, he looked into my eyes and asked about my soul, my *pheelosophee* of *layfe*." We both laughed at her Gallic accent. "A little bit different than an Italian, right?"

I decided to ignore her dig—although she would not have meant it unkindly toward me. She, and Jack especially, did not like my most recent former love, who happened to be half Italian.

"Actually," she paused and looked out the window a moment, "he's a lot like an Italian. He's got another girlfriend."

"Well, that's a non-starter," I said, and immediately regretted it. Lili dissolved into tears, and Lili never, ever lost her grip. This is the woman who told the vice president's wife that she could not close the restaurant on a Saturday night simply because the second lady wanted to have a table for four; the woman who ordered the renowned Belgian guest chef to *get over* the lack of non-pasteurized cheese ("Take it up with our FDA!"); the woman who informed the honorable gentleman from Wyoming that his nubile date crawling under the white-clothed table was not "four-star appropriate," for God's sake. And here she was, in a dingy Parisian taxi, reduced to the shuddering state of passion betrayed.

She had walked in on him, of course. Appropriately Euro-dramatic. She had taken the train to Beaune to surprise him, and she certainly accomplished that. "And do you know what he did?" she demanded. "He lit a cigarette and shrugged and said I should have called ahead!" She burst into tears, again. "I fell in love with a cliché!"

The taxi driver glanced at her through the rearview mirror, and Lili furiously wiped her eyes and shouted, "*Est-ce que ça vous dérange?*"

This pretty much set the tone for the next ten hours. I cleaned up into presentable shape and trotted over to the Essex offices. The vice president, a real Frenchman rather than a well-connected expat, took me to lunch at a famous bistro. He seemed amused when I ordered the steak tartare. "Do you know what it is?" he asked. Every time I ordered steak tartare, I was asked this question. I must radiate "idiot American."

"Certainly. It's raw meat with an egg," I replied with probably too much indignance. The gentleman chuckled. I bet he didn't chuckle at Philip Cross.

"It was not so long ago that I dined with an American who asked for 'steak tartare, well done'," he said.

I was briefed on the current Essex deals through the Paris office, which seemed especially focused on energy efforts ("We single-handedly keep Air France in business, it seems"). And then, the vice president told me, "We are very, ah, private. Only occasionally, this is a situation. But," he shrugged, "that is life. It can be managed."

"Do you have a list of problem-child reporters?" I asked. The vice president, for all his apparent worldliness, blinked at me.

"I don't understand," he said.

"It's American slang," I replied, explaining the expression but then giving up. My mind was fogged with jet lag and disjointed thoughts on oil.

"But yes, American slang from the American girl, who prefers raw meat for lunch." The vice president smiled thinly and paid the bill.

As much as I value a face-to-face meeting—even to the point of disdaining text messaging (to Jack's eternal consternation)—I stood on the buzzing Paris boulevard wondering why I had just hauled six hours across an ocean for a one-hour lunch. I shook my head. Essex must have more money to burn than I thought.

One night in Paris. The last time I had been there, I ended up not only with a broken heart but with the remains of my ego squished across boulevard Saint-Germain. So I knew the manic ecstasy of a woman trying to forget. Lili's cheeks were flushed when she greeted me at the door of her jewel-box apartment, and she talked very fast. But there was now a marvelous distraction.

"John Jaures is in town! He's here—on his way back to

Washington," she said. "I told him we'd meet him for dinner. He was really happy to hear you were in Paris, too."

I smiled and sank into the turquoise-colored divan, which I was sure Lili bought because the cushions matched her eyes. Oh, Jaures. He had been a swaggering former war correspondent eager to make his name as a political reporter back when I met him, nearly two years ago, an ambition that served us both well. Consultants need reporters, and vice versa. Jaures had done well enough in Washington to land the coveted slot of Beijing bureau chief for his newspaper. And then, after nailing a story on illegal arms trading in Asia, a television cable network had raided his talents. It isn't uncommon to go from print to television; in fact, once upon a time, that was the expected trajectory. But Jaures didn't look like an on-air reporter. He was ragged, hated to shave and refused the smooth lure of makeup. It had been a rough tenure so far. I knew all about it. But if anyone could prove a worthy distraction from the woes of the heart or a less-than-stellar business meeting, it was Jaures. He was charming. Half the hemisphere could attest to *that*.

Jaures promised to meet us at the Taverne Henry VI, a wine bar patronized by the political and judicial elite, tucked in the shadow of Nôtre-Dame. The owner, magnificent in suspenders, remained anti-tourist and he definitively did *not* speak English. Not once, in the years I have been going there, had the man uttered so much as a *bonjour* to me. He just gritted his barnacle teeth when I walked through the door; to Lili, however, he smiled.

The formica tables were placed in a jumble under unflattering bright lighting. No trysts happened here. Faux-wood paneling is never sexy, and, frankly, neither were the people in the bar, whose cheeks sagged in jowls instead of soaring high. We squeezed up past the men in red sweaters and wool coats, their scarves artfully tossed over their necks (even Parisian *men* have a talent for this), ignoring the surface noise of a vivid argument over a newspaper, and we ordered champagne while we waited for Jaures.

I didn't recognize the man in the dark blue suit at first. A few more wrinkles around the edges and scattered gray hairs, the usual attire of a tattered T-shirt and limp trench coat gone, John Jaures stood before me, smiling a bit. "What's this, Kate?" he asked. "You don't know me anymore?"

I had forgotten he was lovely, in a rough way. Thin-pressed television did not convey this adequately. Jaures was hardly the bloodless battle bunny that many of his kind become after too many cocktails of adrenaline and testosterone. His forehead was strong, his pale gray eyes glittered, but the lines around his full mouth were soft.

"It's the suit," I said. "It threw me off."

"Hand-tailored!" Jaures exclaimed, stretching his arms which allowed me to see the stitching. "I got three of these when I was in China. Seventy bucks each. What do you think?"

"That you're lucky it hasn't ripped wide open yet," Lili said, handing him a flute of bubbly.

"Hey, I work for cable." Jaures leaned over and bussed her cheek. Me, he grabbed by the face and planted a juicy one on my lips. "That's for both you and Jack," he said with a wink. "So, what's good here? I've been sucking down baijiu so long, I think my taste buds are pickled."

"You've got champagne. Start there." Lili suggested. "In bubbles, there are no troubles!"

Jaures went through two more glasses before he mentioned why his network was bringing him home. Not that they hadn't liked his work in Asia, and in the Gulf region, too. He was on a hot story, he said, an amazing and mind-boggling one. He thought he might get a special-project status, something that would allow him to take time to unravel it all. His eyes were very clear as he said this, and he smiled the slow, easy spread of a man who has glory within his grasp.

"I'll bite," I said. "What've you got?"

"Bastards," Jaures grinned. "Bastards that you wouldn't believe. People so greedy, so overreaching, so devoid of normal human consciousness, it is *wonderful*. I had no clue people like this really existed."

"You did work in Washington," I reminded him.

"Who's saying they're not in Washington?" Jaures asked. "They're in D.C., they're in China, they're in Paris. They're like some pandemic, spreading their disease around the world."

"Monsters," Lili said distractedly. She was more interested, for the moment, in the quality of the paté before her. She rolled it around in her mouth before winking at me in approval. But Jaures liked the comparison. He nodded vigorously and said, "Yeah! And I'm going to get them, and it is going to feel so good."

"It's a bad time to be a gadfly," I murmured.

"Who said that?" Jaures asked, laughing a little.

"Our new client," I said.

"It's a big one," Lili told him. "Our kiddos are going corporate on us."

"We're diversifying," I corrected, and then, turning to Jaures, "We've been put on retainer by the Essex Group."

"What?" Jaures said, his glass midway to his lips. "Are you serious?"

"They're paying us a ton," I said proudly. "That's why I'm here. They asked me to come all the way here just to meet their team in Paris."

"Kate, you're out of your mind," Jaures said. He slammed back the champagne. "You *both* are out of your minds."

Lili and I exchanged a glance. "I've been called worse," I said with a light shrug.

"Have you signed a contract?" Jaures asked.

"Ye-es," I hesitated, because Jaures had never been so snappish with me.

Jaures pursed his lips. He leaned back in the cane-backed chair and sighed. "This is off the record, Kate," he said, "and only because we've been friends for a while. The people I'm investigating? It's the Essex Group."

I stared at him and felt my stomach drop. Lili slowly pushed away the paté and dabbed the corners of her mouth with a cloth napkin.

"Well," she began a little too gaily, "how about dinner?" And, dazed, I followed her and Jaures out of the wine bar.

We ate in Les Halles. The oysters were served fresh and in brine, exactly the way I adore them, but I felt ill as the meaty bits slid down my throat. The steak was bloody and served with crisp, salty fries, but I looked at the sharp knife and wondered if I should be holding a weapon in my hand, what with Jaures jabbing away at me every few seconds.

"But I met with the managing partner," I said to Jaures. "He seems nice."

Jaures snorted. "*Nice*! Where's the tough girl I used to know?" He chewed his slab of beef until pink juice dribbled down his chin.

"They're an investment group," I said.

"Did you do *any* due diligence before you signed on?" Jaures returned.

"I did due diligence on my new boyfriend, and he's cheating on me!" Lili exclaimed. This worked. We did not speak about the Essex Group for the next hour. We drank intently and damned the romantic flaws of Frenchmen instead.

It was as we were spinning down the rue Vielle du Temple, just around the corner from Lili's apartment, on our way to the stained marble bar shaped like a horseshoe, when Jaures whispered in my ear, "My darling girl, nice playmate you've got. You do know who you're climbing into bed with, don't you?"

"Oh, shut up," I said in my wine-soaked haze.

But Jaures just laughed, a big, empty sound in the middle of this narrow street crowded with Euro-hipsters. Lili, in painless oblivion by this point, flung open the wood-and-glass door and cried out, "*Je voudrais une coupe du champagne!*" The long-faced bartender sportingly held up a bottle, and the little group of patrons clinging to the midnight hour, with their artfully messed hair and corduroy jackets, laughed and clapped, blessing the crazy American girl with the near perfect French accent.

"Why couldn't you stick with politicians?" Jaures asked me as we followed Lili and squeezed up to the marble.

"When have I ever limited myself?" I said as I ordered a Calvados.

Jaures asked for a Maker's Mark. The bartender looked askance, but he slid over a glass of the amber liquid regardless of whatever low opinion he held for it.

"You're still young, Kate," Jaures told me.

"Well, thank you very much." I threw back my glass for a long moment. "I thought friends weren't supposed to take cheap shots."

Jaures smiled wryly. "You're absolutely right," he said, and so we ended the evening, completely and utterly numb.

I woke up to spend my final hours in Paris with a metallic taste in my mouth and a shuddering headache. The magic land of no hangovers, my ass. I wadded up my sweaters and pants, raided the minibar for bottles of water, and pulled myself together to meet Lili for post-debauchery coffee.

We both were quiet. I leaned across the wood table and considered the heaviness of European milk. No nonfat to be had. I stirred the coffee, miserably.

"Jaures was a little hard on you last night," Lili said. I did not reply. My head hurt, and I did not know what to think.

"Do you think he's right?" Lili went on. "Are these guys really that bad?"

"I would say no," I answered dully, "but maybe he knows something I don't."

Lili's cell phone rang. It was Jaures, asking for me (curtly, in my opinion) to meet him at a certain café.

"It won't take long," he said. "You'll make your flight in plenty of time."

I went, of course. Jaures was, above all else, my friend. I rubbed my brow and walked through the shuttered meat district, then careening past a string of bakeries, the sweet, yeasty smell filling the cold air, and then down the rue Montmartre, a street you would never stumble upon. It was in a business district of the city. Every possible shade of gray—slate gray, shadow gray, yellow gray—was slapped on the

buildings in the jumbled section of town where the unremarkable Café le Croissant stood.

Jaures was at the wooden bar, nursing an espresso. He
pressed his cold lips to my cheek and hugged me. Then he pointed
across the street to an artless concrete mass that wouldn't have
looked out of place in Washington.

"Guess who owns that?" he asked. The vibrant blue letters
of *Le Figaro* meant nothing to me, however. "The Essex
Group."

With a sigh, I waved to the bartender for a coffee of my own.
A powdering of snow brightened the street outside, and the
few passersby stamped their feet and blew on their hands. I
wondered distractedly if this was typical in late January. "I
don't know," I said.

"You know they're smart," Jaures said. "You know a lot of
the group's affiliates used to be in politics. They acted like businessmen when they were in government, and now that they're
in business they act like the government."

The ruddy man behind the bar pushed a small white cup my
way, and silently I dumped in two lumps of sugar.

Jaures looked at me and took me by the shoulders. "Kate,"
he began, "these guys pay off governments—that's how they
get their deals. They have their own armies. People who get in
their way disappear. There was a middleman, a banker in Aus-
tria, who was laundering money for them. One day, he just
didn't show up at the office. His house was stripped bare. No one
has any idea where he went—or if they do, they're not talking."

"Laundering money?" I repeated.

"Many times, in many places," Jaures said impatiently.
"They don't pay much in taxes, let's just say. They've got fake

corporations funneling money to real corporations, bribes spread all around the world. They think they're untouchable, and they probably are."

"But you think you can get them," I said.

"I think I can," Jaures answered slowly. "I've been trying to talk to someone on the inside, anyone. Once, at the Dairy Queen in Beijing, I met a guy who worked for them, but when he heard what I did, he suddenly had to leave."

"And are you asking me to get you someone?" I felt sick— from the previous night, from the conversation.

"No," he said. "With a contact of a contact, I'd like to get through to someone there who counts. But I'd rather have my friends—you and Jack—a million miles away from them. This is going to be a very big story when I break it."

"How close are you?" I asked.

Jaures paused for only a moment. "Very. This story's got everything: staffers on the Hill getting payoffs, arms deals, tax-payer funds being corrupted, Essex makes for a hell of a villain."

"Well, good for you," I said.

"I'm saying all this because you ought to know who you're signing up with," Jaures said.

"Oh, thank you," I retorted. I felt a kind of suffocation in my throat, and as my temper rose my ears were ringing. "I think overall Jack and I have conducted our business with more ethics than anyone else."

"It's not you, honey, it's the crowd you're running with," Jaures snapped.

"Good luck with the quest," I said dryly, dropping the cup with a clatter. "I have to make my flight." I pulled on my coat and wrapped a red woolen scarf around my neck several times.

I marched out of the café, stomping down the sidewalk with righteous indignation at Jaures—a television hack—telling *me* that I had sold out, that I was consorting with dangerous, unsavory types, with only a stitch of guilt about treating a friend badly. Of course, I felt much worse about it on the flight home. Jaures was only trying to help me, and no matter how nicely Philip Cross presented himself, I had to defer to a tried-and-true friend instead of a fat paycheck. I ripped the plastic wrap off the coarse airline blanket and thought, "It will be better back in Washington. Jaures can go through his story with me, and we can handle everything together then."

2
The Absinthe Fairy

I hadn't been in Paris long enough to suffer from jet lag, but still, I was groggy as I stood in the taxi line at Dulles airport. The air was just frigid enough to bite my cheeks, and the uniformed man coordinating the procession of yellow-and-white cars barked unintelligible English tinged with a Persian accent. The taxi system at Dulles was monopolized by Iranians who had once been very important men under the shah. A taxi might seem far below them, but they had the lock on the market there. As I yawned, thinking that they probably raked in more than I did, I reached the front of the line. That's when I heard a voice as rich as clotted cream ask, "Pardon me, but are you headed downtown?"

I turned toward a blinding smile. "Ye-es." I blinked.

"Do you mind if we share?" the young man asked. "It'll be faster."

The stern taxi captain waved jerkily at me, and I shrugged in the young man's direction. He grinned again and leaped in front of me to open the taxi door. He had a runner's narrow shoulders, his chin ended in a point, *and* he had a British accent, but otherwise he was only a few notches above the usual crowd in the Washington airport.

"Two stops, please," he told the driver. I gave my office address; he gave his. It sounded oddly familiar, but then, all the buildings in downtown had businesses stacked one on top of the other. The young man turned to me as we zipped down the icy highway.

"I'm sorry about this—I almost always have a car waiting. I did not mean to intrude." He held out his hand. "Wolfgang Lawrence."

"You're kidding," I said, taking it. His fingers were long and uncalloused.

"Unfortunately, no," he laughed softly. "My father wished it on me. A saint, or something, not the composer."

"There was a Saint Wolfgang?" I asked.

"Known as a model bishop, ready to correct as well as direct the flock entrusted to him." Wolfgang paused. "There was also a Saint Lawrence, patron saint of chefs. Cooked alive in the end, I'm afraid. Put on a giant skillet and grilled for giving away the church's possessions to the poor. His only words were, 'Turn me over; I'm done on this side'."

"Oh, come on!" I burst out laughing. "Now you really are kidding!"

The young man raised his hand. "As God is my witness, and he should be with two saints to my name. I swear to it."

"Do you have a middle name?"

"Yes. Donovan."

"Is he a saint, too?"

"My mother's maiden name," he said. "You're safe with that one."

I sized him up in a long moment. He had an open face—he got plenty of sleep at night, that was for sure, because his green eyes shone and his complexion was ruddy. He wasn't my usual type—I preferred men with dark hair, and his was blond, and his fingernails were even tidier than mine—but I liked his air of refinement. This guy, I thought, would know how to order wine.

"Well, Donovan, that's what I'll have to use," I said. "Anything else is too gruesome."

The next inquiry in the ritualistic order of things—in Washington, anyway—was to discuss who we worked for. In what had to be a first, however, the matter never came up. Instead, Donovan talked about Paris. By coincidence, he had been on my flight, but in business class, not surprising since he was wearing a much nicer suit than mine.

"Holiday or business?" Donovan asked.

"A quick business trip," I replied. "And you?"

"Only business, unfortunately." He shrugged his shoulders as if it was a waste of time to do anything other than stroll through the Louvre.

The taxi carefully turned down the street where I worked. The city was hushed by a thick layer of snow. Washington never handled weather issues well. Wheezing plows scraped through the streets only occasionally; there was the inevitable panicked run on kitty litter in the grocery stores. (Washingtonians scattered it in their driveways to provide enough traction to pry out their cars, and woe to the cat owner who really needed it.)

"I'll see you again," Donovan called out as the driver handed me my bag.

"You think so," I said. But I smiled, thinking this was an

excellent sign of things to come. I would call Lili and check on her, and when Jaures arrived in Washington in a few days, I would apologize to him for my bad behavior and we could figure out the rest accordingly. Surely the Essex Group wasn't the malignant entity he made it out to be, so there was no need yet to burden Jack with what Jaures was doing. Let the man take it up with Jack himself.

The office was warm, a bouquet of tulips on the reception desk. Jack must have cashed that first check from Essex, I thought. He never would've sprung for flowers otherwise.

"Kate?" Jack called out to me. He was in the kitchen. His baby. When Le Sénateur had closed and Lili left town, Jack decided that we needed to take care of ourselves, what with all the late nights we pulled during the height of election season. The kitchen was a jewel—better than what either of us had in our own rented apartments—from the gleaming stainless steel refrigerator to the professional-grade range, and the insanely expensive Rancilio cappuccino machine which had been a summer intern project: "Find me the best," Jack had instructed four sweet-faced college sophomores, who might have thought they'd be spending their time clinking whiskey tumblers with congressmen. Then, when the machine arrived, the magnificent chrome gleamed so perfectly, perched in the corner of the black countertop, that Jack could not bring himself to touch it. He was worried he would break it. Instead, he used the stained plastic coffee machine I had picked up at a garage sale in Virginia.

My partner looked up at me through the lashes that were the envy of women throughout the mid-Atlantic states, and asked in a strange voice, "How was Paris?"

"Fi-ine." I reached for a ceramic mug. Maybe Jaures had called ahead, told him about our tiff, or his "scoop."

But then, Jack asked softly, "Have you seen the news today?"

"I just got off the plane," I replied. Jack put his hand on mine, not a foreign gesture, but his voice was tight.

"Kate, Jaures is dead. They fished his body out of the Seine this morning."

I did not faint. I did not sink to my knees in howling grief. I saw the redness in Jack's eyes for the first time, contortions of pain in the lines worrying his brow, the pale and drawn complexion.

"How?" I asked, because it wasn't enough to hear the words *Jaures is dead.*

"He was shot in the head. His hands and feet were tied with twine."

It did not seem possible that these words were true. Maybe they were in some alternate world, where the sky was green and the grass was blue. Jaures, who had survived Kosovo and Haiti and Afghanistan and any number of other wars, who had been shot in the arm and beaten up, Jaures, who showed up in the world's most fashionable city in a *suit*, for God's sake— Jaures was *dead*?

I burst into tears. Jack drew me to him, and I sobbed until I shook uncontrollably.

Television being television, Jaures's network milked the moment for all it was worth. There was a ratings war on, and the death of a correspondent was always good for a day cycle. The bland anchorman, droning with mock humbleness, said, "And now this reporter would attempt to say something about John Jaures. He is dead. His body, bound with twine and a bullet hole in his head, was taken from the River Seine in Paris today. For more than a year he had been the chief Asian correspondent for this network. He was a brave and amiable man." The bitter rind of a talk-show host, who had inexplicably risen through the network ranks, pontificated, "The French police have no suspects, although they are following a lead that Jaures was working on a story about Islamic terrorists." The panel of experts hastily assembled to ramble on about the perils of international stories. The U.S. government, it was said, was even considering issuing a travel warning to France.

No one called me or Jack for comment. The one reporter who did check in was Crispin Mulch, and he did so only to express his condolences. "I know you were all very good friends," he said. Mulch was a two-time Pulitzer winner who wrote a syndicated column. A jolly sort, with a round black face, round eyeglasses, and round belly, Mulch liked to wear purple, because the color framed him perfectly for the television cameras. He was often called upon for punditry, and Mulch maintained that "it isn't easy to light a black man." He was a member of the Gridiron Club, a regular at the White House Press Club gala dinner, and commanded a speaking fee of ten grand per appearance. I liked him—we often had lunch together on the roof of the Hotel Washington.

"I guess you know, my dear, that we won't let this go without our own investigation," Mulch went on. "The network says they're going to do one, but it might not be a bad idea to have one of our own looking in to this."

"Well, if the network is going to do one," I began.

Mulch sighed. "Unfortunately, the networks have a short memory for our colleagues who fall in the line of action. I'm considering putting together a blue-ribbon panel. The best of the best."

"I think Jaures would have liked that," I said.

"Yes," Mulch said distractedly. "I wonder what he was working on."

"He was going to write about the Essex Group," I said. There was nothing to protect now. No hot story, no big prizes, just the flat emptiness of a life wiped out.

"That would have been very interesting," was all Mulch said, which I thought was rather chintzy of him. Didn't Jaures at least deserve more than a round of vague pleasantries?

Mulch had been kind enough, I suppose. But I still wished that Jaures had lived long enough to finish his story—at least to give Mulch and his colleagues something to drool over. That would have been the way Jaures would have wanted to go out.

Jack had first met Jaures at the bar at the Hay-Adams, a venerable hotel across the street from the White House. Jaures had been fresh to Washington, Jack was just in search of a good French 75, the potent champagne-and-cognac cocktail named after the Gallic machine gun. So that was where we went, after we shut off the lights after a useless day of work. It seemed like an appropriate course of action.

Unfortunately, owing to recent hard times, the bartender there was no longer making French 75s. He was, however, concocting American 47s—New Mexico sparkling wine and Tennessee apple brandy. We shuddered, but ordered them anyway. I am not sure we were too discriminating.

"He was standing there," Jack said, nodding across the bar at a corner occupied by a portly man. "He had just been to a lecture at the National Press Club by that blowhard TV guy, the one who hosts the crappy show now? The one who liked to call himself a war correspondent? Jaures came up to me and said, 'Lemme get this straight: That guy pretty much said all writers oughta go to war and get killed, and if they don't, they're big sissies.' And then I told him, 'Yeah, and now the TV guy's drinking over at the Cosmos Club.'" This was the most exclusive place in town. Jack laughed at the memory. "Yeah, Jaures had a few words about *him*, all right!"

He trailed off, staring at the corner of the bar until the man standing there noticed. Jack looked away. "Jaures was good. He was a nice guy, and he was good at what he did."

Jaures once brought me an orange for a birthday present. He had scrawled on the peel, in black ink, "To Kate, With Love." I might have considered it the gift of health, except that he told Jack it came with the bag of Chinese food he had ordered the previous night. I promptly told Jaures he better damn well improve come Christmas, which he did.

I thought about him, about the smell of his skin. This would have been an odd thing to bring up to Jack, who would have taken it the wrong way. But when I first met Jaures, I had noticed immediately his apparent aversion to wearing any other fragrance than his own sweat. When we had stood pressed together around the horseshoe bar in the Marais, I noticed a light, genteel scent of lime on his neck, a sweetly odd choice for Jaures to make, as if it would have given him a bit of polish in that stupid, cheap Chinese suit. It must have been the television thing, I thought, and I stared intently at my fingernails, clutching the end of the brass rail. My eyes started to itch with tears. I hated to cry.

"Jack, when I saw Jaures in Paris, he told me about a new story he was working on," I began, my voice cracking. "He was investigating the Essex Group."

Jack glanced around the room, because I hadn't exactly whispered the words, and Washington was notoriously small. The magazine reporter who tracked down a president's mistress had discovered her when she blabbed away to her friends about the affair in a booth behind his at a local bar. So Jack was careful to lean in to my ear as he asked, "Are you sure?"

"Yes." I brushed my eyes with my fingers. "He was pretty mad that we were working for them."

"What else did he say?"

"That we should get as far away from them as possible."

Jack did not say anything. He stared out the window of the bar, which had a beautiful view of the White House. The bartender had finished his laborious preparations, and slid over to us two flutes of his patriotic bastardization of a classic. Jack lifted his. "To John Jaures, who never polished anyone's apple."

He cleared his throat gruffly, and, nodding, I clinked my glass against his.

Later we went to an Ethiopian bar in Adams-Morgan. This was the place we had all gone just before Jaures left for Beijing. Bars in Washington locked up at one a.m.; this place stayed open until five, but only for those fortunate enough to make it through the door before midnight. The owners locked the doors after that, and then the service really got wild.

I ordered the absinthe, because long ago, in one of our frequent e-mails, Jaures and I admitted we had always wanted to try it. The real stuff was served up here, brought in from Spain, one of the places where they still make it, wormwood and all. You will forget, you will see, you will sleep. Or so Jaures told me. Sugar was burned in a spoon, poured into a glass that glistened like a jewel, and, ever-so-slowly, I drank it, and gagged violently. It was horrible stuff, moonshine for Europeans. I leaned against the cold steel bar and tried to clear my stinging throat. Somewhere in the room, drums played relentlessly. Thick laughter curled up in the haze of cigarette smoke. I blinked, and rasped again. Broad, red, and purple faces receded in the dim light. I heard French, I heard Portuguese, I heard languages I did not recognize, all jabbering around me. I thought I might have started crying. I felt wetness on my cheeks.

"Don't cry," I heard a voice in English. "You'll be all right."

I blinked and turned to look: There, smeared in my vision, was John Jaures—my dear, lovely friend, nursing a Maker's Mark.

"I'm sorry I was mean," I managed to mumble, not even wondering how he could be there.

"I know," Jaures said, and then I saw that his hands were pinned behind his back, chafing under the binding of twine. And then his eyes closed, and his face went from pale to gray. Blackness swirled around him, but just before he disappeared into it, I saw, right in the middle of his forehead, so perfectly symmetrical, a hole torn by a bullet.

I must have screamed. Hands—real hands—came to my aid, comforting me and rushing me into the cold air outside. I gasped as if I couldn't breathe. I heard the bartender ask someone, "What bullet? What is she talking about?" And I realized I was saying, over and over, to no one in particular, "He saw the bullet coming, he saw the bullet coming."

Despite a painful throb behind my eyes the next day, I marched into Jack's office, up to where he sat rubbing his eyes over morning coffee. My coat was soaked with snowflakes and my fingers were red as I stood in his doorway and announced, "I think we should check into the Essex Group a little more."

Jack looked up, confused. I tried again: "Jaures was going to do a story about them."

"I heard you the first time."

"What do you think?"

"God, Kate, what do you want me to think?" Jack opened his palms to me. "I think we should let the police do their job. I think we've already signed our contract. I think one of my best friends is dead, and I don't know *what* to think beyond that." He ran his hands through his hair, despondent. "I need to turn this over in my mind a little, get things straight."

I pressed my lips together and nodded. "Lili's getting his things from the hotel and from the police. Maybe she can find something." And I went into my office to pop back a few aspirin.

Lili pretended to be Jaures's sister, because of course the police weren't about to turn over a dead man's effects to just anyone, but a pretty blonde who spoke their language was decidedly not just anyone. Lili was also determined. "He was my friend, too," she told me when she called.

"The police gave me his watch," she said. "It stopped at twenty after twelve. That must've been when they got—when they got rid. . . ." Her voice faltered, and I was glad she couldn't continue. My eyes had filled up again.

Lili cleared her throat. By the time she arrived, the charmless cubby of a hotel room had already been tidied by housekeeping and sorted through by the police. There was just one oversized black suitcase in which Jaures carried his life. Lili said she crammed in the Chinese suits, the Iron City Beer T-shirts, khaki cargo pants, four different pairs of jeans, a plastic shaving razor and a bottle of lime-essence cologne, all of which she planned to send on to his mother's house in Pittsburgh.

"I think Jack wanted to take everything to her himself," I said. This was true—he didn't know what else to do, because a phone call or letter seemed so insufficient.

"I'll send it all to you, then," Lili said. And then, after a beat: "There's something else. There were some notes from him that I got in the mail today. He must have sent them to me before . . ."

My face felt very hot. "Why?"

"He only wrote 'for safekeeping'. There's a—there's a sentence here I think you'll be especially interested to hear."

I cleared my eyes with the back of my hand. And then, Lili read aloud over the echoing transatlantic line: *"Philip Cross; Essex Group oil and energy division."*

"He was specifically tracking Cross?" I asked, a horrible prickly feeling creeping up my scalp.

"This is the only mention I see," Lili told me, and then she paused a moment. "You don't think this is anything too bad, do you?"

"No," I quickly replied, but I asked her to overnight the notes separately from everything else.

I do not believe that the political world is stocked with

greedy fiends. Most of the men and women who slog through the channels are not paid particularly well and have a sense of obligation to answer to a calling higher than just themselves. But some of the folks who drift into the business, well, the same cannot be said for them. There are the people who gunned down a Moscow bureau chief for an American newspaper outside his office one day after he published an article about the richest men in Russia and how they controlled the country. Or the people who took out the Mexican magazine editor, who was shot to death after publishing an ongoing exposé on the mayor of a border town and his ties to a drug cartel. These are extreme cases, of course, and we'd all like to think that such a thing could never, ever happen to one of our own.

I once met a former agent of the Special Air Service, a bull-necked Scot who told me that the world was divided into "goodies and baddies" and that it was often difficult to tell the difference. I did not want to think that Philip Cross was a "baddie." His résumé was too bright for me to imagine there were any cracks in his facade. It was also long. I leafed through the file that my sharp hipster of an assistant (her hair was a shaggy bob and she had a silver stud through her tongue) had compiled: former assistant secretary of homeland security, a trial lawyer, a failed candidate for the U.S. Senate, a graduate of Princeton and of Harvard Law School. Two marriages, three kids, and four houses (Warwick, Philadelphia, Georgetown, and Aspen). He sat on the board of the Kennedy Center, gave every year to the children's hospital, ranked number fifteen of the top one hundred most powerful Pennsylvanians, and supported a mathematics camp.

I sighed and flipped the file closed. Philip Cross couldn't be a baddie. Did baddies sponsor mathematics camps? Cross must have just been part of an enormous investigation by Jaures, and even the best investigative journalism wasn't conclusive very often. A gut feeling here, a rumor there, a barroom conversation. There was nothing concrete, though, only that Jaures was dead, and I couldn't even tell him I was sorry for being a jerk. I put my head down on my desk and wept. I hadn't known until now just how much a person could cry.

3

The Voie Sacreé

The French government announced, in what must have been the most rapid investigation of a murder ever, that John Jaures had been killed by "terrorists." No specific terrorist, mind you, just simply, nebulously, "terrorists." It sort of made sense. Jaures had spent enough time in and out of dicey-sounding places like Tashkent and Kiev and Lahore to rack up a strong set of enemies. This theory was immediately accepted by most American officials and certainly much of the press, which then turned its laser-like powers of investigation onto the burning question of whether or not the new Speaker of the House was gay. Still, for one night, the lead headline was, JOHN JAURES, MURDERED BY TERRORISTS.

But an extraordinary thing happened: Despite the acquiescence of the U.S. government and a majority of the press regarding the murder of John Jaures, Crispin Mulch, with all his connections, managed to pull together a "blue-ribbon committee" of assorted media luminaries to launch its own investigation. A lot of commotion about the committee was stirred up in the journalism circles. The Internet rapidly popped with postings for and against it, but mostly with admiration. Mulch had

gathered the head of the news department from Jaures's network, the Washington bureau chief of the *New York Times*, and
the publisher of the *Washington Post*, among others, to partic-
ipate, and they issued a statement: "The committee's purpose
is to do everything within its power to see that the murderers
of John Jaures are arrested, brought to trial, and convicted."
There had been another "blue-ribbon committee" long ago,
formed to investigate what was called the first death of the cold
war. That committee ultimately failed, because the journalists
assembled had been too close to the officials they were suppos-
edly investigating. I was sure that the Mulch Committee, as it
was called, would do a better job. It even hired a private investigator in Paris, a former police detective. I was reassured.
This was going to be resolved properly.

Meanwhile, I had my own matters to contend with. Philip
Cross and his partners decided that as the Essex Group had
foregone hosting a reception during the inauguration ("The papers were still writing about one of our deals," he explained to
me), it was therefore necessary to do so now. The congressional
calendar was kicking off, so the time was right to lubricate the
rank and file. Vanzetti/Boothe was asked to handle it. "A dip of
the big toe," Cross e-mailed me.

As we routinely organized fundraising receptions for clients, this wasn't too different for us, though our nerves might
still have been stretched tight because of Jaures. Still, you always want to please those who sign your checks, and an Essex
associate had decided to make us her personal project.

"My name is Celerie Worth, and I am Philip's most trusted
colleague," she announced over the phone, the words falling in
a stilted rush. "I want to meet with you to discuss the details of
the function."

"We've got it covered," Jack informed her. He looped his finger through the air and mouthed "OCD nut" to me.

"You are the event *sieve*," she replied severely in what had to be the only time we have ever been called a cooking utensil. To underscore this, Celerie came to our offices, on a Saturday afternoon, to explain what she "expected" of us. She was short, almost stubby, with a dirty-blond bob and close-set eyes. Her lips were almost nonexistent and her jaw jutted forward, away from the red turtleneck tucked neatly into a matching cable-knit sweater.

"Philip and I are *very* close," she said immediately, in her screechy voice, even before Jack had managed to pour us cups of coffee. "He's my mentor—we work extremely well together. He's told me that I'm like a daughter to him. So you can imagine how much I want everything to go very, very well." She looked us up and down. It made me want to hit her.

"All right, Celerie," Jack said, his patience strained from lack of caffeine. "What do you have in mind?"

Celerie had a lot in mind. She wanted the invitations hand-delivered ("We don't do that," Jack told her); she wanted a velvet rope outside ("We can do that," I told her); she wanted a particular brand of gin ("Not our area," Jack said); and she wanted the event held in the Capitol. "I wouldn't advise that," I said.

"Why not?" she demanded, fixing her glare on me.

"I understood, *from Mr. Cross*, that this was to be a 'dip of the big toe.' I don't think that having a cocktail party in the Capitol—"

"I know *exactly* what Philip wants, and he *wants* the Capitol," Celerie snapped. "The Senate Reception Room."

The vaulted and frescoed Senate Reception Room, where

Civil War widows once gathered, usually hosted book parties for members of Congress who published "mysteries." But a party thrown by a company that did an enormous amount of business with the federal government? Well, this would be a first. Maybe even a little unseemly. We got the room, of course. A former vice president of the Essex Group was now the honorable gentleman from Illinois, and so it was no problem after all.

My job was to be the minder for Cross. The Essex Group had its own spokesmen and assorted lackeys for protection, but Cross had specifically asked for me to accompany him. "I want you to be my eyes and ears," he said at the start of the event. "You're my girl here." Jack's duty, after erecting the requested velvet rope, was to mingle. He looked a little bored while I made my way to the Big Guy, who had charmingly placed his gold nametag on the lapel of his jacket. I smiled at this unexpected modesty. It was his party, of course, so everyone would already know him, wouldn't they?

"Ready, Mr. Cross?" I said as we walked across the Minton tiled floor, Celerie watching enviously from the caviar bar.

Cross leaned in confidentially, whispering, "I hate these things." I smiled again and nodded, because he was the client, and that was my job. Cross patted the shoulder of a veteran network correspondent, one I had watched as a kid and who my father admired. The man jerked around and beamed while balancing a giant boiled shrimp between his thumb and index finger, and he said in his famous voice, "I want you to know your replacement over at Homeland Security is not you."

This seemed like a colossally dumb thing to say, considering the man had a reputation for intelligent repartee.

"Aren't you kind," Cross said. "I just hope you put him through the same scrutiny you did me."

"Never mind," the famous correspondent said, ignoring me and the rest of the rabble. "You got off easy."

"I did, and don't think I don't know it!" Cross laughed, cuing the correspondent to issue a chummy guffaw.

Cross plucked a martini from the silver tray of a passing waiter. "How's the book coming?"

The correspondent was radiant. "The mystery is coming along very well." Of course it was a mystery. "The best parts are between the head of Homeland Security and this extraordinary television correspondent."

"I'm touched," Cross replied dryly. He cocked his head slightly to the right, and added, "You know, I have always believed that you and some of the others ought to spend a year or two in government to round out your perspectives."

"I was at the State Department for two years, in the Embassy in Moscow," the correspondent quickly piped. The boiled shrimp nearly slipped from his grasp.

"If I'm asked my opinion and you won't prohibit it, would you permit me to mention you as a possibility?" A strange smile oozed across my client's lips.

"*Yes*." The correspondent was breathless.

"They may not have enough imagination to think of it themselves."

"You know my area of interest," the correspondent added, sensing that Cross was beginning to move away.

"Indeed, I do." Cross stepped to the side. He gestured just barely to me, and I moved closer in case interference was needed.

"The fundamental thing is to carry on a policy that gives Israel the best chance of surviving—"

Cross continued forward, nodding.

"—and maintains a strong, growing, viable American position in the Arab world!" called out the correspondent. "Call me! It has been your position, too!"

Cross kept nodding and weaving his way through the lush crowd. He was almost immediately clutched at by the tobacco-stained fingers of a husky man who couldn't have been more than fifty but looked pallid in his pinstriped suit. "Phil, Phil, honest to goodness, I appreciate the fact that you're taking along one of our boys next week on that swing through Asia. I'm going to put a fine one—I'm going to put Tommy Slater on. Do you like him?"

"I like him very much," Cross said pleasantly. "He's a fine man."

"Yeah, he's a good boy," the man wheezed. "I think a hell of a lot of you, and I'm not complimenting you to get our boy on an airplane, either."

"No, you wouldn't," Cross agreed.

We kept circulating. I had thought I knew how it was done, before I walked around with Philip Cross, but now I felt like syrup had been poured all over me.

Cross didn't need a media strategist with him as much as a bodyguard. I did nothing. I just smiled and waltzed through the throng with the senior vice president of the Essex Group. Cross evidently considered it a job well done, because he shook my hand enthusiastically and exclaimed, "My girl, all right!" I wondered for a moment if I was being patronized.

An hour later, I pushed a lock of hair behind one ear while I surveyed the room. My client was safely retired for the night; my work was done. I slung my satchel over my shoulder and hobbled down the shiny floor. My feet had grown swollen in my new high heels, which I had bought because I thought I appeared sophisticated in slim, three-inch suede. I looked great, but I was crippled. I leaned against the wall, and tore the offending shoes off my feet.

"Well, hello there." The unmistakable, rich voice of Wolfgang Donovan Lawrence caught me with one shoe off. His eyes crinkled at the corners as he smiled. "Quite a party."

"You were there?" I tried to regain some poise.

"Indeed I was. It was an office-wide requirement." He looked at my stocking feet and said, "I was going to ask you if you wanted to have a drink, but perhaps I should offer to carry you to your car instead."

I laughed and sheepishly crammed my shoes back on. "I'm making a very bad professional impression."

"I wouldn't say that," Donovan consoled. "I thought you were rather marvelous in there."

"At what?" I asked. "I just followed my client around, mutely."

"And you looked terrific while you did it," Donovan proclaimed.

"Hi!" Jack boomingly approached us. "Jack Vanzetti, Kate's partner." He firmly grasped Donovan's hand in the time-honored custom of trying to crush another man's bones.

Donovan didn't even wince. "*Donovan* Lawrence." He winked at me, and Jack raised his eyebrows in my direction. "Vice president, Essex Group."

"Oh." That changed things for Jack, slightly.

"One of many," Donovan added. "Well, Kate, we'll have that drink—or perhaps dinner?—later this week, if you have the time."

"I'll have the time," I said.

Donovan strolled down the hall, whistling.

"A Brit?" Jack demanded, rolling his eyes. "Why do you always have to have an accent?"

"He's no Roberto, if that's what you mean." I thought Jack's reference to my half-Italian ex was unnecessary, especially considering how Lili had gotten in her licks a couple weeks before.

"You want to get a drink?" Jack said. "Let's go get a drink."

We passed Celerie on our way out of the Capitol. The dome lit up the Hill like a candelabra, the American flag cracking back and forth in the crisp air. Celerie looked sullen, but maybe that was her natural expression. "Did our colander abilities work out all right?" Jack asked.

"For now," Celerie said stiffly. And Jack and I chuckled the block and a half to the bar where a legendary bloated senator once had an infamous ménage-a-trois with two waitresses in the pink-sheathed private drinking room.

Jaures's papers arrived from Paris the morning after our Essex fest. Lili, true to our arrangement, had sent them separately, and as a greeting to me she had scrawled a smiley face on one of her personal notecards.

"Whaddya got?" Jack asked, walking in my office to hand me a steaming cup of coffee.

In the jumble of papers there were crazy diagrams and arrows, knots of names. But there was also a memo, jotted in Jaures's scratchy penmanship, which he must have meant to type out and e-mail to his boss. I slowly turned it over in my hand.

"According to this, a memo about Jaures's story."

"Tell me." Jack settled in the suede chair across from my desk. The Essex Group, Jaures had written, was on the verge of a major oil deal in Russia. Last September, while Jack and I suffered through our losing streak, and Lili moved to Paris, and Jaures drank baijiu in ramshackle street-side bars, none other than Philip Cross himself had flown key staffers on the House Armed Services Committee to France on a private jet.

"Christ!" Jack exclaimed.

"You're going to hate this part," I said, skipping ahead a few lines. "In Burgundy, to a chateau. A first-class, all-expenses-paid, trip, and guess who whipped up the little dinner?"

"Don't," Jack warned.

"Gerard Boyer from Les Crayères."

"*No.*" Jack's hero. He owned every cookbook the man had written and had attempted to make every dish. "Let me get this straight," my partner began, "Cross flew out these guys in September, at the height of budget time on the Hill?"

"Interesting the committee chief would let them go," I said.

"Interesting, my ass," Jack muttered. "The chief of staff probably went, too."

Capitol Hill staffers, even those on committees, don't make a lot of money. Most of them pull down sixty grand a year, although press secretaries and other senior staff can earn in the low six figures. But they have a bit of power. They can earmark money for projects, and they can hide that money amid other choice projects, knowing that representatives will never read every line of a fifteen-hundred-page bill before voting on it.

"Jaures says here that a Russian company called Perun got twenty-three million dollars allocated to buy arms from them," I told Jack.

"What kind of arms?" he replied, as if this was something we discussed every day.

"A type of gun," I said, and looked further down the memo. "But Kalashnikov isn't just an arms company, it's primarily an oil company. It's got the rights to the fields in Siberia, and controlling interest in the fields near Tashkent."

Jack looked at me. As we had both watched the coverage of Jaures's death on his network, we knew that Tashkent was a place he had often visited.

"So with the deposit of all those millions in taxpayer funds . . ." Jack began.

"Those would be bribes!" I interjected.

"Whatever," Jack continued. "Don't tell me what comes next."

But there it was in the memo, in Jaures's own words: "Essex emerges from that weekend in France with a sweet deal: Kalashnikov gives them first dibs on developing the oil fields under its control. And what other companies does Essex have controlling interest in? Companies that are in oil development. This is a deal worth hundreds of millions—probably billions—and it goes straight into Cross's pocket."

My mouth went dry as my eyes traveled over the words, again and again.

"Cross who?" Jack asked. "Our Cross?"

I thought about when Jack and I started our company, when we were young and sharp and knew what it took to win a race. And I thought, "Oh my God, we are in way over our heads."

Now, I am a firm believer in economic growth through competitive private enterprise, and I do think that this growth should and does rely on individuals of initiative, merit, and intelligence. But the enormous potential of what Essex could do went well beyond this. It was what my father would call "big rich." It wasn't about paying off a credit card or a mortgage, it wasn't even about wintering in Aspen and summering in Montauk. This was a world of unchecked power. Who *were* these guys?

Instead of ripping my brain out about it, I went to my fellow K Streeters. We all know what everyone else is doing, even if we can't quite prove it.

"Essex fucked me over," said my pal Pete, who worked for a bipartisan firm. "One of my clients is part of the wealthiest family in Turkey. He owns all the phone companies, several power plants, stuff like that. The family's business practices— I don't really listen when they talk about it, stick my fingers in my ears, I just don't want to know. They cut a deal with a tele-com company here. The American company gave the Turkish company one-point-two billion dollars to buy equipment made by their company, and in the American company's books, it looks—to the shareholders—like the U.S. company did one-point-two billion in business with Turkey. Earthquake then strikes Turkey. Telecom company can't pay back its loan right away. American company swoops in for the kill—they want the Turkish company's assets. Who reps the American company? Essex. They get the vice president, yeah, *our* vice president, on the phone. Next thing I know, the Turkish government's de-clared my client a terrorist suspect and seized forty billion of his assets, including all the telecom stuff. I deal with this on one day, but this is what Essex does *every* day."

Later, at a consulting company I almost joined before start-ing my own, my friend Sally wagged her finger at me. "Ooooh, smarty-pants girl, You gotta be kidding! Essex is raking in every former muckety-muck in the world. There're others, but

Essex has the lead on them. You wait—it's gonna get worse, the more competition there is. Essex and the rest are gonna go real dirty."

After hearing all this, I stared at the Jaures memo and wondered what had been wrong with me, thinking all these years that a congressman or a governor was naturally imbued with power.

Forget what you see on television, the screaming pundits who sling insults against "treasonous liberals" or "nutcase conservatives." The *real* big boys privately light their cigars and scoff at such antics. And why not—the court jesters would never, ever breathe the rarefied air of major power and money. Partisanship and ideology are for amateurs. I started laughing, hollowly, because, in terms of business, Jack and I were right to go after a corporate client like Essex. It didn't really matter who got elected next time around, or even who sat in the Oval Office. Essex would always be on top.

I am not a do-gooder. If I was, I would be toiling for a nonprofit, drinking fair-trade coffee in a shabby office, wearing faux-leather sandals and long floral skirts. I like to make money. I like to walk through the halls of power. I don't deny anyone the right to turn a profit. But this was different. This method of "doing business" was wrong, and quite possibly my friend had been killed because he knew it was wrong, too, and was going to prove it.

Ethics, of course, is an ephemeral term in Washington, or anywhere, for that matter. There are those who believe "good" and "bad" are black-and-white terms. I have always been a shades-of-gray kind of girl, and when it came to ethics, well, I weighed the pros and cons by paying attention to someone's motives. I had survived in Washington because I figured that someone's intentions determine the true nature of their actions. My mantra is: *Why* is *who* telling me *what*? Cross was very big on telling me I was his "girl," that I was going to be huge, that my time was coming. Why, I now wondered, would a powerful guy like that pay all that attention to me? I was cute, but not that cute.

Then again, if there was one group that needed to maintain its public image as Masters of the Universe, it was definitely the Essex Group. Keep 'em scared—"bad time to be a gadfly," and things like that. I felt my temper rising. They were bullies, at the very least, and the worst was something so horrible, it hurt even to entertain the thought.

I left the office early. I desperately needed a long run to relax—my house to Mount Vernon and back again. Fifteen miles. The slice of asphalt was clear of ice, and I idly watched squirrels scurry across naked tree branches as my breaths came fast and sharp. I wondered if squirrels suffered much in this weather, but then, only people feel sorry for themselves.

I ran hard enough to wipe myself out. I was sprawled on my overstuffed sofa, wrapped in a blanket that my grandmother had crocheted for me, when my phone rang. I almost didn't reach for it. My limbs felt sore and heavy.

The voice that spoke was wondrous and high. "You are a bitch."

I bolted upright. "Who is this?" I demanded.

"This is Nina Scott Lee."

"I'm sorry?" I had never heard this name before, and I wasn't quite used to being insulted like that.

"I'm a friend of John's," she said. Then, very direct: "Are you the reason he was killed?"

"*Pardon me?*"

"You're working for Essex, I found out. You must've pissed off someone there."

I was speechless. What could I say to that? I just sat there, the phone dangling in my hand, which angered Nina Scott Lee even more.

"Hello? This is an expensive phone call. I'm calling from Paris."

I found my voice at last. "I think you're assuming way too much. And I have never heard of you. Jaures never said anything about you, and—"

"Maybe I'm not assuming enough," Nina Scott Lee barreled onward. "Maybe they meant to hit *you*. Or, did you have him killed because he was investigating Essex and you wanted a big fat contract with them?" Nina sucked a deep puff off a cigarette. I could hear the angry intake of breath.

"Who the hell are you?" I almost shouted.

"I'm a friend of John's, and I'm investigating his death, and I'm going to write about it, that's who I am. I'm not backing down from this. If I have to ask you some things that make you mad or uncomfortable, too bad for you. You're still alive; John is not."

"I was his friend, too!" I exclaimed.

"Funny way of showing it, playing along with his killers."

"You are way out of line," I shot back. "Get your facts straight."

"Are you or are you not working for them?" Nina demanded.

I paused, and then cursed myself, because this allowed Nina to plow ahead. "Exactly!" she shouted.

"Screw you!" I shouted back. "I've never heard of you! Jaures never mentioned you, and I don't know who you work for! You're just some little freelancer on a fishing expedition, and I will not be drawn into a pissing match with you!"

And with that, I hung up on her. It was ten minutes before I realized, with some horror, that I'd sounded as self-righteous as Philip Cross.

4

The Value of Good Manners

I could play a tough girl, but the fact was that I hated being called a bitch by another woman. I expect the word from men—"bitch," of course, being the favorite backslide to any prickly situation involving a woman; a bad date, a bad meeting, the wife didn't make turkey pot pie. But I take special offense when the slur comes from a fellow female, particularly one who worked with words for a living.

And, I thought as I angrily jerked my car into the parking lot the next morning, she really went after my qualifications as Jaures's friend. My loyalty had never been questioned in that area, and to have a stranger do so!

Nina Scott Lee. Who the hell was Nina Scott Lee? I got to the office a couple hours early just so I could poke around. The reporters I called had not the slightest idea of her. "What kind of name is that? A lounge singer?" one offered. The Internet coughed up a few articles she had written, with datelines like Sierra Leone and Baghdad. I called a newspaper she had filed for, a family-run Mississippi paper, whose editor summed her up in a heavy tone: "She's *difficult*." Well, then. I shouldn't be bothered by Nina Scott Lee, who was, by one account, kind of a nut.

"Hey." Jack waved as he sauntered past my office.

"Hey yourself." I must have sounded glum, because Jack backtracked.

"You all right?" he asked.

I thought about Jaures, and the last time I saw him, and I tried to squeeze out the reverberating accusations of Nina Scott Lee. "Do you think I'm a good friend?" I asked Jack.

"Sure." Jack shrugged, and squinted suspiciously. "Why? What do you want?"

"I got a call from an old pal of Jaures last night," I said, rubbing my forehead.

"I imagine we'll be getting a lot of those," Jack replied.

"This one thinks he was murdered."

"No kidding. The police think he was murdered," Jack said.

"Well, she's blaming *us*."

"That doesn't make any sense," Jack said sharply. "We were his friends."

"Her argument is that because we're working for the company he was investigating, we're not very good friends."

"That's bullshit." Jack said. "She must be crazy. Jaures wrote and broadcast a lot of dangerous stories. He could have been killed by anyone. So *that's bullshit*." He was shouting now, startling our assistant into dropping a bundle of pens she had gathered from the supply closet.

"Maybe," I began hesitantly. "I mean, I think we should check into what Jaures wrote in his memo. Just in case."

Jack breathed deeply for a few moments. "I agree it all looks weird," he said. "But I'm telling you, Kate, I can't play this 'what if' game about his death. He was—" Jack's voice caught, and he quickly cleared his throat "—my friend, no matter what some crazy bitch in Paris is saying."

"I hate that word," I reminded him.

"But she's earned it!" he reminded me, jabbing the air with his index finger, before stalking off to the kitchen for a cup of coffee.

Our assistant had put together a massive file on the Essex Group. One bright résumé after the other, pleasantly bland faces, people with families. I flipped through the pages, wondering about those men and women who toiled beneath beige-colored walls, drinking mineral water and mapping out conquests. Nearly five hundred people around the world worked for Essex. They surely had defined concepts of good and bad, and they must have dreams for their lives and their children's futures. I pursed my lips at this thought and pushed the file aside.

Jack likes to say that I "fall in love with the meat," that is, I become a true believer in the person espousing the ideals. His mentor, a strapping Louisianan who whipped up gumbo as well as he devised an ad campaign, taught him that it is generally considered bad form in Washington to lose professional detachment. I didn't know any other way, though. During a campaign, I would get to know a candidate—often his or her family and close friends as well—and meet with the press and organize town hall meetings, and all this felt like it meant something. I respect even those who have deeply held ideas that I disagreed with; honor among equals, noble conviction, and such. I didn't know what to think of Essex. The closer I got to them the more flaws I found, and Nina Scott Lee kept popping into my head like a Greek chorus.

It was very inconvenient for my conscience, then, that I had babysitting duties for Essex later that afternoon, over the phone, this time, minding an interview that Cross would have with, of all people, Crispin Mulch. I sat at my desk and wondered what Mulch was up to—maybe his committee had come up with something. He had hired that investigator, and it had been a few weeks. Essex is your client, I reminded myself, you are here to protect Cross, not dangle him like bait just because you have some concerns.

I called Cross's office, smoothing my voice with some effort as I assured him that I would be on the line during the interview. I felt a bit silly; Cross had obviously done enough of these to handle one on his own, but if the Essex Group wanted to pay us for this little duty, that was all right with me.

Crispin Mulch started with mechanical inquiries, the usual. I might have yawned a few times while he cut through the niceties. And then:

"Let me read a quote of yours, three years ago, to the *Washington Post*: 'The Word of God gives no authority to the modern tenderness for human life. It is necessary in all Eastern lands to establish a fear and awe of the government. Then, and only then, are its benefits appreciated.' What Eastern lands were you referring to?"

"Philip, if I may, for a moment," I broke in, instantly alert, "remind you that the agreed-upon perimeters of this interview do not mean you have to answer for something you said years ago, or even specify. All you are supposed to do is explain your position at the Essex Group. Of course, if you want to answer this question, Mr. Mulch will understand that it is on background."

"Then I will leave it at that," Cross said.

"But the 'Word of God'?" Mulch tried again.

"On background, if at all," I said again.

"I was not speaking in terms of religion," Cross said.

"What were you referring to, then?" Mulch asked.

"We can spend as much money in government funds as we would like in these countries, but we would only assuage ourselves," Cross said. "It isn't government money that works in emerging nations; it is private investment."

"On to the matter at hand," Mulch said. "The president is a good friend of the energy industry. You're heading up the energy and oil division of Essex Group. It's feasible, then, wouldn't you say, that you, a close personal friend of the president, could personally become very rich off of policy decisions he makes. A marriage of private and public investment, if you will."

I coughed. "Philip, maybe you want to take a couple moments to think about this, and of course keeping in mind that the interview is strictly off the record."

"The president," Cross began, unruffled, "is an honorable man. To imply he would manipulate national policy for monetary gain is unseemly, Crispin. You realize that."

"His uncle and his brother are investors in the Essex Group, aren't they?" Mulch asked.

Again, I spoke up. "Realizing again this is off the record, Philip, maybe you want to walk Crispin through the relationship between Essex and its investors."

"We have thousands of investors," Cross said, and he left it at that. Mulch spent a few more moments with harmless inquiries, and then it ended. Mulch hung up, but before Cross went, he paused a moment and said to me, "That was good, Kate. Good, good, good." He said this almost absent-mindedly, like the chant of a teacher to a pupil.

Some learn faster than others. Jaures, for instance, re-deemed himself for my birthday orange when he went over-seas. He spent a Christmas in India. The pity of the life of a foreign correspondent, but somewhere between the stew of Mumbai and the steaming greens of Cochin, he picked up token gifts for his closest and mostest. Jack got a full array of spices ("Eighty of the known spices are from India!" Jack liked to ex-claim—a fact he obtained from the menu of a local Indian restaurant). My present arrived six months later ("I have no explanation for that," Jaures had ruefully e-mailed), a palm-sized bone carving of Saraswati, the goddess of knowledge. Saraswati presided over a stained green table in the entryway of my apartment, serenely greeting me each evening with an open left hand, her right firmly encircling an oil lamp. I had been to India years ago, courtesy of my father's most adven-turous brother, who felt his niece needed to see a developing country, and it had always pleased me that the symbol of knowledge was a woman. I also liked the aesthetic. It was as if when I walked through the door, Saraswati was urging me, "Stop, think about your day a moment."

But that evening I didn't even have a chance to consider it—I rattled through the door, keys jingling, and into darkness. Maybe because I was discombobulated from the interview with Cross, but I immediately smacked my forehead into the sharp corner of a bookshelf that I had forgotten about, reeled back into the hall table, and heard the clatter of something hitting the floor. Damn it all, I thought, as I reached a lamp switch. There she was, the goddess of knowledge, face down on the hardwood floor. I gingerly turned her over. Her left hand was broken off, and the lamp of reason was chipped.

I was horrified. What did this mean? That I was deluded?
Doomed? It was terribly early in Paris, but I called Lili, anyway. "It only means you're clumsy," she said in a soft voice.

"I damaged the goddess of *knowledge*," I stressed.

"You're not Hindu," Lili reminded me. "This isn't a sign."

Hardly convincing, coming from a woman who knocked
wood after every other sentence. And now my head throbbed
like hell. It hurt even to think, let alone sift through the pile of
mail scattered around my entry hall, having been shoved
through the narrow brass mail slot. I was slumped against the
wall, tossing various envelopes into "must read" and "circular
file" stacks. They were the same old stuff—a postcard ad for
broadband wireless, a sorority newsletter, a magazine. The title of that last one had glowing block letters that stung my tender eyes: *Yellow Belly*.

Never heard of it. I was always getting free magazines and
innumerable catalogues, so this one might have been trashed,
unread, except for the tiny print at the bottom of the cover that
caught my eye: IN TIMES OF NEED, VALUES RECEDE. That was
intriguing enough. I laid with it on my sofa while I put an
icepack on my forehead.

Yellow Belly was more a pamphlet than a magazine, a list of
over one hundred fifty journalists, writers, film directors, pro-
fessors—people who allegedly had been involved in questionable endeavors, such as lecturing about the follies of the war on
terrorism. The publication was careful to mention upfront that
this was not to be taken as a blacklist; rather, it was an "educa-
tion initiative."

The information set forth in the following report is taken from
records available to the public. The purpose of this compila-

tion is threefold. One, to show how the un-American have
been able to carry out their plan of infiltration of the radio and
television industry. Two, to indicate the extent to which many
prominent members of the press and artists have espoused
unpatriotic causes, regardless of whether they actually believe in, sympathize with, or even recognize the cause advanced.
Three, to discourage the press and artists from naively lend-
ing their names to unpatriotic organizations or causes in the
future.

There was one name on the list I immediately recognized:

JOHN JAURES, journalist, print and broadcast

I blinked several times—because my head did still hurt, and
my eyes could be reading this wrong—but my heart and stomach seemed to fold into one. Who the hell were the morons publishing this crap? It wasn't enough that the guy lay in the
ground decades before he was supposed to? If someone didn't
want Jaures out there, mucking around, well, they'd won.
There was no reason to keep such a dirty paper in circulation.
But, as Cross had observed at our first meeting, times were different. Plenty of people unapologetically saw a need to develop
and distribute a list of "yellow bellies."

Drinking a glass of red wine might not have been the best
course of action, but it would make me feel better. I stood on
my terrace with a half-filled glass, looking at the slush of the
Potomac under the moonlight. I breathed deeply, the cold air
stinging my lungs and, I hoped, spurring my brain to action.

There was a perfectly historic reason for *Yellow Belly*. I had
read Carlyle, at the insistence of my grandfather. I knew that

the great, enlightened Scotsman had concluded that the solution to agitation was oppression—by a king, preferably, along with compulsory labor and military training. So, I thought, anyone who agreed with this, which many people did these days, would endorse a *Yellow Belly*. All the better to keep the masses in line.

I brushed my fingers across the raised lump on my forehead, and suddenly the red wine tasted musty. I drained the glass over the railing of the balcony. The John Jaureses of the world. They were not simply unappreciated; they were chewed up and spit out.

The president of the Essex Group, a mysterious entity known as Harcourt, married for the fourth time at the end of February. The ceremony itself was low-key and quiet, held in the drawing room of his Georgetown mansion, but the reception was an affair meant to dazzle. The entirety of the Corcoran Museum was reserved, the stark gray facade sparkling with silvery lights and the wide steps manned by uniformed violinists who rubbed a tango. I know this because I had one of the embossed invitations in my hand. Jack wasn't with me. He had flown to Pittsburgh, to bring Jaures's belongings home to his mother.

I had never met Harcourt, but that wasn't the point. As I handed my blue wool coat to a smiling young woman—a student, probably, hoping to network while scraping up drinking money—I looked around at the glitterati of the city, the senators and congressmen and the "famous, for Washington" types who included the lush-lipped network correspondent who loudly mentioned to her companion, "I was having some nipple concerns with this dress, so I used Band-Aids," and the meaty editorialist, who made the talk-show rounds to pontificate on the sanctity of marriage while he was having an affair with a socially connected married woman and—unbeknownst to her—her daughter, too.

I was used to this crowd, but then the White House chief of staff walked by me. I looked twice over my shoulder to double-check. It was. I sucked in a deep breath because, unexpectedly, I was in rarefied air.

Suddenly, behind me, I heard a woman's cultured voice saying, "Well, you know the chief justice officiated."

"The chief justice?" I couldn't stop myself; the words just poured out.

"Of the Supreme Court," the woman said, glaring icily. I realized I had made the unforgivable faux pas of inserting myself, unwanted, into a conversation between the wife of a famous and beloved newspaper editor, and the editor himself. He was nothing like the dashing journalistic hero I had read about in various books. He was bent and wrinkled now, but he still grinned at me just as he reportedly did with all women. This was, naturally, *another* black mark for me in the increasingly narrowing eyes of his wife. She seized him by the arm and dragged him away from my clutches. I felt sore and embarrassed, although none of the shiny important people around me even noticed the moment. I shifted uncomfortably from one heel to the next, until I remembered the woman became the editor's wife (his second) after many infamous late nights on top of the long oak table in the editorial boardroom.

I plunged deeper into the cavernous room. I tried nonchalantly to smooth my wrap, which was nothing compared to what these women were wearing: the long strands of enormous pearls that bore the heavy sway of heirlooms, dangling elegantly below lips laced with tiny lines from too many late-night cigarettes. I was used to parties, but ones that were a few notches less intense. I was just a kid from Chicago in a gray satin dress I bought off the rack. But I was stuck. Jack would never forgive me if I left, especially before a thorough sampling of the food.

I picked my way through the crowd, which was lush and sticky with power, and headed toward a yellow-sheathed table stacked with *fruits de mer.* "Oh, hello." It was Celerie Worth. Her legs stood apart, nearly splitting the seam of her skirt, and she was armed with a martini. "You're here, too."

"Yes." I reached casually for a crab claw.

"I came here with Philip," Celerie said. She viciously tossed her bobbed hair to the left. "He said a *lot* of really nice things to me."

"Good," I said, wishing I knew someone—anyone—else at this gig, instead of enduring another round of girl-to-girl smackdown.

"He told me again that he thought of me as his daughter." Celerie put her hand to her heart for emphasis. I paused, wondering how, exactly, to reply to this, when a rich and warm voice broke in.

"Have you had a drink yet?" Donovan Lawrence leaned between us and grinned. Yes, indeed, there is a God.

"Hello, Donovan," Celerie chirped.

I knew Celerie was just another one of the multitude of over-educated, highly ambitious women trapped and frustrated inside the Beltway, but I still wanted to smack her on her smug little nose.

"I would *love* a drink," I said to Donovan, who took my arm, and we left Celerie standing by the jumbo shrimp.

"Enjoying yourself?" Donovan inquired, and I caught a faint whiff of spice from his neck.

"Not really." I smiled at him.

"It's our own special torture," he said. "Every few years, Harcourt gets married, and he has one of these events to show off the new toy."

"That's a terrible way to think of a wedding reception," I said, feeling like I needed to stick up for the new wife.

"Take a look for yourself." Donovan nodded toward the center of the room, festooned with piles of saffron- and cream-colored flowers, amid which stood the man named Harcourt, a surprisingly squat figure with thinned gray hair and a bulbous nose. He looked not unlike a troll. And his hand, swollen with arthritis, squarely rested in the small of his wife's back. She was willowy and exquisitely built, sheathed in a silk evening dress that clung and plunged.

"Do you know him?" I asked Donovan.

"I rarely see him," Donovan replied. He asked a gloved bartender for two glasses of champagne. "I primarily work with Philip Cross. Our divisions in the company are clear-cut. We do not overlap much."

An orchestra was swelling to Count Basie, but no one was dancing. It was such a waste of good music.

"Ah, Miss Boothe!" None other than Philip Cross himself patted my shoulder as he joined Donovan and me. He struck much closer to my idea of a Master of the Universe than Harcourt did, but perhaps Harcourt was smarter, or luckier. Cross smiled genially, and clapped an arm around each of us. "Come with me. There's someone I'd like you both to meet."

He led us across the crowded room, nodding at each side to

the myriad he knew, and up to an older couple, who beamed at him. It was the famous editor and his awful wife on whose conversation I had eavesdropped.

"I think you both know Wolfgang Lawrence," Cross said. The editor nodded rapidly; his wife was more effusive.

"At the White House, the dinner for the prime minister," she said in a special tone she must reserve for plummy men. "We sat at the table next to yours."

"That was the first time I have ever tried Texas wine," Donovan said, and they all laughed. I continued smiling idiotically—it was an outsider's only defense.

"It's not every day you see a wine label with 'Lubbock' on it," the editor said.

"And this is Kate Boothe," Cross continued. "Our bright comer."

The editor shook my hand, and his wife did not seem to mind the attention shown to me this time. In fact, she was transformed. "So you're at the Essex Group?" she asked pleasantly.

"No, Kate has her own company," Cross said. "We're just one of many clients, keeping her busy."

"What kind of company?" the editor asked.

"Consulting," I began, but Cross interrupted.

"She did the Gold affair, if you remember."

"How could we forget?" the editor's wife regarded me with some interest. "And now you've got Essex as a client."

"Her favorite client," Donovan said with a wink.

"Of course," I replied in kind.

"You should dine with us," the editor's wife said to me. I was so startled that I looked around, as if to check who else she was addressing. "We give dinner parties every month."

"Stew parties, this time of year," the editor said. Then, to Cross, "I never know what she puts in 'em."

Their dinner parties were legendary—gatherings of the most important. It was said if you dropped a bomb on their house during one of their dos, you would wipe out the machinery of the country. And I was being invited!

"Kate, give them one of your cards," Cross urged. And, because it was Washington, of course I had my business cards on me at a wedding reception. I handed one to the editor's wife, and she carefully put it in her clasp purse.

"We'll look forward to seeing you around our table," she said, and I felt the kick of a small victory.

I wasn't misplaced in the room, after all. Gaiety swirled around me, and I chatted and minced with the best of them. I could hear snowplows wheeze through the streets—ice must have slicked the sidewalks, too—and I knew that I would hate to plunge back into the cold outside.

5

Agenda? What Agenda?

Jack returned from Pittsburgh, and looked older for it. "I don't know how a mother buries her child," he said in a flat voice as he dropped his bag in his office. Jaures's mother was a retired bookkeeper, confused about her son's life as well as his death. He had moved away right after high school, she told Jack, and only occasionally returned home from the far-flung places he trawled through. His younger sister, about whom neither of us had heard before, was more forthcoming. "He left us because he thought he'd become a rock star," she told Jack, who reminded her that Jaures was a journalist. "Yeah, but don't journalists *think* they're rock stars? All important and cool, like we give a damn?" she shot back. "Now he's dead, and was it worth it? He was only thirty-six, and there's nothing to show for it all."

I was quiet while Jack told me all this. I forgot all about the triumph of Harcourt's reception, which seemed stupid and empty now. Jack gave me an acidic smile and held up the copy of *Yellow Belly* that I had left on his desk earlier in the morning. "Well, Jaures made an enemies list," my partner said.

"That's something." He sighed and probably would have gone into his office to ruffle through all the paperwork that had accumulated, except that our assistant brought me a lovely bouquet of irises. Jack raised his eyebrows as she handed me a small card. *Dinner?* was written on it in beautiful penmanship.

It was from Donovan Lawrence. My assistant stared. "Nobody does that in Washington," she said.

"Nobody does this anywhere," I corrected, turning the card over in my hand.

"Maybe because he's British," suggested my assistant.

"Maybe because he wants to get in your pants," suggested Jack.

"Oh, for God's sake!" I wadded up a page of newspaper from my desk and threw it at him. The flowers were distracting, though. Jack regained his old grin.

I decided that one formal gesture deserved another. I wrote on a thick piece of stationary, *I will happily dine with you at eight o'clock on Wednesday.* And I had it delivered by courier, just for good measure.

Washington is a cloistered world. Just like any other one-industry town, like Los Angeles, for instance, there is a language understood by the denizens, there are tribes and there are geographical demarcations. Consultants, for instance, had K Street to work in, the Virginia or Maryland suburbs to reside in, and the restaurants of downtown Washington to eat in. The top layer of the various industry offshoots—the media, the Hill people, the executive branch—had its own rituals, including sharp gatherings and events at certain clubs or drawing rooms. But once in a while, something occurs that upsets this balance.

The bloggers invaded. These barbarians of journalism pumped away at their blinking screens, spilling screeds of conscious-ness, bile, and, in a few cases, excellent reporting. I love these folks, because they could always be counted on to shake things up. They are the latest version of the grand American tradition of pamphleteering. Every kind of ideology, personality, and irony is represented in cyberspace. I strongly believe in perus-ing several web sites on a daily basis, although Jack disagrees. He thinks bloggers, on the whole, ought to be committed.

But it is an extraordinarily influential way to reach people (mostly the younger ones) who were already suspicious of newspapers and television reports. It hadn't taken long for the political parties to notice. "Give me a blog!" had been the top request of my candidates last cycle. But some in the system took this a step beyond. For every "real" blogger, there was a hack with a web site, employed by a political party to churn out the party line under the guise of "independent thought."

Some of the more stalwart members of the media main-tained privately that bloggers are nut jobs with too much time on their hands. "They're not *real* journalists," a worm-faced magazine columnist once grumbled to me when one blogger—a favorite at White House press conferences—was revealed to be a male prostitute, both sexually and politically.

"Well, he was a *fake* reporter," I pointed out. Most bloggers come up with stuff the rest of the media didn't cover. What stuck in the craw of that magazine columnist was the self-appointed watchdog status that bloggers assume over the mainstream press.

"As if they're the guardians of unbiased journalism!" he snorted.

This, however, was the prevailing opinion in the gilded

newsrooms around town. So the feud was running high when a blogger calling him- or herself (you never really knew for sure) Ida Tarbell posted on the Internet: "What massive conglomerate is behind the load of crap known as *Yellow Belly?* None other than the Essex Group. That's right, the Evil Empire long ago added a printing business to its roster, and decided to use it. The question is, why? Could it be because one of the listees was in the middle of a hardcore investigation of their dirty dealings? Handy, then, that the listee turned up dead."

"Um, Kate," said my assistant, hesitantly alerting me to the results of her afternoon web surfing.

"Oh, shit!" Jack shouted from his office.

My heart sank, and I told myself that this could not be true. If it was, wouldn't the so-called real media be on the case? But I knew the answer to that. The real media would never touch it—they too might end up in a future issue of *Yellow Belly*—until the general narrative warranted coverage. For now, the general narrative required only perfunctory calls to our firm for comment. One of their own had gone down, but "this happens when you are a war correspondent," as went an opinion spewed on a talk show by a petty female magazine writer with owl-glasses, who once told me that she never, ever traveled on assignment unless the magazine express-shipped her luggage ahead to her hotel. So I wasn't worried about coming up with a non-substantial answer that protected our client and bought us some time. I was dreading what to do if this latest was true. We just couldn't be working for such people—that is, against Jaures.

Jack and I quickly convened in the kitchen.

"We've got to continue doing our job," Jack said, but he wasn't too enthusiastic.

"Bloggers aren't always right," I said, but I knew better. They might not get all the facts straight, but, not unlike a tabloid, they usually were on to something.

We called Philip Cross's office on the conference phone. Celerie Worth took it.

"It's a complete lie," she shot at us. Jack and I exchanged a look over his desk.

"What part of it, Celerie?" he asked.

"All of it—and I don't appreciate your attitude."

"We're all on the same team here," Jack tried again, but he was starting to flush a bit.

"We're just trying to get the facts straight before we move ahead," I added. "Is Philip available?" A sure-fire way to set her off, but anything to get past an irate gatekeeper.

"Philip has asked me to handle this," Celerie said.

"All right," I began, "does Essex own the company that prints *Yellow Belly*?"

"No," Celerie quickly replied.

"Does Essex have controlling interest in it?" Jack asked. "Any interest?"

Celerie paused. "That doesn't mean *we* published the magazine."

"Celerie," I said, rubbing my forehead as Jack pretended to pound his fist into the phone, "help me out here."

"There's no agenda," she answered. "It's an unfortunate co-incidence."

Later in the afternoon, I gave a statement to Crispin Mulch, who, like a lot of mainstream journalists who also wrote the occasional book, had a blog of his own.

"Come on." I told him. "The Essex Group is held responsible when the Red Sox don't make the play-offs. The publication of *Yellow Belly* is as connected to the Essex Group as the roving Beltway boy-hustlers on board the fake 9/11 Pentagon plane are connected to the CIA."

I hated myself for uttering this, although Mulch got a laugh out of it and added that, indeed, it was a *tad* conspiratorial of the blogger called Ida Tarbell.

"We haven't turned up anything about *Yellow Belly* in our investigation," he said. "And oh, by the way, we have a new member of the commission. He says he met you the other night." The famous newspaper editor, of course. He had joined the investigative brigade.

"We're becoming hip!" Mulch exclaimed. "If this continues, we'll have to start charging an initiation fee."

"Have you come up with anything yet?" I asked.

"No, but we've had some very good meetings," Mulch told me. "I'm sure we'll have something soon. We've got an investigator in Paris, and one here, too."

Meetings are de rigeur in Washington, land of a thousand commissions. Still, I was a bit disappointed. All those amazing investigative minds gathered together, and nothing yet to report. I was relieved when Jack decided we should finish off this terrible day with drinks.

Donovan called me on Tuesday to ask if I could leave the office at six the following evening. He had a special restaurant in mind, he said. Jack found this hilarious—"Special restaurant? Let me guess: his house?"—but my partner rose to the occasion. He even saw me to the door, just as Donovan roared up in a red-and-white 1968 Porsche convertible. Jack's jaw dropped. "They're making more at Essex than I thought," he murmured. He appreciated cars, having spent every extra cent he had on an Alfa Romeo years ago, and on countless visits to the mechanic ever since.

Donovan strode up the walkway. "Good evening, Kate!" He certainly looked the dashing Englishman, camel-colored coat and tweed cap. He peeled off racing gloves to shake Jack's hand. The look on Jack's face was priceless. I could almost see him thinking, "Racing gloves! *I* need those!" But what he said was, "Is that yours?" He nodded at the car.

"Ralph? Yes, all mine!" Donovan exclaimed. He took my hand and kissed it.

"Your car has a name," Jack observed, a funny, tight grin crossing his lips. I kicked him, subtly I hoped, in the back of his left calf.

"After my uncle. He always wanted this car, and when I got it, well, how could I not name it after him?" Donovan crooked his arm in my direction, and I slid mine through his. "Anyway, we've got a bit of a drive ahead of us. I promise to bring her back in one piece."

"Uh, yeah." Jack waved his cell phone my way, meaning I could call him anytime, and I waved back at him. I could see him reflected in my passenger-side window, standing on the sidewalk under a yellow streetlight and shaking his head.

Donovan took me to the Inn at Little Washington, a restaurant routinely voted the "most romantic" in Virginia, and a two-hour drive from the city. The only people I knew who had gone there did so for their anniversary—their thirtieth. The heavily flowered room and terribly expensive multicourse meal was decidedly not standard first-date fare.

"Are you expensing this?" I asked, and Donovan smiled as he ordered us champagne.

"I thought I would make dinner with me worth your time," he replied.

Worth my time! Sixteen chefs and assistants sweated away for fewer than seventy-five people in the dining room. The atmosphere laid on the gentility a bit too heavily for my taste, with its plush banquettes festooned with rose-colored lamps. It was as subtle as being slammed over the head with an iron frying pan. But, Jack once told me that eating at the Inn was the closest to having sex he had ever been without actually, well, you know. I couldn't help but be impressed when Donovan ordered the tasting menu, plus wine, for both of us. This guy was doing it up right.

I had consumed gorgeous meals with intriguing men before. But still, if I hadn't read the Jaures notes, if I hadn't been berated during a transatlantic phone call, if I hadn't become suspicious of *Yellow Belly*, I might have fallen into the bath of that warm lamplight and emerged a charmed woman. I could almost hear my mother's voice, "But Kate, his face is inoffensive, he's taller than you, he's got a good job—so, what's the problem?"

"Do you like being at Essex?" I asked him.

"I should hope so," Donovan replied. "I put in a ninety-hour week for them."

"Sounds like dedication to me," I observed.

"Golden handcuffs," he corrected. "I like my car."

"Would you ever leave?"

"Haven't considered it before," Donovan said. "I work for one of the franchise players in the business, many of the right people know him. You've seen what it's like."

He took a sip of wine. "How do *you* like working for Essex?"

"It's interesting," I said. "Nothing like a campaign."

"Just wait," Donovan replied. "They haven't even started with you yet."

"What are you saying?" I held my glass in midair.

"Think of it this way," he began. "You've passed through the crossroads, chosen a route, and now you'll find out what that means. On the one hand, it means meals like this. On the other hand, it means you have no proper life in order to have meals like this."

"That doesn't sound worth it," I observed.

"Oh, no?" Donovan grinned. "Have you had the cheese course here?"

He smoothly ordered up a selection for us, and we finished the evening with a 1970 port. And afterward, ever the gentleman, Donovan drove me back to my apartment building where in the thin hours of the night, he raised my hand to his lips before speeding off home. My assistant was right: Nobody did this in Washington.

I drove to work the next morning listening to a thick, familiar voice on talk radio. A reporter I had known long ago, when he was a better man, was speaking with the zeal of a someone who, after years of dwelling in bottom-feeding anonymity, had honed his pundit persona. I idled in traffic that had stalled to allow a motorcade to pass, so I had plenty of time to be assaulted by his new message.

"We ask God to bless us and this great country of ours," he was saying. "These are dangerous times. Danger, and the effort every individual must put forward—becoming part of a group as a whole, for instance—in order to face an imminent menace, means that it helps to believe God is on your side. And I believe He is. One reporter was murdered in France—"

I flinched, but did not turn the station.

"—He was typical of the latest crop of journalist elite: rash, brash, and possessing dangerously misplaced righteousness which might, even, have gotten him killed. His death should be a lesson to all of us—that none of us are bigger than the whole. And that the whole is the nation . . ."

I had to flick off the sound. This hack, who once described Putin as a "cozy bear of a man . . . someone you could have a nice chat with," dared to say that Jaures's death was his own fault? He should be so lucky to have the honorable career that Jaures did! Furthermore, this man had *known* Jaures! I knew then that *Yellow Belly*, insidiously crawling through the ranks, was at work.

All that week, I took a long, unvarnished look around me. In my office, I watched as the stale crusts—the usual visages of esteemed journalists—trooped onto political talk shows to yammer on about the risks and the morality of their profession (this, from a circle of people whose idea of covering a war is to invite the Secretary of Defense to a dinner party). I also saw the airless marble corridors of Capitol Hill teeming with hard young faces that swung through a season of bloated cocktail parties and receptions, glutted on Swedish meatballs and stupid with cakes. I watched the starched people pouring out of their gleaming offices along K Street. And I noticed, with a shudder, the copies of *Yellow Belly* tucked under arms during rush hour.

One morning, while I should have been preparing a television briefing for one of our congressional clients, I wondered what happened to the movie that was supposed to have been made from a series of articles that Jaures had written during the Gold affair. A movie producer who fancied himself politically savvy had actually optioned the series, and a famous director had been attached to the project. I had the producer's number, and I was put through to him right away.

"It's been canceled," the producer said shortly. Movie projects, of course, fall through all the time for all sorts of reasons. But then the producer added, "I scrapped it after the fucking call from fucking Washington."

"What call?" I asked.

"Not a good time for this kind of movie," the producer said.

John Jaures was being slowly besmirched and then erased. No one would remember him, let alone question his murder. Except for the Mulch Commission. Its investigation could punch its way through; I trusted Mulch to see to that. He was a respected, prize-winning journalist.

And then, two days later, as if on cue, I was suddenly summoned to Paris. The private detective hired by the commission, a former policeman with the inspired name of René Hardy, wanted to speak with one of the last known individuals to see John Jaures alive.

It was to be a very brief visit, Jack emphasized. We had our Essex work, and there were plenty of other clients filling out our dance card. I had no intention of staying in Paris longer than I had to—the city had nothing good to offer me, except for Lili, of course. She was delighted when I called. She even insisted I stay with her.

I packed my hard-shell suitcase, bought last year in Italy because I thought it made me look chic, and was changing my dollars for euros at the currency exchange in the shining, bustling corridors of Union Station (I don't trust ATMs overseas), when who should approach me but Philip Cross.

He was getting off a morning train from Philadelphia, his long black coat folded across his arm, the edge dragging along the floor. He nodded at me by way of greeting and asked, "Off to the Continent?"

"Yes. Paris," I told him, not wondering how he knew, because such a man made a point to know.

"Not for long, I hope," Cross said. Then, with a twinkle, "I understand there's a young man counting on a second date."

Oh dear. I was not usually one for mixing office and romance, so I quickly replied, "I didn't know he worked for the Essex Group when I met him—"

"Please, Kate," Cross waved off my concern. "We're all big boys and girls here." He smiled. "I'll look forward to seeing you in a few days." And then he nodded formally and wished me a safe journey.

6

The Grand Industry

I have said before, on the basis of some experience, that the great lottery in life is the airplane. Seat assignments are fluttered through a system that spits out your fate. Across the aisle from my narrow coach-class seat (because Jack did not believe in six-thousand-dollar tickets) was a familiar face, craggier than I remembered, but immediately recognizable from the long, ropey scar on the throat. The visage that had launched a thousand ships—and fighter jets.

Yes, the lobbyist Joe Morgan did very well for his defense contractors, on whose behalf he trudged through the airless halls of congressional office buildings and endured witless remarks by men in badly cut suits. Morgan himself favored dark blue, with pressed trousers and open-collared shirts—all the better to intimidate, because who would question the advice of a man bearing the physical mark of military experience? Certainly not the majority of Congress, whose members had strenuously avoided serving during wartime, if at all. Joe Morgan's gait, therefore, carried weight.

I had known him for years. Consultants and lobbyists often

crossed paths, and we had a history of mutual helpfulness. But, now, Morgan's broad, pale brow was knitted with consternation, and no wonder: a tow-headed boy, probably about four years old, was rolling his toy car up and down his arm.

"Where is your mother?" he asked the child, who promptly pointed in my direction. Morgan turned and broke into uproarious laughter.

"You *have* been busy, Katie," he said.

"Uh, I'm not—" I sputtered.

"I'm right here," a tiny blonde said tiredly. She heaved an overstuffed bag onto the seat next to me. "My husband is up in business class."

"And you let him get away with that?" Morgan asked.

"We tried to get seats together back here," the woman ignored his comment, "but I'm hoping one of you won't mind switching with us."

Morgan was up before she even finished. "Window or aisle?" he asked me, pulling a leather weekend bag from under his seat.

As he wedged through the passengers who were settling into their places, he grabbed at the arm of an already harried flight attendant. "Any chance of getting a beverage now?"

She regarded him witheringly. "We don't serve before take-off in this class of service."

We *were* flying a British carrier, after all. Morgan growled but said nothing as he buckled himself in. He tucked a pillow behind his back and wadded up the airline-issued blanket for extra padding.

"Paris doesn't seem like your kind of town," I observed.

"Paris is not my final destination," he replied, and he shut his eyes tightly. Well. One does not press those who are capable of killing us. Besides, he would eventually spill it—Morgan was remarkably open for someone whose former occupation demanded a high degree of secrecy. He once told me it was either talk or burst from the increasing pressure in his chest.

So, it was somewhere over the Atlantic, after he had devoured an ersatz steak (he shrugged—if it tasted like meat, it might *be* meat) washed down by two scotches, that Morgan turned to me and said, "They've called me back in."

"Who has?" I asked as I picked at a dull slab of salmon.

"Uncle Sam. Who do you think?" Morgan went to work on his third scotch.

"But you're retired."

Morgan laughed irritably. "I can walk. That's all they wanted to know. Stop-loss. DoD's using special ops for everything. You name it, we're there. The new military." He laughed again, this time with bitterness. "Guys who were trained in Russian, who specialize in that part of the world, are being sent to Malaysia. Malaysia! Guys who've been working on the drug war, they're over in Venezuela or some other fucking place. There aren't too many of us, Kate. It takes a long time to train them, takes a lot of money. DoD's running out of them, so, they're calling back people like me."

"To do what?"

"Missions." Morgan stared at the seat in front of him and then shook his head. "I spent fifteen years sleeping with one eye open. Now here I am again, but with a bum knee, a gut belly, and a shot liver. You would've thought I'd done my duty to my country." He looked dolefully at the plastic cup of scotch.

"How long is this mission supposed to last?" I asked.

"It's the 'War on Terror'; there's no end to this thing," Mor-

gan said. "At least, not for me. They've told me to expect to get
sent out on a regular basis indefinitely. Eh, well." He took a
drink. "For about fifteen years, we had a nice time of it. That's
all changed now."

"What about your lobbying business?"

"It's still there." Morgan shrugged and rattled the ice in his
glass somberly. "The grand industry has always been a political
necessity."

"Eisenhower," I said.

"Don't be naive," Morgan said. "Before Eisenhower. He
coined the phrase, is all. And it's the 'military industrial com-
plex'." He cackled. "Sounds like a fucking mini-mall." He
paused a moment while the engine hummed. "Could be worse.
I could be one of those poor bastards who go private."

I had heard about the former special forces troops who,
upon retiring, signed six-month contracts as mercenaries with
various private companies. A hard two hundred grand for six
months' worth of sitting in the sand or the mud or wherever
their companies sent them. Good money, but, as Morgan
snorted, "Once you start down that road, with that crowd,
there's no getting out. You'll get calls for twenty years, middle
of the night, and you can't tell 'em to go fuck themselves."

The lights had already dimmed in the cabin, and there didn't
seem a whole lot more to talk about in the stale, dry air. So it
was only seven hours later as we gathered our bags to leave
the plane that I asked Morgan about the Essex Group. He was
a defense lobbyist; Essex had a lot of defense companies among
its holdings. I should have struck the information motherlode.
But Morgan only glanced at me sharply.

"Why would you want to know about them," he muttered.

"Jack and I are working for them," I said. Morgan didn't so much as twitch. "On retainer," I added.

"I'm sure they're making it worth your while," Morgan said.

The passengers uncoiled into the aisles. Morgan nodded for me to go ahead of him.

"Let me tell you something I learned in the military," Morgan began, ducking in close to me. "A man doesn't die from the first blow. He dies from the second or from the third. Those blows come while he's stunned from the first and thinking, 'This can't be happening. I can't be hit. I can't be dying.' And before he knows it, he is. That's one of the first things they teach you in the military. It makes you adjust your way of thinking."

"How sad to live that way," I said.

"Sad," Morgan agreed, "but useful. You continue to live."

"Unless they shoot you between the eyes," I said pointedly.

"They don't care how they get you, as long as they do," Morgan said, and I kept my mouth shut.

French customs discharged me into Paris. The roiling sky baptized me for my latest visit, as I had no umbrella, wandering through the streets after stowing my suitcase at the hotel in the Marais.

I reported to the Mulch Committee's investigator straight away. I was curious as to what he knew. But if René Hardy knew anything, he wasn't telling me. He had a pinched face, a thin moustache and a reedy voice. As he fumbled with a stack of paperwork, repeatedly asking when I came to France and why I came to France and who in private business I knew in France, I became less heartened. This investigation, at least, wasn't off to a flying start. Hardy lit a cigarette, and I was released.

Lili nearly screamed when she heard my voice. "I'm at La Tartine," Lili burbled. "Come meet me."

I was extremely tired. The airport-to-interview rush had kept my adrenaline running longer than usual, but now my muscles felt heavy with jet lag and I had my usual post–transatlantic flight pallor. I did have a sure-fire routine to beat it, though: Eat shortly after arrival, take a two-hour nap, then stay up until at least ten, swallow a melatonin, and *voilà!* I'd be straight-up all right by morning. But I wasn't staying in Paris long enough to make the routine worth it. And, hell, who couldn't use a glass of red wine and a plate of goat cheese?

La Tartine was on the busy, proletarian rue de Rivoli. Lili and I had sat there once before, watching the riders in the Tour de France blur by. The wine bar hadn't changed much since Trotsky (allegedly) drank there; it was quite literally yellowing with age. Old men in hand-knit sweaters and tweed caps, nary a beret in sight, gathered at the bar, punctuating their arguments by jabbing the air with their cigarettes. A bemused woman in a black apron watched them over assorted bottles. There were fifteen different wines served by the glass and an equal number of cheeses to match.

Lili had commandeered a table in the back, and she was there with another American, a woman. The latter looked up at me from under a mass of jet-black curls and curtly nodded a greeting. She had sturdy shoulders, clean fingernails, and a strong jaw. Quite handsome, actually. Of course she was a girl, but she had the slightest masculine air. When Lili introduced us I nearly threw up.

"Helloo, darling, I want you to meet Nina Scott Lee."

"How ... interesting," was all I managed to say.

"Is it?" the girl said as she raised her eyebrows.

"Nina's a journalist," Lili elaborated. She patted my hand as I settled in next to her.

"I'm aware of that," I said, and added with a slight edge, "but what I haven't been able to figure out is, for who?"

"I work for hire." Nina Scott Lee didn't miss a beat, although Lili did look from her to me and back again, puzzled.

"What do you write about?" Lili asked pleasantly. Ever-ready Lili, always prepared to diffuse a moment.

"Death," Nina Scott Lee said flatly.

My theme for the day. I raised my eyebrows at this, and Nina Scott Lee added, "Last month I was on maneuvers with Hezbollah."

"That must have been . . . something," I said, unimpressed.

"They don't think like you or me, that's for sure." She shoved a piece of bread into her mouth. "So. You're Kate."

"I am."

I kept my eyes on hers. A strange gleam crept into her dark eyes. Nina kept chewing the bread, and she turned to Lili without even swallowing and asked, "Where's the toilet?"

Nice segue. I tried not to glare at her.

"Downstairs. It's Turkish," Lili warned.

"Easier than in the desert," Nina shrugged, and she tossed her hair as she clunked out of the narrow, unsteady chair.

I waited until the girl had disappeared down the steep stairs.

"How do you know her?" I asked Lili, my very best friend, the traitor.

"From here," Lili whispered. "She was having a drink. I just met her a couple days ago."

"She called me a couple days ago!" I exclaimed. "Yelling something about how Jaures's death was my fault."

"*Yours?*" Lili was shocked. "But that makes no sense."

"Thank you." I uncharacteristically slurped my glass of wine.

"God, Kate, and do you know where she's been? She's been to southern Iraq, Chechnya, Sierra Leone—you can't believe the places. She doesn't even live in Paris. She kind of lives wherever."

So Nina Scott Lee was a war junkie, moving from conflict to conflict with no fixed address. I think the chronically transient are avoiding one reality or another. Anyway, with that loaded passport, it would take more than a Turkish toilet in Paris to faze this girl. The first step in the torture of women, Joe Morgan once told me, is to deny them a bath, and Nina Scott Lee looked to be the type that didn't mind skipping them on a regular basis.

"And you know what?" Lili lowered her voice even more. "She was in jail in Peru for a year—for killing a man!"

"What?" That stopped me. I wouldn't want to be in an American jail, let alone a Peruvian one.

"She told me she didn't really do it."

"Oh, good."

"But she also said there's not much she's afraid of now."

I would think not. I decided to grudgingly admire her. I am afraid of a lot of things, and I happen to like baths very much.

"And you'll never believe—" Lili began, but she spied Nina coming up the steps and quickly snapped her mouth shut.

Nina ordered another glass of wine, a thick and chalky Cahors, and turned to me.

"I'm not sorry about calling you," Nina said. "I'm never sorry about things like that."

"What are you sorry about?" I asked, my voice stumbling a bit. I wasn't used to chatting with an alleged murderess.

"I'm sorry John is dead," she replied.

"We're all sorry about that," Lili told her.

"Yeah. Well. John and I knew each other a long time ago, when we were in Bosnia." The expression on Nina's face drifted into a memory, and she smiled slightly. Her front teeth crooked inward.

"He was a very nice guy," Lili said sincerely. She lifted her glass of wine, and with only the slightest hesitation Nina followed. "God bless 'im," Lili could toast in twenty-three languages, but of course she had to choose the one expression that Nina would object to.

"Don't tell me you believe in *God*." Nina wasn't completely humorless; she barked a laugh at this.

"I have no problem admitting that I believe in God," Lili said. "I believe in the Buddha, I believe in Allah, I believe in all things these days. Kate here believes in Saraswati."

"Yes, but I broke her arm and the lamp of reason," I reminded Lili.

"Bad sign," Nina said.

"Anyway, you're wearing a gold cross around your neck," Lili pointed out to her.

She frowned. "Yes. But not because I believe there is a God dictating life and death, or I'm on a crusade or anything. It keeps away the evangelicals, and it's—it's my good luck charm, I suppose."

"Everyone needs one of those," I agreed.

Nina looked at the cross for a moment. "They haven't arrested anyone for John's murder," she said abruptly. "That's why I'm here. I'm going to write about who killed John. Why he was killed." She lit up a cigarette, a French one. They might be worse for your lungs, but they certainly smelled a lot better than American brands.

"The inspector hired by those Washington jerks is useless," she said, exhaling. "He's too easily reachable by government officials and too susceptible to considerations of high policy to be the right guy on the job."

"I wouldn't call Crispin Mulch a jerk," I said. Nina raised her eyebrows.

"Really? How about a sell-out? You think guys like him are going to do a hard-hitting investigation on the very people they have over for dinner parties?"

"What about his television network? They're doing an investigation," Lili said.

"Oh, them!" Nina snorted. "How good of a job do you think *they're* doing? They've budgeted twenty grand for an investigation, and do you know how much they've spent? Nothing. They're owned by the same company that John was investigating!"

"The Essex Group?" I asked, looking fleetingly at Lili, who was working very hard to maintain a neutral expression.

"Typical conglomerate. What are there, three companies now that own most of the U.S. media? No, you can't trust them at all."

I understood the sentiment. I didn't know much about Jaures's own network, but I was aware of strange happenings at others; the self-important president of one, who had decreed that no Palestinians would appear on "his" air because "they're all terrorists"; the network that sent out a memo to its correspondents urging them to be "more patriotic" in their coverage; the major network that routinely hired fresh college grads as baby stringers and pumped them into war zones like Iraq, where these hapless, hopeful freelancers routinely were killed. News was a loss-leader industry, and corporations that dabbled in it were not to be believed.

"This wasn't a random act, and it wasn't a 'terrorist attack.' I also find it hard to believe, although the investigator freak disagrees, that it was an *affaire d'amour*. John could be a cad," she continued, "but he had discretion. Somebody had him killed."

"A hit?" I asked, pressing her. There was weight in that word, and my stomach felt tight and hot.

Nina might have recognized the dread in my eyes, but she did not acknowledge it. She hacked off another chunk of cheese for herself with the same primitive gesture that Jaures showed when he ate. How *did* these people live when they were in Bosnia? Lili coughed away a laugh, and I stared at Nina, who in one quick, clumsy movement had brought back the ghost. I suddenly, emptily, thought about Jaures, and how he would never again shovel food into his mouth and make me roll my eyes at his lack of manners.

"Why not?" Nina said, chewing on one side of her mouth while crumbs tumbled out of the other. It was quite a trick. "He probably knew more about the Essex Group than any other American reporter abroad. He was coming home. He was murdered. It might be that he knew too much."

I said nothing. I could only stare with alarm as Nina went on. "We journalists are quite expendable. There's rarely an investigation. There's a teeny bit of outrage at first, maybe a recap of our work, and then we simply disappear from memory. If we're 'lucky' we get an award named after us." She leaned across the table, so close that I could smell the sourness of the tobacco on her breath.

"The Essex Group is a multibillion-dollar company. Their investors have trillions. Do you know what that kind of money does? People disappear. All the time." Her brown-black eyes blazed with the injustice of an outsider, and she pushed her chin up and out.

"People disappear," I echoed.

"A sacrifice for the greater good of the bottom line," Nina said. "We're just numbers to them."

"But murder?" Lili asked. "That's what you're saying, that the Essex Group is capable of murder."

"Do *you* think that's going too far, Kate?" Nina asked me intently. I didn't have a chance to answer before Nina leaned forward and grabbed me by the wrist. The contact startled me. I nearly upset the tiny table.

"It's not only the Essex Group," Nina continued. "Look, we're talking about energy sources here. And hidden within those deals are arms deals, terrorists become investors, and so on. All sorts of black-hearted types are involved, and otherwise-straight people are involved with them because when it comes to money like that, everyone loses their heads."

Nina stabbed out the cigarette and pulled on a black pea coat fastened with giant silver safety pins instead of buttons. "Think about it," she said, pointedly, to me. "*Again.*"

I kept my eyes on my wineglass until she left La Tartine, while Lili murmured, almost to herself, "I'd be wearing a cross, too."

An e-mail from Jack was waiting for me when I returned to the hotel and logged on to my computer. He had forwarded a long dispatch, the last one Jaures ever sent his producer, a cowardly man who had not passed it along to his network because, as he wrote Jack, "The crunch is coming." What crunch? His colleague was dead, but he couldn't withstand a little corporate pressure? But then, reading through Jaures's message, I realized, Jaures had been expecting a crunch, too: "Now that many correspondents are writing such critical stories on the dominant faction of the Essex Group, there are any number of vague hints that 'somebody is likely to get hurt.' There's nothing but bad paper on these guys."

I think best when I am in motion. I clapped shut my laptop and headed out into the black and wet night. Scattered tourists struggling with soggy paper maps picked their way through the soaked gravel near the Louvre, and the air was chilled just enough so that I could see my breath. I wondered if Jaures had ever, at any point, directly contacted Philip Cross. If Jaures felt that someone was "likely to get hurt," surely he must have had more than mere conjecture to go on. Maybe he called up Cross, perhaps they had an argument, possibly Cross had gotten worried.

But then, what if *Jaures* was wrong? What if he was chasing a story that sounded good, but was really only a dead end? Journalism was pockmarked with such scars, and, worse yet, false stories that networks or newspapers chose to air or to publish, which ultimately tarnished their credibility. Certainly, that could be a possibility here.

The rain beat steadily upon my hair, rivulets running down my neck, soaking the threads of my wool coat and the cuffs of my sweater. There are some who might find this romantic, to be drenched on a frosty night in the winter-dead garden where royalty once lived; I call those people students. I was miserable, and not just because my socks squished in my sneakers.

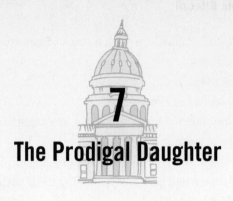

7

The Prodigal Daughter

The street plan of Washington was laid out by the same guy who designed most of the boulevards in Paris. The wide streets, marble bridges, and swirls of traffic circles could inspire awe, I suppose. Sunk in sullen, dark February, the city looked to me to be made of jutting bones, the whiteness of the buildings stark, the monuments cold.

I returned to a flurry of roses (*You were missed*, read the card, paid for and issued by Donovan)—white roses, which I had always taken to mean death, but which my assistant assured me were dreamy. Jack took one look and asked, "So are you seeing him?" And when I answered in the affirmative, my partner returned, "Is he gay?" Classic.

There was an e-mail from Cross: "Did the Frog put you through the mill? Welcome back. Loved the new stuff Jack sent over." And there was a message from my mother. My father was coming to town in a couple of days and wanted me to join him for dinner.

"I met Nina Scott Lee," I told my partner, rubbing my eyes and yawning. He kindly handed me a cup of coffee.

"Crazy?" Jack flipped through a stack of newspapers, scanning the headlines.

"High maintenance."

"Did you show her the e-mail?"

I shook my head. Jack pressed his lips together and said, "Probably best you don't, for now."

"Maybe the Mulch Committee, though," I said.

The committee had been busy, aligning itself with investigators in the U.S. as well as France, if reports in the newspapers were to be believed. I immediately called Mulch to compliment him on his efforts. He laughed, reflecting that it didn't say much about his "loyalty" in certain quarters. All of a sudden, poking into the Jaures *issue*, as Mulch said it was becoming known in certain circles, had been discouraged. Work from the inside. That's what Mulch had been told by a source at the State Department—don't do anything public.

Then, Mulch's voice turned silky. "I wish that Jaures had let one of us know what he was working on. Maybe we could pick up where he left off."

"Yes," I said vaguely. If there was a journalist to pick up the mantle of Jaures, it had to be Mulch. He had the panache and the reputation. And he was heading up the only investigation into the murder. But I said nothing. I had never heard that note in his voice before. If I hadn't liked him, considering how long I had known him, I would have thought he sounded greedy.

The blogger named Ida Tarbell slammed away again in cyberspace. She seemed to really, really enjoy her job:

The world's most powerful man—no, not the president . . . the head of the satanic cult known as the Essex Group—threw a mighty hissy fit yesterday when tracked down by this brave young blogger and asked about the rag known as *Yellow Belly*.

OL' HAM HEAD: How did you get this number?

I.T.: Did you name *Yellow Belly* yourself? Because you're jaundiced?

OL' HAM HEAD: (pissed) How did you get this number? Hello? Who are you? I'm hanging up!

I.T.: Constipated?

OL' HAM HEAD: (very pissed) I don't know who you are or what you think you're accomplishing by—

I.T.: All that crap can back up in ya. There are pills for this. Drinking the blood of fresh babies doesn't seem to be working.

OL' HAM HEAD: (very, *very* pissed) You must embarrass your parents! (hangs up)

Oh, yes, Mr. Harcourt, I do. When you fly screaming out of the underworld to feed on their souls, they will tell you all about it.

"Does his head," Jack asked, "really look like a ham?"

Celerie called immediately. She felt *someone* ought to be doing the rounds of talk shows, namely us. But we had time to ponder the talk-show option. I wasn't too eager to publicly defend the company, and as no phone calls had come in from mainstream reporters, I figured I had some time to sift through things. Bloggers and assistants could be ignored.

But nothing would stop that woman when she felt her boss, though unmentioned in the blog, had somehow been maligned. Celerie called and called, and then she e-mailed and instant-messaged until my assistant begged me to do something.

"Silence is the strategy," I said to Celerie as soon as she answered her phone.

"But this says—"

"Silence earns us no press and keeps the language in the realm of the wackos," I went on. It felt deliriously good to interrupt her. "If we speak out, this expands, and suddenly we're above-the-fold and in regular cable rotation."

"You can't sit back and do nothing," Celerie finally snapped.

"You can't attack everyone you think has wronged you," I said. "That's not how media strategy works."

"You're pretty stupid," Celerie said nastily. "That's *exactly* how it works. And loyalty matters, Kate. Period." And then, to my surprise (because women who wear turtlenecks and matching blazers generally have good manners), Celerie hung up on me.

Essex summoned Jack to Las Vegas, where a slice of the company was holding a meeting. Jack was thrilled—he thought this made up for me getting Paris. "There are some great restaurants in Vegas!" he exclaimed. I would rather go to New Jersey a thousand times than to the land of over-stuffed tourists and chain-smoking gamblers with exhausted kids in tow.

Later, at the time of day when Washington truly comes alive, as Jack was excitedly explaining over French 75s the virtues of a particular tuna tartare to be found at a restaurant on the strip, each of us had a shoulder clapped by Donovan Lawrence. "Hello, Jack! Hello, love!" he kissed my cheek. "Having a drink?"

"Why, yes," Jack replied, only slightly civil. He rolled his eyes at me.

"Here for a meeting with the boys myself," Donovan said. He squeezed my arm and nodded toward a partially hidden table surrounded by men in vibrant shirts. "Something of a club. Play cards, chat about football."

"You mean soccer," Jack said.

"Soccer," Donovan agreed. "I heard you're going to Las Vegas. You play cards yourself?"

"Uh . . ." said Jack. He had once played poker and got thoroughly cleaned out by Jaures, who was able to use Jack's beloved Alfa Romeo every weekend for three months as a result.

"Good luck! And I'll take care of our girl while you're gone." Jack just looked at me.

"Kate, why don't you come to my place for dinner? It's a bit humble, but I'm a whiz at ordering take-out."

"Love to," I said, and Donovan kissed my cheek again, shook Jack's hand, and was off to his "meeting."

"I don't get the guy," Jack muttered, staring at Donovan's disappearing figure. "He's not your type."

"I didn't realize I had one," I said.

"You like men who can cook," Jack said.

"Oh, well," I winked at my partner. "Just think of it as reconnaissance."

Jack shook his head and finished his cocktail.

The American embassy in Tashkent was bombed that afternoon. Wire services reported that "embassy officials could not be reached to comment." As if embassy protocol was, upon being bombed by terrorists, to wait around for the press to call. I usually wouldn't have paid much attention to this news bulletin—I had a pile of memos waiting for my initials before being zipped out to a few clients—except that Tashkent, among other places in the Middle East, had popped up so often in Jaures's files. I made a note to my assistant to find more information on the place.

My father liked to visit our office. I guess some sort of parental satisfaction is derived from seeing a brass plate with your family name engraved on it and hung outside a brick building. It was, at least, a tangible sign that his daughter was doing all right. My father insisted on meeting me in my office, from which we could walk to the Ritz-Carlton, where he was to see his Big New Client.

"It's kind of snowy outside," I mentioned, glancing out the window at the ice clinging to the pane. My father was still ensconced in the relative warmth of a taxi cab, just off his three-hour flight.

"Cold weather builds character," said the man who swam in Lake Michigan even in the dead of winter.

"Sure, Dad," I murmured. What else was I going to say?

My father looked exactly like a Midwestern lawyer, with his square suit and lack of cufflinks. His eyes showed only the slightest trace of weariness, and he had gained a little more weight since I last saw him. He was eating out a lot these days, he told me, entertaining his rainmaker of a client and avoiding my mother's culinary attempts in the peach-checked kitchen. My mother, the woman of a thousand power suits who had always made a point of *not* cooking, now tried to follow Julia Child, usually wanly. She made a soufflé once and forgot the egg whites.

I waved farewell to my assistant and took my father's arm. The air was damp and cold. The worst kind, in my opinion. I would most certainly wake up tomorrow with a sore throat.

"Well?" my father asked, looking me up and down in the lamplight. "How was the trip to Paris?"

"Not very useful," I told him honestly.

"You holding up all right?" My father did not look at me; he never did when asking questions that could elicit an emotional response. "Remember that no one ever said you had to take the death of a friend stoically."

"Oh, Dad."

There was a time, when I was a little girl, when I did cry a lot. I blame those jags on switching elementary schools. I went from a tender, safe school where I had loads of friends to a snobby cloister where a horrible little blonde named Michelle Matusek stole my lunch every day because she knew it would make me cry. Alarmed, my parents sent me to a therapist, who asked me questions like, "Do you like the beach?" and "If you could live anywhere, where would that be?" I solved the problem myself by bringing two lunches and bashing Michelle Matusek over the head with one of them. I didn't cry much after that, until Jaures.

"I'm fine." My tone was sharper than usual, because I didn't have it in me to recount everything for my father, then and there. "So, what does this new client of yours do?"

My father seemed relieved to switch topics, too, now that he had performed his parental duty. "International business. The only profitable area these days. You might find him interesting."

"Maybe," I said doubtfully. I had been dragged to meetings like this my whole life, so what was one more? Both of my parents worked, but they never considered day care—after all, I was an only child. So, at a relatively young age, I spent hours in the midst of adult wheelings and dealings, staring blank-eyed at the table, the wall, the carpet; ignoring the blather; scrunching my toes up in my shoes and flexing them out.

The lushness of the Ritz wrapped around us as the bellboy nodded and smiled. I straightened my shoulders. My father took me by the elbow, guiding me down a hallway past the concierge desk and the businessmen huddled over small, round tables.

"You've had good news," my father said. "Your mother told me about the Essex Group."

"Yes," I said. My father smiled affectionately at me, and then drew himself up. We had entered the main room, the same place where Jack and I had sat with Philip Cross. My father and I headed toward a slightly older man, who looked like he lived in a tree. He was thin and rangy, his collar frayed, and his graying hair haphazardly cut.

"Joe Joffre, my daughter, Kate," my father said, and the gentleman, who my father estimated to be worth fifty million dollars, nodded at me. "Kate is a political consultant."

Joffre didn't look remotely interested. "Sure, sure," he muttered and popped several pretzels into his mouth.

I knew I was at the table gratuitously, mostly so my father could call the moment "visiting with my daughter," but I was enjoying watching Joffre polish off the silver bowl of nuts and olives while detailing his numerous adventures in the wild, wild world of energy deals. The longer he talked, the more I thought about the board game Monopoly, and how the secret to winning is to buy the utility companies and the railroads. Remain uncommitted to any special way of making money, become a speculator, rule by the imperative of accumulation.

Joffre had known some real characters, all right, men who made and lost fortunes, negotiated with Bedouins ("How many dates can you eat before you want to fry up a camel's ass?"), dabbled in arms deals. High-stakes stuff, well beyond my realm of experience. It was an effort to keep my eyes from widening at every word. But then Joffre began, "There was this one fellow, a good man, Abdul Haq—" and I couldn't help but interrupt.

"You knew Abdul Haq?" I asked. For I had known him, once, as had Jaures. It had been one of the first things we had shared.

Joffre regarded me with interest, but my father shot me a look.

"You were starting to tell us about the pipeline," he prompted Joffre. But Joffre, a man used to having his way, wasn't so easily deterred.

"Haq was an old friend of mine," Joffre said. "For a time, I lived in a house he owned in Peshawar. It was a kind of boarding house, you might say. The man who ran it officially worked as a television journalist. But we all knew—everyone knew—that he was bankrolled by the CIA."

Joffre chuckled to himself. Dad raised his eyebrows at me ever so slightly over his highball. The wacky world of geopolitics and CIA covers. No wonder journalists weren't safe anymore.

"Haq didn't live there himself. He was the patron, you see, so most everyone there had some sort of a connection to him. Did you know him?" Joffre asked me.

"I only met him one time, at a dinner here in Washington, years ago," I admitted.

"Sometimes one meeting is all you need," he said. "Understanding a man is not tough."

Understand a man! I stifled a choking laugh. How much did my friends like Lili spend on tarot card readings to divine the thoughts of men? I had a session once. I did not learn much. The reader said I was "blocking."

"You're on your way to Jordan?" My father prodded, trying to steer the conversation back to something useful.

"By way of Paris." Joffre paused for what was for him a long moment. "I read in the papers there was an American murdered there about a week ago. A journalist. No suspects, they say, but what do you expect from the French police?"

"That journalist was my friend," I said, my cheeks burning.

"Well, that is a sad thing. You never forget your first friend who is murdered. It's the ones after that you become numb to." Joffre grimly plucked the olive from his martini glass. He rolled it between his thumb and forefinger before tossing it into his mouth. "The *first* friend who was murdered?" Who *was* this guy?

"What can you do." My father was growing anxious. "The pipeline is through Afghanistan, is it?"

"Yep. All that natural gas in Turkmenistan." Joffre glanced around for one of the ancient waiters to replenish the snack supply. As this was the Ritz, it didn't take long.

"It's a multibillion dollar deal for anyone willing to do it," my father said.

"Six billion, was Unocal's estimate," Joffre said dismissively. "They tried it, a few years ago. They even brought those backwards bastards out to Sugar Land. Think about that one! What a game of cowboys and Indians!" Joffre slapped his knee. "Then an Argentinian company got in on the action. They tried to work it through the Saudis *and* the Taliban. Suckers. No wonder their economy went belly-up."

"You're trying to build a pipeline?" I asked. "You've got all those warlords. What company in the world would insure a pipeline?"

"It's a mind-fuck over there," Joffre said. "It's the same in the oil game, except they've already got money. Those princes have more oil and more greed than they do brains."

"How did you make your money, Mr. Joffre?" I asked. I didn't mean to sound impertinent, but I was curious.

"The stock market, kid," he said. "International finance."

"And you lived in Pakistan," I said.

"If you're going to take the risk, you have to educate yourself very quickly to get taken seriously in some corners of the world. There are no big rewards without big risks. You want safety? Make quilts."

"Absolutely," Dad agreed.

"Manifest destiny," Joffre said. "Twenty-four/seven business; anywhere, anytime, do a deal. In 1950, ninety-five percent of U.S. business was domestic. What do you think it is now?" He pointed at me, and at once I got performance anxiety. I stared at him, and Joffre expansively swung his arms. "Come on, kid! This is your chance to shine!"

My father nodded almost imperceptibly, and I thought fast. "All right," I began, "considering all the ranting and gnashing over the loss of American jobs—"

"An election chestnut," Joffre smacked his lips as he ate another dripping olive.

"I would think that the domestic side of business accounts for less than fifty percent," I guessed.

Joffre laughed uproariously. "Try eighty-five percent domestic. What does this tell you?"

"That a lot of politicians just lost their campaign slogans," I replied.

"That the potential to go global is explosive." Joffre crooked a finger at me. The man was all edges.

I leaned in toward Joffre and asked, "What's your interest in a pipeline?"

My father winced, but Joffre didn't seem the slightest bit perturbed at the inelegant questions of a young woman. "I have clients that like energy deals," Joffre said.

"I have a client that likes energy deals, too," I said. "They're not a very nice group."

"Sometimes you run across people who you believe are moral retards," he said. "Often, these are the people you will be making money off of. Sometimes, you can make a lot of money off of them. And usually, they will be very happy to help you make as much money as possible, because this is a motivation they understand. That's what sitting at the big table is all about. You don't have to be in the game, you know. You can always leave. A lot of people do just that. They clock in at their jobs and out again, buy a nice car and raise kids, and get consumed by the concerns of the day-to-day, and they are very happy."

He was right. How many young men and women like that had I known from my early days in Washington, the ones who shared group houses and threw keg parties and went to bashes like Taste of the South? They arrived in town waving new college degrees and after an average of three years of working seventeen hours a day, seven days a week, for paltry salaries and after a round of realpolitik left their idealism reeling, many ran screaming for their home states.

Not me, though. I didn't want to leave town. I liked waking up to my job, because I didn't just clock in and clock out or push papers or get consumed by a regular, normal, elusive job that left no trace of my existence. I did understand the rules.

"Is there a third way?" I asked, only half joking.

Joffre laughed. "If you find it, let me know." The rainmaker stood. He was very tall, or perhaps I was just extremely tired. "Nice to meet you. Good luck."

"We have dinner reservations at the Watergate," my father reminded him.

"Dinner? I've eaten now." The silver dish stood empty for a second time. "Why bring a sackful of money to the Watergate when you can eat here for the price of a martini? C'mon, Boothe! You were only gonna bill me for the dinner later." And Joffre cackled as he sauntered out of the bar.

I dined at the Watergate in his stead. And well into my plate of grilled pheasant, I wondered, "How *do* we live with the selves we end up with?" You make a choice: Sleep with the devil or come to Jesus. Sometimes, it happens without you even noticing. I wondered if my moment already had come and gone, and I was firmly set upon a certain track.

I was waiting for my father at the front of the restaurant, where the padded walls were hung with florid Williamsburg paisley, when a tiny, anemic woman approached me. Her long face was pinched and her straight brown hair was parted precisely down the middle. She said in a quiet, urgent voice, "Miss Boothe." It wasn't a question. "You're a friend of John Jaures."

"Yes," I replied uneasily, glancing around, but no one was paying attention.

"I'm the agent assigned to the Mulch Committee over at the State Department."

I was dumbfounded, unused to operatives announcing themselves to me. Her bony hand clasped the sleeve of my coat as she leaned toward me and whispered, "Don't believe them!

I've told the Mulch Committee repeatedly, a cover-up is taking place! The whole truth has not come out!"

Then, just as quickly, she withdrew. She was so nondescript that even in such a public place, she disappeared easily into the chintz and the correctly attired crowd. I could only stare at the space she had occupied, and when my father came over and asked if I was ready to go, I was speechless.

8
Roulette

Jack returned from his Vegas jaunt brandishing fingernails that had been buffed and manicured. "Oh, you have got to be kidding," I said when he sauntered in to our office kitchen, wiggling his fingers at me with one hand while he grabbed a coffee cup with the other, because this was too much, even for him.

"How else does one play a ten-thousand-dollar hand of poker?" he casually replied.

"Tell me it wasn't your money," I pleaded, because Jack could count on his fingers the times he played blackjack.

"Sort of . . . not." He poured himself a cup of coffee. "The Essex boys spotted me, but I finished the night up five grand."

The Essex *boys*? I tried not to raise an eyebrow, but I am even worse at poker than Jack. He glanced at me and grinned.

"Just think of it as reconnaissance," he said.

Snarky jerk. I started to tell him about the odd run-in with the so-called State Department agent when our assistant appeared bearing a sheaf of pink message slips and still wearing her phone headset. "Kate, Donovan called about dinner; Jack, Mandy called before you got in; and both of you were nominated for a Polli." She touched her headset, which was buzzing. "Vanzetti/Boothe, please hold." She dashed back to her desk. We really needed to consider upping her salary.

A Polli! These were the highest awards in our field, and we had not won one yet. Jack shook his head. "What for? New Jersey?" he asked, puzzled.

"So, who's Maaandy?" I dragged this out in just the right tone to elicit a shudder.

"Someone I met in Vegas," Jack said casually.

Our assistant barked a laugh. "Ha! She told *me* she was your fiancée!"

"Get a little drunk?" I asked him.

"Well, she *is* a wine angel," Jack told me. "At one of the best restaurants there. It's very cool. She gets in this harness thing and when you order a bottle of wine, she rappels up and down a tower of wine bottles, and she wears a black catsuit."

"Wow." I tried not to laugh.

"It takes a lot of coordination," he insisted.

"What did she do before she was a wine angel?" I asked. "There must be some sort of training involved."

"She was the mascot of the Rio Hotel," Jack said. "Rio Rita, the Girl from Ipanema."

Now I did laugh, knowing full well that ninety percent of the men in Washington would have given Jack a high-five on this one. The other ten percent probably already knew her.

"She told me she started out in the circus," our assistant interjected. Jack shot her a look.

"What did she do in the circus?" I asked, slow and delicious.

"She—" Jack began, as if searching for the right tone, "she rode the elephant."

There were so many things I'd have liked to say, that Jaures *would* have said, at that moment, something like, "What appropriate training for a girl with our Jack!" But I didn't have to. Jack took one glimpse at my face and shook his index finger warningly.

"You know," I began, "if it was my restaurant, I'd have wine devils, too, in pits. And every night at eight and ten, the angels and devils could pelt each other with corks. What do you think?"

Jack threw a newspaper at me on his way to his desk.

Ida Tarbell struck again in the blogosphere:

Is it true that American authorities in France circulated the story that a 'terrorist hit team' was heading for Paris? This is the story that filtered through French authorities investigating the murder of John Jaures. Some voices say that from the start, the French, who have their own problems these days with their Muslims, plan to convict a person who fits the 'terrorist' profile. You put it together, dear reader; I'll pack for Gitmo, which is where I'm surely headed after telling you that if the authorities were serious about this, they'd ask themselves why a certain journalistic cabal is on the payroll of a certain nefarious company. Good thing I happen to look spectacular in orange.

I was pondering Tarbell's plain red-and-white web site when my cell phone jangled.

"Nina Scott Lee here." The brisk voice crackled.

"Oh, *God*."

"Did you know that everywhere there's a war or a little insurrection, your Essex pals are there?" Nina said, ignoring me. "I've seen the reports. Bosnia, Chechnya, Rwanda, Burma, Pakistan, Iraq, Iran, Libya, Indonesia—"

"I get the idea." I held up a hand tiredly, even though she couldn't see it.

"Doesn't that kind of bother you?"

"What? That they're making money?"

"Think about the former president, the one who's a partner at Essex," she said, quite righteously. "What hat does he wear when he tells the king of Saudi Arabia not to worry about U.S. policy in the area, especially when Essex *loves* oil deals?"

"You're sounding like one of those partisan blowhards Jaures and I always made fun of," I said.

"Do a little reading," Nina said, and she clicked off the line.

Not because Nina Scott Lee unsettled me—more because she unleashed my competitive urge to be well-informed—but I did spend the majority of the morning checking into the world of oil. It was clear, after many mind-numbing hours poring over Web sites, that oil is not bought and sold like other commodities, within the confines of traditional balances of supply and demand. It is a determinant of well-being, of national security, of power. And it was clear that the Essex Group loved the oil business. They had a majority stake in the companies that had landed recent multibillion dollar contracts in the gulf region. I rubbed my eyes and wondered who I could call on for guidance on this.

"Jack, Mandy's on the phone again!" I heard our assistant call out. Girls come, girls go, in the flow chart that is Jack's dating life.

I went back to my oil notes and began to type out an e-mail

to Crispin Mulch, who, after all, was supposed to be investigating Jaures's death: "Please tell me what progress you have made, if there are any leads or even tips that have gone nowhere. I feel that—"

"Kate." Jack stood in my doorway. "There's . . . something." He grimaced and then said, "I'm engaged, sort of."

I started laughing—I couldn't help it.

"No joke, Kate," Jack said, flushing slightly. "I really am."

"To who?"

"To Mandy."

"You mean that was true?" My jaw might have come unhinged. Engaged! For real! And to someone I didn't even know! "Were you drunk?"

"Were you when you hooked up with Donovan?" Jack snapped, unnecessarily in my opinion, considering I wasn't the one out of matrimonial control.

"I haven't 'hooked up' with him," I said, "and I certainly never said I was going to marry him."

"I'm not getting married, I'm only engaged." Jack returned to his office and slammed the door.

"This," our assistant observed to me, "is very weird."

I was too surprised to do anything other than bend my head down again over the oil industry research. The world could be spinning off its axis. Jack was engaged, and I was suddenly interested in economics, a class I had flunked three times in college.

Jack didn't leave his office for the rest of the day. I picked over my notes, clicked again and again on Ida Tarbell's blog, just in case she had posted something new. "*A certain journalistic cabal . . . a certain nefarious company . . .*" I thought about the thin woman I met at the Watergate, the one who I hadn't told Jack about yet because Mr. Engaged was currently not speaking to me. I sighed and tapped my desk with a pen.

If you don't trust your own judgment, it's a good idea to have someone whose judgment you can trust. I decided to call my former mentor, whose honesty and instincts were impeccable, and who had done a high-profile stint at the State Department a few years ago. She was at the Department of Defense these days, involved in military intelligence, an area that I wouldn't want to penetrate even on my most curious day. (Who wants to know *that* much?)

I was very careful about what I asked her. When it comes to the Pentagon, you have to phrase your questions precisely, otherwise you will end up with a useless reply. It was the way things worked over there. My mentor was a former professor—she had been hard on me in college and hadn't let up since, so she would not be one to cut me a break.

"How do you think the Mulch Committee is doing?" I asked.

"I would not know," she replied. "That is going through State."

I had expected to hear "fine" or, "I understand it's fine." Not such a direct bump across town.

"I understand State has assigned an agent to the case," I said.

She paused a long moment. "It may be that the agent was too good at her job."

"She didn't tell them what they wanted to hear," I suggested.

"That's right."

"There's a cover-up," I said, my voice rising an octave.

"Now, Kate," my former mentor began, "it may be that for . . . some people . . . your friend's death was extremely useful."

"And there's only one conclusion that is acceptable," I murmured.

"That's right." She cleared her throat. "I've got to go now. You seem to be doing just fine."

Just fine! I was practically hysterical as I hung up the phone. The sense of betrayal shuddered through my body. Crispin Mulch had sold out! They had all sold out! And if Ida Tarbell was correct—and at this point, why the hell not?—the Mulch Committee sold out literally, and of all the multinationals in the world to the Essex Group, the biggest and the baddest swinging dicks in all of politics!

Jack stared at me when I burst into his office, screaming this at the top of my lungs, which are quite expansive thanks to my marathon running.

"What are you saying?" he asked.

"We've lost. There's nobody we can trust, they know everybody—they really do have them all on their payroll! Our friend was killed by them and they want everyone to forget a murder ever happened!"

It was an undeniable fact: Washington twisted itself around and through the Essex Group so thoroughly that cells must have been joined and matched at this point.

"The committee hired some guy in Paris as a shill?" Jack's expression of astonishment grew even more intense when I told him about the thin woman at the Watergate and her confession to me.

We did not collapse in consternation; we did the one thing we did best. We immediately repaired to a bar.

All of our big moments happened in bars: when we conceived the company; when Jack met Jaures; when the tide turned during the Gold affair. We chose a wine bar—a new one, because this way we wouldn't be noticed. We already knew an inordinate number of bartenders in Washington.

The light was dim and the table small. We crouched over it, huddled with our French 75s, the real kind, thank God, because we badly needed to feel numb and fearless.

"Well, what do you think Jaures would do, up against people like that?" I demanded. "He told me he had 'a contact through a contact.' They must have set him up—"

"Kate," Jack began, "the French say he was killed by terrorists."

"Do you believe that?" I asked. "Do you really believe them?"

Jack stared at his drink. "No."

"We are becoming silent partners in a killing," I whispered.

"You don't think I know that?" he rasped back. "But what can we do?"

I leaned back against the velvet upholstery. "I have no idea." And then I quickly amended, "*Yet.*"

Jack glared at me. "Well, start thinking fast, baby, because there's so much money flowing through this thing, under the table—hell, *over* the table, they don't give a flying fuck! That's all this is about. Goddammit!" He slammed his fist against the wood, rattling our drinks. "And I *love* our fucking paycheck!" He ran his hand over his face and down his chin.

Washington wine bars do not often entertain high-running passions, so Jack attracted a few glances. But the cosseted crowd would only be really interested if we were known—

elected officials or name journalists, people they could trans-
form into a nifty anecdote. We were just political consultants,
and I hadn't been on television for quite a while. No one looked
at us for too long. Except one person.

Celerie. She was at the end of the bar, with an enormous
pink martini and several empty glasses in front of her.

"Where's human decency in this?" Jack asked me, his voice
carrying. "What are we becoming here?"

He might have gone on in the same fine, self-aware fashion,
except that Celerie had heard him. I knew, because she glared
at him in the venomous manner of the righteous drunk, and she
stormed over suddenly and jabbed a finger into his chest and
demanded, "Have you ever sucked a cock?"

God only knows what part of his soliloquy she heard, but
Jack nearly jumped out of his suit. For once, he was rendered
speechless. Celerie launched into him again: "Have" *jab* "you"
jab "ever" *jab* "sucked" *jab* "a cock" *jab-jab*.

"Uh, no, I haven't," Jack finally managed.

"Well *I* have," Celerie announced, "and let me tell you a secret: *Women . . . don't . . . like it*! But we do it. Why? Because
we want that diamond bracelet or that Mercedes. And that's
why I suck corporate cock. To keep my boss in business. You
get it?"

I did, although Jack looked mighty confused.

"Is she telling us she's blown Philip Cross?" he asked me
quietly. "Or is she saying women really *don't* like it?"

"It's what we are doing, Jack," I told my partner, and for the
first time, Celerie smiled at me.

"Now you're getting it," she said, and she stumbled back to
her perch.

Jack grimaced like he had been sucker-punched. I felt a little sorry for him. I reached over to pat his hand. "It's not every day you get engaged and *still* have your oral abilities questioned," I said.

"I'm going to be ill," Jack said.

My cell phone rang on our way out of the bar. It was our assistant, who told me that Philip Cross had called and asked me to meet him—in Brussels. He told her he had some people he wanted me to meet, part of my European duties.

"You can't go," Jack said. "Not after what we know. These guys . . ."

The wind whipped through the street while we waited for the garage attendant to bring us our cars. I pulled my coat tighter and made the one call that I knew would help. I woke a very disgruntled Joe Morgan, wherever he was at the moment, and begged him to go to Brussels.

"Jesus Christ, Katie, there'd better be a helluva dinner you're inviting me to," he grumbled, but he agreed to go. He said he was just a short train ride away, and I didn't think to ask him why.

9

A Very Small World

I had never been to Brussels. I marveled as it unfolded in a chain of traffic circles, wrapping around narrow stone buildings embellished with swirls and curves. If Washington were reconceived in art nouveau, it would look like Brussels. Here, too, were the plain-suited bureaucrats I knew so well and loved, the harried reporters, the lobbyists and foundation members, fashion-free haircuts and necks wrapped in obligatory scarves. My thoughts on other matters were dark, but the city itself I liked immediately.

Joe Morgan had messaged me to arrive early. That way, we could meet up well before I went to dinner with Cross and whoever else the Essex Group had on their devil's list. Despite the transatlantic flight and the anxiety bubbling in my stomach, I was in a pretty good mood. Morgan represented a degree of safety, I suppose, even for Jack. My partner stopped worrying long enough to regain his interest in food. I had a text message waiting for me upon landing: "Wittamer chocolates, baby; get some if you can!" I obligingly asked my cab driver to swing by the pink-sheathed chocolate shop in the swanky Sablon, just so I could dash in and buy a few raspberry truffles. Once back in the car, however, I couldn't resist. I devoured them, smoothing the centers across my tongue, one after the other, but I did message Jack a chocolate report (with a special *bonjour* to Mandy). What he sent back to me would be too impolite to repeat.

Morgan had asked me to meet him outside a restaurant in the Grand Plaz called the Golden Cup. And this was where Brussels had Washington beat, because we sadly lacked a cobblestone square in the center of gold-leafed buildings. Shops offering chocolate and lace (what else?) were squeezed side by side, and wooden platforms offering an al fresco experience were neatly laid out in front of the various restaurants. The air was brisk, but not so much that I couldn't bear a glass of champagne outside. I was fifteen minutes early, after all. No fewer than four different champagnes were offered by the glass, and the prices were better than in Paris.

I snuggled in my red wool coat, my fingers tapping the flute, took a deep breath for the first time since I had landed again in Europe, and waited for Morgan. Only a few people were about in the Grand Plaz. Did cocktail hour occur later in Belgium? The square was so hushed that the ringing of my cell phone nearly caused me to topple my glass.

It was Nina Scott Lee. Her tone of voice was arch and her breath was ragged as she inhaled a cigarette. She skipped the perfunctory stuff like "Hello" and "Sorry I called you a nasty name" and got right to the point.

"Ooo-kay, here's what I've got," she began. "Our Johnny really pissed off your Philip Cross."

"He's hardly *my* Philip Cross," I said dryly.

"Whatever," Nina plunged on. "I found the kid who Jaures hired to translate for him in Baghdad. He's living outside Paris now. He met John when our guy went to Iraq for a couple weeks—tracking deals."

She let that hang for a moment so I could appreciate her journalistic fortitude.

"Does Perun mean anything to you?" Nina asked.

"Party at a château, thrown by Essex?" I might have sounded a bit smug about my access to the Jaures notes.

"You think you might be able to find out what congressional staffers were there?" Nina asked. "The kid told me John told him that Essex was tossing out promises of six-figure contracts to all of 'em."

"In exchange for a hidden line item in the defense budget," I murmured.

"You got it!" Nina stretched the vowels, sing-song.

Graft theoretically did not happen anymore on Capitol Hill, at least not among staffers. When Congress passed ethics rules, under considerable pressure from the public, the members made damn sure that most of those rules applied to staffers, not to themselves. I really hadn't heard of any instance as blatant as what Nina alleged.

So far, we had bribes, taxpayer dollars used to purchase equipment from a Russian company even though the same equipment was made by American companies, the enormous price tag appearing to be a down payment on a potentially much bigger deal involving oil. Jaures had been right: It *did* shape into a Splendid Story. All those painstaking hours of following the money, lining up sources, mapping out routes, were worth it.

But then, Nina exhaled and added, "The kid said something else. John confronted Cross."

"What do you mean?" I went very still with dread.

"The kid says it happened in Baghdad. Johnny went there briefly right before Paris. Gets better. You want to know what he said? He told Cross, and I quote, 'This will finish you. I'm going to blow this story sky-high when I get home.'"

What a colossally stupid thing to do, I thought. It was a wonder Jaures had survived in Paris at all. He probably went to Cross to interview him, became increasingly frustrated by the unctuous protocol assumed by high-level government types (even former ones, who parsed every word of every question), and lost his temper. Jaures would've been fed up and on his way home. He might have felt like he could say anything, because what was Cross going to do to a reporter—kill him?

I closed my eyes, sitting back, allowing the horrible realization to rush over me. It was Cross all along. He might not have pulled the trigger, but he had a lot to do with the bullet.

"The kid's not going on the record. He says he's afraid something'll happen to him." Nina sounded disgusted. "I can't use a word of it." She paused. "Where are you? Washington?"

"No, I'm in—" I began, but then a shadow came over me and I heard a brusque voice say, "Miss Boothe, what a pleasure." I looked up into the hard, handsome face of Philip Cross himself.

I nearly swallowed my tongue.

"I have to go," I finally managed to Nina, who handled this marvelously. She clicked off without another word.

"You're in town earlier than I expected," Cross said, still standing. "How do you like the hotel?"

"I haven't checked in yet, but I'm sure it's lovely," I said truthfully. One thing about a corporate client: The accommodations were a far shot better than the places I stayed during campaigns. Cross looked at me for a long moment, then scanned the square. Not far from him stood a broad-shouldered man with a squat neck and a windburned face. He could have been in a tuxedo and would have still looked like a veteran of any country's special forces. Cross followed my line of sight.

"I meet with NATO when I'm here," he said. "I have to be careful. These times we're in."

I nodded like I understood—and I did, sort of, because now I knew Cross hired privateers. He checked his watch and smiled at me thinly.

"Miss Boothe, I'll see you at eight. The restaurant is called Comme Chez Soi. You'll see an old friend of yours tonight, I believe." He left me in the Grand Plaz, the bull-necked man with him.

Joe Morgan text messaged me an apology for standing me up ("couldn't be helped"), and then e-mailed me a secure document. He wrote, "The password to open this is the name of the airline we flew." Easy enough. I tapped in "British Airways." Password rejected. I tapped in "BA." Password rejected. I tried "Imperial Airways." Password rejected. I sat literally scratching my head, and then tried a simple "British." Password accepted. Leave it to a girl who got an A in copyediting to make a simple task impossible.

"I'll get there as soon as I can," Morgan had written.

The woman you met in Washington is a tool—the Mulch Committee is giving the administration cover to send someone to France to provide pressure and direction to come up with a politically correct solution to the case. She was too honest and complained about a cover-up occurring and was removed. Her replacement is connected to the State Department and used to work in the oil and energy division at the Essex Group. The

Mulch Committee has been told that the "national interest" is served by providing only one narrative: John Jaures was killed by terrorists. They have been given government and embassy hand-outs; all programs they produce are vetted and corrected by the State Department. The corporate parents of the publications are informed and on board.

My hands found my face, and I rubbed my eyes furiously. I closed the document, and sat back in the armchair of my blandly elegant hotel room, wondering how I was going to get through dinner. I was entirely on my own in this absurdly swirly Euro-capital and having dinner with the Prince of Darkness himself.

The restaurant was in a quiet square, stuffed into a narrow townhouse. Its name, Comme Chez Soi, translated as "Just Like Home"—if you happen to be a prince. Every inch was papered in Michelin style: oozing rosy light and the kind of white-clothed comfort that important people loved to surround themselves with. I was ushered to a table in the back, where Philip Cross was seated, with another gentleman who looked vaguely familiar. I stopped a second, and then wondered what fresh hell I had stumbled into.

"Hullo, young Boothe," bellowed Joe Joffre, star client of my family's law firm. He was happily plowing through a plate piled high with bread.

"Joffre here might want to do some business with us," Cross said as a waiter pulled out a chair for me. "I had no idea your father was working for him."

I suddenly realized that wasn't true at all, and that the whole reason for hauling me across the Atlantic—again—was to prove a very expensive point: *Yes, kid, there is no one I do not know or don't have access to.* He must have heard from Celerie about my questions regarding *Yellow Belly*. She might even have told him about her run-in with me and Jack. I felt very small and very stupid.

"The world intersects in strange places," I finally said, and in the brightest note possible. This pleased Cross. He even smiled.

Joffre snorted. "Sure. At the Petroleum Club at Air France." He gulped his martini. "How's your father?"

"Fine. Very well. When did you last speak with him?" This was just all my dad needed, having our business interests intertwined.

"Before Baghdad but after Amman," Joffre replied, as if I had been privy to his schedule.

"Racking up the mileage," Cross smiled.

"Aren't we all these days?" I said, and this remark earned me a sharp glance from Cross. I turned to Joffre. "How's the pipeline going?"

Joffre stopped eating bread. "Well, funny you should ask, young Boothe. Seems I've got some competition." He jerked the butter knife in Cross's direction.

I could imagine the conversation I was going to have with my father: "Did you know that *your* guy is up against *my* guy for that billion-dollar deal?"

"Not competition," Cross corrected. "A potential partner."

Joffre looked distinctly displeased, and I could have sworn I heard him mutter under his breath, "Partner—ha!" But I could be wrong. Cross appeared nonplussed.

A waiter appeared, and Cross ordered for all of us in French. This also perturbed Joffre. (Me, too, but then I had never seen the political big-swinging-dick contest extend to menu selection.) He scowled and might have uttered a reprimand except that at that moment, the sommelier appeared with a 1982 Chateau LaTour and presented it to Cross, who nodded his approval. Joffre, however, announced, "None for me. I'm going with scotch."

Tiny porcelain plates, sparkling with caviar, were set in front of us. Joffre regarded his with distaste.

"China's looking interesting these days," Joffre said suddenly. "But probably not your scene, Cross. Not like the 'stans."

"Pardon me?" I raised my eyebrows.

"Ol' Cross here has been spending his time in Azerbaijan—which I suppose isn't quite a 'stan, but hell, what's the difference? 'Jan, 'stan, po*tay*to, po*tah*to, mercenary, contractor." Joffre regarded Cross with a roguish, but not quite nice, grin. "Uzbeki*stan* is the big one."

"There are many potential opportunities," Cross agreed icily.

"And whatever you can do to sew 'em up." Joffre tossed back his scotch and waved to the waiter for another. "I appreciate the meal, Cross, but not the thug tactics."

"We can work together on the pipeline," Cross said. He was unruffled. "It's a stronger deal with the two of us in it."

Joffre lowered his narrow chin and looked at him. "I once knew a cross-eyed midget in New Orleans," he said, "and I thought, if I could pimp her out, I'd be a millionaire." He paused. "Doesn't mean I did it, though."

Cross laughed, though mirthlessly. "We can discuss this again," he suggested.

"Yeah. Round two. See you in France." Joffre sounded as confident about Cross as I was in Jack getting married. Joffre stood up and threw his napkin on his chair.

"No dinner?" Cross gestured at the next course, oysters drowned in broth.

"I've got a plane to catch," Joffre said, and then he winked at me. "Young Boothe'll tell you: I never eat in places like this." He clapped me on the shoulder as he left the restaurant in one sweeping movement.

It was just me and Philip Cross and a bottle of very expensive Bordeaux.

"Thug tactics?" I asked.

"A misunderstanding on strategy," Cross corrected.

Cross handled silverware beautifully. Most Americans, myself included, stab and saw. Europeans delicately cut individual pieces, arching the knife and barely tapping the fork. Cross ate like a European.

He made sure to keep my glass full, and although I pride myself in the regenerating powers of my liver, the wine and the warmth of the restaurant, the richness of the food, the shock of seeing Joe Joffre, and the rising need to understand just what Cross wanted me to comprehend about his world prompted me to blurt out, unceremoniously, "You know that some people say the Essex Group killed John Jaures."

Cross merely lifted his eyebrows. His media strategist had just displayed an astonishing lack of tact. He was probably reconsidering our retainer fee.

"What do you think?" he asked slowly. The waiter set before us two chocolate soufflés.

"There are also rumors about Essex's involvement in the investigation. You must be aware of the accusation out there—that Essex is doing its best to squelch any outcome that might be unfavorable to it." The wine was really making me reckless.

"Come now, Miss Boothe, what kind of a business do you think you're in? You understand how it works—I know you do." Cross touched his enameled cufflinks. "We are concerned with perception, yes, which is why we hired you. As for the unfortunate death of the reporter, we have no dog in that hunt, as the president himself might say."

"I've heard," I began slowly, "that there are a lot of mercenaries out there who could be hired for the right price."

"It was terrorists who got that reporter," Cross said firmly. "That's what the report says, and that's what the State Department and even the Mulch Committee say."

"But it could've been a mercenary," I said doggedly. "Frankly, I'm surprised the Essex Group hasn't been suspected or accused of hiring one. If I was a reporter—if I was Ida Tarbell, even—I'd be connecting those dots right now."

Cross stared at me, and my bravado wilted. His voice went dead quiet as he addressed me. "Don't you understand we are in the middle of a war? You are a smart young lady from a good family. If you keep on this track you will ruin your career." And then he gave me that empty smile of his.

The waiter cleared away our coffee cups and dessert spoons. Cross folded his napkin.

"If you are ready," he said, "I have a car outside. We'll take you back to the hotel."

He and his security team—I didn't think so. Joe Morgan once told me the way his kind stayed alive was to listen to their fear. Well, mine was screaming. So: How to get out of this?

"Will you pardon me?" I rose to my feet. I needed a moment

to think, and where else than the sanctuary of the ladies' room. Cross stood and nodded, and I wandered around the narrow, carpeted hall for the staircase that led down to the restrooms.

I was definitely out of my league. Unlike Nina Scott Lee, I am not exceptionally brave, although Jack has remarked that it can take a lot to make me panic. I have scoffed at anthrax scares, have marched my staff out of the office during bomb scares, have flown despite security alerts. But this—well, I didn't actually think Cross and his buddy were going to kill me. That would be a stretch, and it wasn't as if people wouldn't notice if I turned up dead, and— Suddenly I thought: What if this was the kind of logic that led Jaures to his death? A rush of cold horror nearly overwhelmed me, and my foot slipped on the staircase.

I lurched forward and broke my fall with my face. I heard the shouts of waiters as I tumbled head over heels, a heap of carpet burns and rent cashmere, and then I smacked my forehead on the solid wood banister, which soundly knocked me out.

I woke up in a hospital. I was told I had a hairline fracture on my left ankle and a slight concussion, with stitches sustained from my forehead meeting the banister. Trust these doctors to do the stitching right. I fingered my own pattern of Belgian lace, tiny and precise, in the clean bed with only the medical attendants around me. Undoubtedly, I had a painkiller coursing through my veins as I felt fine and light. My clothes were folded neatly and stacked on a chair near the bed.

One of the attendants called out (in Flemish, I suppose, since the vowels were lush) to a doctor, who was at my bedside presently.

"You are awake," he said in English. "How do you feel?"

I opened my mouth to speak, but couldn't with the rush going through my head. My eyes must have narrowed with dismay, because the doctor nodded.

"Yes, you will have some discomfort speaking as a result of the concussion, I am afraid."

He might as well have said I'd have trouble breathing. I glanced around, helplessly. How was I supposed to reach Jack? A text message would in no way get my point across effectively.

"I am sorry. I must to ask you a few questions," the doctor said. "Do you have insurance? Your friends did not know."

My friends! Who would those be? The doctor showed me the signature on the admittance slip. Philip Cross. "Because if you do have insurance, then we must keep you here for five days."

I raised my eyebrows. I didn't want to be stuck in a hospital in Brussels with Philip Cross knowing I was there! I needed to get out. I needed to get to Jack, I needed to talk to Nina Scott Lee and Joe Morgan and—

"If you don't," the doctor blandly continued, "as you are not a citizen of the E.U., we must release you immediately."

My exit strategy. I pulled a sad face and regretfully shook my head at the question of insurance. This did not surprise the doctor, who like most Europeans probably felt superior to the slipshod American methods of healthcare coverage. He pursed his lips and padded away. A few minutes later, an attendant brought forms for me to sign, and with my signature (and a bottle of antibiotics pressed into my hand), I was free to go.

I strode out the door. A cold night wind blasted my cheek, and I hailed a cab for Midi station.

10
Sleeping on a Volcano

Ex-boyfriends can be good for some things, especially when you know that they feel guilty about how they dumped you. I was once terribly in love. That the object of this love happened to be half-Italian was probably my mistake. He said beautiful things, wrote lovely letters, and did help me out of a jam or two. But he also broke my heart in the worst way possible: He met up with me in Paris, poured me a few glasses of champagne, and told me he was getting married. *Grazie* to you, too, pal. Nothing ever worked out for me in the City of Lights.

I hadn't spoken to him in nearly two years. I was feeling a little woozy when I reached the train station, as if I had been shot up with dozens of vaccinations. I bought a ticket for the first train pulling out. It was going to Milan.

He was the only person I knew in Italy, and I used the phone on the train to make the call. I sat in the booth, missing my toothbrush, as the night rushed past me. I listened to one ring, then two, then three.

"*Pronto?*" a woman's tired voice asked. There it was.

"May I speak to Roberto, please?" I resolutely used English, although I did know that much Italian, at least. A string of invectives poured forth from the other end of the phone. It was a little late in the hour to call Roberto, especially as we hadn't spoken in so long, but that couldn't be helped. A deeper voice, one that I recognized, murmured in the background. And then, finally, Roberto.

"Yes?"

"It's Kate." I was very businesslike.

"Ye-es," he said slowly.

"I need you to meet me in Milan," I said.

He paused. "That will be very difficult."

"Roberto," I began, but then my voice chocked up on me—from the pain, from despair, I don't know. But he heard it.

"Are you all right?" he asked.

"No." I leaned my forehead against the cold steel in the phone booth and crossed my fingers.

Roberto immediately replied, "Tell me what time you arrive."

Roberto Picchi, grandson of an Italian diplomat and the estranged son of a Chinese ambassador, purchaser of my Vespa, and generous font of information, left the ranks of journalists two years ago, having written about architecture as much as he wanted to. He joined the family business and became a diplomat. The East-West combination in Roberto's blood lent him considerable appeal to any global effort, and the Italian president had courted him especially. He was the best person to turn to now, with Morgan off sending me password-protected documents that were hard to open and the press corps filled with moles and my partner engaged and six thousand miles away.

Still, I limped off the train into Milan's stern, fascist vision of a station and wished that I had a change of clothes. I had gotten no sleep. My hair was pulled back in a stringy ponytail. I had circles under my eyes and a red gash on my forehead. Hardly the grand entrance you hope for when you see a former significant other. I couldn't even summon a jaunty smile; I was already throwing back handfuls of the painkillers the hospital gave me. A few more of these, and I was going the way of one too many radio talk-show hosts.

Roberto was at the end of the platform, waiting for me. The station was icy, the metal tracks screeched under grinding wheels, and pigeons fluttered under the soaring arches of stone, steel, and glass. His long black coat was buttoned all the way up and a striped scarf was knotted around the collar of his shirt. His hands were in his pockets. He looked exactly, devastatingly, the same. Blue-black hair falling across his almond-shaped eyes, marble-smooth skin broken by fashionable stubble. I had seen this face in Italy a thousand times, and loved it.

"Hello," I whispered, because that was all I could manage. The old thudding in my chest began again, but I chalked it up to anxiety rather than anticipation. I was not the weak-kneed type, and I had other, larger problems.

"Kate." He politely kissed my cheek. "The car is outside."

As we walked to the parking lot—me, a little more slowly than usual—he peppered me with questions: Did I have somewhere to stay? No. How long was I here? No idea. Where was my luggage? Why didn't I have a coat? Didn't I realize it was very cold in Milan?

I answered as best I could without telling him everything. Roberto must have noticed my evasiveness, because we didn't stay in the city long. He immediately hit the *autostrada*, peeling out into the concrete industrial towns that surrounded Milan, not saying much as signs flicked past us. Rho, Vanzago, Parabiago. One long, dreary stretch of jutting chimneys and walls.

We turned off the highway onto the winding local streets and into a wildly unattractive place called Canegrate. Northerners in Italy didn't seem as aesthetically inclined as their Tuscan or even their Umbrian counterparts, but then they might argue it was their proliferation of factories and no-nonsense work ethic that kept the country moving.

"I called ahead. There will be no one there but us," Roberto said, and he stopped the car at a dirty, salmon-colored building. I saw it was a wine bar, unremarkable from the outside but lit just enough on the inside for bottles to glisten from shelves. The room was warm when I entered, and my shoulders suddenly felt less tight.

The proprietor smiled and called out a greeting to Roberto. He shook my hand and quickly produced a bottle of Amarone, which he set on a tabletop painted with a vineyard scene, along with two glasses and a plate of cheese and cured meats. The man disappeared down the winding steps into the cellar. Evidently, he knew his cues.

"This is a strong drink this early in the day," I observed. I had had such a wine before, in Rome, with Roberto, and not so long ago.

"I thought we might need it," Roberto replied. He peeled off his coat and thick leather gloves, and it was then that I saw the gold ring, glinting on his finger.

"Oh," I said. What else was I supposed to say? I touched my forehead where the stitches were. The wound throbbed dully. "Who is she?"

"Her name," he said as he poured the wine, "is Francesca."

"Have I met her before?"

"No. She lived in Chianti."

"What does she do?"

"She comes from a very old family," Roberto said. "One of the oldest in Tuscany."

I got it. She was landed gentry. Well, that was the sort of person who fit into Roberto's new life; I could not begrudge him such a match, even if it sucked the breath out of me. What good would I have been at arranging flowers, meeting and greeting, fading into the background?

"How long have you been married?" I asked.

"Almost two years." He looked at me significantly. "We were married the week after I saw you in Paris."

"Oh," I said. It was curious how I didn't feel anything.

"So," Roberto said, by way of prodding me along. Of course. He did have other obligations.

"John Jaures is dead," I said.

"Yes, I read an item about it."

I didn't know how else to plunge into it, except to brush back my bangs with my fingers. He could see the skin around the stitches was mottled blue and yellow. "And my ankle," I said. "I fractured it."

"How?" Roberto's jaw tightened.

"I was trying to escape, sort of." At his look of disbelief, I gave him the scattered facts. Roberto listened intently, as he always did, leaving his glass of wine untouched. A few times, the proprietor started up the steps of the cellar, then, seeing us deep in conversation, retreated again.

Roberto reached across the table and touched the wound lightly with his fingers, sighing.

"Oh, Kate," he said. Yes, oh, Kate, what in the world had I followed blindly this time? He thought twice before he said, heavily, "My family has some money invested with the Essex Group. Many people I know have. I never met anyone from the company, but they are well-known, considered reputable. There is even a former Italian prime minister on the board— although, I suppose, we have enough former prime ministers to fill several boards."

I did not crack a smile. Once, I had adored joking about Italy's fickle political system. Roberto sighed again. He stood up, shaking the table a bit, but kept his face carefully still.

"Francesca is in Rome, packing. We are moving to Bucharest. I am to be the new ambassador to Romania," he told me. Another pause. "What can I do for you?"

There it was. I cleared my throat. "First, I need a place to stay. Cross is still in Brussels, or he might look for me in Paris. I need to be here, until I figure out the next part."

"When does that occur?" Roberto asked.

"Depends upon how smart I am," I answered, and I felt a tiny bit of my old audacity return.

Roberto, of course, knew someone in every part of Italy. He called a friend while en route to her house nearby, and nodded at me in affirmation. An elderly woman, who, Roberto informed me, had known his mother long ago, was waiting outside her door when we arrived. He spoke to her for a moment in rapid Italian (I caught only a few words, like—significantly, in reference to me—*amica*), and she waved an assent. "Mathilde will give you everything you need," he said to me as he climbed back into his car. He did not kiss my cheek good-bye, a breach of etiquette. And then he roared away on the five-hour drive back to the apartment near the Piazza Navona, where I had once lived with him.

The air was damp and chilly, hanging in a shroud over the empty street. There was no sidewalk—the buildings grew right to the edge of the street, with yellow walls and gray doors. There was no zip of a Vespa, no grinding gears of a car— just silence. The town was very near a major metropolitan area; everyone must have been at work. Then Mathilde hugged her cardigan to her and motioned for me to come in.

She didn't say much, this woman of aristocratic mien, with a high forehead and white hair clipped back from her face with two bobby pins, a look usually seen on the Upper East Side of Manhattan or the Lido in Venice. I thought perhaps she didn't speak English, but then I was in no shape to talk anymore. My ankle ached and my head hurt. She led me through an icy terracotta hallway and opened a frosted glass door to show me a large *sala* with a blazing fireplace of carved stone, a painting of Paestum above it. A sofa, covered with a dark blue flowered sheet, was in front of it, a stack of books serving as an end table. Our arrival must have interrupted her tea; an elegant, silver-trimmed cup, steam still sputtering, sat on top of the books.

She led on, through another hall off of the main room, past a dark kitchen and several closed doors, finally to one that she opened, flicking on a light. I shivered. These Europeans and their piety about resource conservation. Heat and light were two commodities of which I was happily consumptive.

It was a small room, austerely white, with a narrow bed and a hideous modern light fixture made of layers of bubbled glass. But there was also a computer and a phone on a tall, carved table that one could imagine had been used by priests to read illuminated manuscripts. With jabbing fingers, she indicated that these were for my use. She then waved for me to follow again, this time into a bathroom. She turned on the shower and pulled a towel from a cupboard. I *was* a little grungy. And I was in Italy, where there is no excuse for that.

I scrubbed myself back to civilized life. Mathilde must have slipped in, because when I emerged, my skin reddened and my stitches tender, I found a pullover and a plaid woolen skirt laid out for me. The skirt was too big, though nothing that a safety pin couldn't fix, and it fell below the knee, far longer than most of my other skirts. Nevertheless, I was presentable. Mathilde was in the main room, wire-rimmed glasses on, reading. The burning wood crackled and split. She did not so much as glance at me.

"*Dormi*!" it was not a suggestion; it was a command for me to sleep.

I obediently went back to my room. With the effort of a clean body and fresh clothes came the sudden realization that I was wrung out. This wasn't the business I had signed myself up for when Jack and I sat in a bar and drew up a plan for our own firm on a napkin when we were twenty-seven. We had even tossed a coin to decide whose name came first. I threw myself on the bed, which was thin and lumpy, and curled around the pillow, wondering if that Washington bar even existed anymore.

Mathilde kept me in virtual seclusion for a day and a half. I learned nothing about her; she didn't talk to me much, if at all, but she fed me *grana*—a hard cheese that Italian parents feed their children to make them grow big and strong—she gave me glasses of red wine (which couldn't possibly be good for someone with a concussion), and she insisted that I sleep. Despite my limited Italian, I learned that the strange desk in my bedroom had been her inheritance from a great-uncle, a man of God. The desk had once been in the Vatican. She summoned a doctor with a crumpled face to come by once to check my stitches and my ankle. By the time Jack showed up, to my surprise and delight, I had repaired considerably. Yes, my own Jack, in tiny Canegrate, an enormous leather bag weighing down his shoulder, his eyes narrow with distress behind those ridiculous purple sunglasses he liked to wear. A miraculous event had occurred: Roberto had telephoned him at our office, and civilities were exchanged all around.

Roberto must have also forewarned Mathilde, because she didn't seem at all surprised to see Jack. She escorted him to yet another closed door, which led to one more guest bedroom. The house of a thousand doors, I thought. It was quite unlike me to resist pulling open each of them, but then I had spent most of my time sleeping.

"How's Mandy?" I asked him.

"How's Donovan?" he asked me. He threw down his bag and examined my head and swollen ankle.

"This is sick," my partner said. "I can't believe Cross did this to you."

"I kind of did it to myself," I said. "Does anyone at Essex know you're here?"

"No. I don't report in." Jack shook his head at the question. "Here. I brought you a sweater." He tossed a swath of orange at me.

I caught it. Jack leaned against the fireplace mantle, his mouth pulled flat.

"I heard from a friend of yours, a journalist. Your Nina Scott Lee."

"That must have been interesting." I smiled.

Jack cocked his head. "Especially when she told me Essex has a deal with private contractors out of London, who do business with people in very shady places."

I nearly jumped off the sofa. I wanted to shout, "*I knew it!*" But I hadn't, really. It had been an educated guess. Jack held up an index finger in warning.

"I'm not saying this company is definitely part of a grand conspiracy," he said, "but—"

"But why not, Jack?" I demanded. "Obviously, there is!"

"But," Jack continued, ignoring my outburst, "I think this is just 'business as usual' for them. They see nothing wrong in their tactics. Screw it, Kate. They killed him. They had to. I'm not a journalist—I don't need three sources for verification."

Jack was right. We were sleeping on a volcano. Jack sighed and settled down on the cushions next to me. He didn't say anything for a moment while he stared out the window at the day's drizzle.

"It's so confusing," Jack said.

"Volvos with gunracks are confusing," I said. "This is not confusing."

"So what are we going to do about it?" he asked. "You've got a better imagination for getting back at people than I do."

"How do you figure that?" I asked.

"You're a girl," he said, and he carefully propped my lame ankle against his leg.

11

The Rites of Spring

One of the more loathsome creatures in politics once told a former acolyte of his that principle is okay up to a certain point, but principle is useless if you lose. The former acolyte followed this advice to the letter, ultimately selling out his boss by passing along information to me that led to the loathsome creature's dismissal. I thought about this now, as my partner slouched in a deep armchair near the fireplace. He had recovered well from jet lag—it was the Essex situation that made his eyes bloodshot.

I had commandeered the flowered sofa, resting on pillows covered with worn Venetian velvet. Mathilde must have come from old money. There was no other way to account for the faded finery scattered throughout her otherwise modest house.

Jack asked me the same question he asked last night: "What do you want to do?"

"Well," I sighed slightly, "we're not going to quit the Essex job."

Jack was surprised. We didn't have to resign or swallow our fury. There had to be a third option, and we could only explore the possibilities as long as Essex felt that we were still on their side.

"Jaures's mother sent me some notes that he had mailed to her, for safekeeping," Jack began slowly. "Apparently, when Cross joined Essex, the first thing he tried to do was score an oil contract in Azerbaijan. Don't worry"—he misinterpreted the consternation on my face (Joffre!) for confusion—"I'd never heard of the place, either. One of the pieces of the former Soviet Union. The guy running the place used to be in the KGB, and he 'ethnically cleansed' the country of Armenians. He's got oil, though, and Cross knew him from way back—they actually went to some college "world conference" together. Cross has been lobbying Congress to lift the aid embargo on Azerbaijan, and if he succeeds, Essex is positioned to get the oil contracts."

"Cross will be worth millions," I murmured. No wonder Joffre took a dig at him.

"Guess what company had some shares of the fields?" Jack seemed to glower as shadows from the fireplace hollowed out his face. "Perun."

"Why am I not surprised." I couldn't even muster outrage. All the lines intersected—Washington tangled through Essex, so why not the rest of the world, too? And why wouldn't Cross be pals with a scourge who was slapped with a label that sanitized inhumanity? It all made too *much* sense, if you really thought about it.

Kate, love—

   I heard about the bad spill you took at Comme Chez Soi— reach out and let me know if you're all right. Your mobile isn't working, and no one seems to know where you are.

—Donovan

I couldn't stop myself from sighing at the e-mail. What was I supposed to do with it? Attentive, polite Donovan, who wanted to have me to his house for dinner, but who definitively was in the ranks of the enemy. They signed his paycheck, after all, and he did have car payments to make. He dealt directly with Cross—he could be the designated emissary, trying to find me and elicit whether or not I was still on board with the team, as it were.

I couldn't bring myself to tap out a reply, not because I couldn't decide if I should trust Donovan but because I had absolutely no idea what to say to him.

I ran cross-country in high school, long ago. Some girls came of age through romances at summer camp; I grew up with each mud-splattered mile and my father yelling *"Fight harder!"* I suddenly wondered what my dad would have to say about all this. I could at least come clean with him, of all people.

I picked up Jack's cell phone, knowing I would be able to catch my father as he walked into his office, just off the Miracle Mile in Chicago.

"Hey, Dad," I began in a wavering voice when he answered, and then all of a sudden I couldn't stop myself from crying.

"You are out of your mind," my father said when I finished telling him about the Mulch Committee, the scene at Comme Chez Soi, about Joffre and Cross. "You're lucky I don't conference your mother in on this. You are out of your mind." It was becoming a catchphrase.

"I don't know about—" I said, but my father broke in, shouting.

"I do, and I am telling you now, you cannot beat the system. That's what you're talking about—and you *cannot* beat these guys. They have more money, more power, more connections, and if they think you are not with them, they will destroy you."

"I'm not talking about 'beating' them," I said.

"Then what is this about?" my father demanded. "Kate, I'm not saying these are good people, but think about what you're up against. They're playing all the angles."

"So I have to find one they aren't," I blurted.

"You are out of your mind," my father said again, his tone this time somewhere between frustration and despair. But all I could think was: "Why *can't* I find an angle? In politics, there's always one available, if you know where to look."

My father told me that there are three reasons why people do what they do: love, apathy, and greed. Veterinarians, for instance, almost uniformly love animals. Most lobbyists I knew were fairly lackadaisical about their jobs and lives; they made a decent amount and paid their mortgages. And then there were those who were in it because they craved something: money, power, property—it didn't matter which. There was always a tender spot.

My "third way," that path to salvation I would, by God, discover and wield in the name of good, would be found in that spot. Now, it is an undeniable fact that I had drifted into political consulting as a result of no particular calling. Unlike a lot of my colleagues, who calculated their way to a six-figure paycheck on the backs of overweening, unsuspecting candidates, I found the business of politics to be a handy way of merely staying solvent. The job also conferred a measure of respect if your winning percentage was high enough. I liked the command of that. I also fondly recalled the Gold affair adventures with Jaures a couple of years ago—a consultant never forgets his first major challenge. It is kind of like going to war: You remember the fear, the camaraderie, the hopelessness, and this seems to give you an edge. Jaures was one of us, and if that did not require a degree of loyalty, I don't know what did.

Of course, Cross—and, by extension, the Essex Group—had a different point of view: Loyalty to them equated loyalty to my country. It was breathtakingly audacious, and only those who believed themselves to be Masters of the Universe would be so bold as to embrace it. So, how was I to find their soft, sweet vulnerability?

I pushed back from the desk and hobbled down the hall to pour myself a glass of wine. Fog had rolled into Canegrate. Occasionally a car sputtered through the emptiness. Jack was sitting on the flowered sofa, flipping through the file of Jaures notes that he had brought with him, and muttering to himself, "Egypt, Turkey, São Tomé." He stared hard at the paper, as if by doing so he might divine some hidden knowledge.

I thought about this while I fortified myself with a crisp white wine. Egypt, Turkey, São Tomé. Emerging economies with relatively stable governments. Money could be made there. The American politicians who made decisions about our interaction with these countries were the same ones who would move on to Essex, where they would then benefit financially. It was so transparent, really. I couldn't believe I never noticed it before. Lateral moves. And what was the cost of a few lives or a few decades' worth of political fallout, in the broad scheme of things?

I must have been talking to myself out loud, because Jack glanced up from the notes and responded, "We don't know enough yet. We don't want to look like the conspiracy theorists."

Jack was right, of course. We were supposed to be competent young professionals.

I wandered back to the Internet. About a quarter of the way into my glass (it was a *very* good wine), I ran across an old article written by Nina Scott Lee, dateline Congo:

In a confetti of medicines, pens, and second-hand shirts, armed looters raged through Bunia's main marketplace. The death toll since Congo's war began in 1998 is higher—3.1 to 4.7 million—than any other ongoing war; combatants are mostly irregular militias, victims mostly unarmed, fighting has gone on for nearly five years. A century ago, most conflicts were between nations, and 90 percent of the casualties were soldiers; today almost all wars are civil, and 90 percent of victims are civilians. Now, here, money trumps kinship. Why? As one militia member, dressed in a tattered suit vest and a top hat, accessorized with the entrails of his latest victim, said "Even where you are sitting there is oil."

Oil. I tapped my fingers on the keyboard, and I considered the countries where the Secretary of State had made a point to visit several times in recent memory: Russia, Venezuela, Ecuador, Nigeria, Malaysia, Saudi Arabia. The president had trotted over for stops of his own. Most of the time, these were cast as cultural missions (the reports would read, "The president and the secretary stood on the site of a slave trading post today. . . ."), but if I was a more cynical type, I would notice that all of those places had one thing in common: oil. And if I was even more jaded, I would recall that other officials from previous administrations had also made visits of their own to these locations, and that a startling number of these former politicos had gone on to work for Essex and other multinational firms. Greed did not differentiate ideology.

Oil. The drug of choice for the developed world. This had to be my angle to play.

In the political-consulting business, winning is everything. If you come in second, even a close second, take that to your local bar and see how far it gets you. And because anything less than first means absolutely nothing, no cost is too great in order to succeed. So I swallowed any pride I might harbor—such as asking stupid questions in the course of due diligence—and I called Nina Scott Lee. She might not particularly care for me, but we were on the same side of this one.

She answered gruffly; I could hear the absurd music of a carnival in the background.

"I have been trying to find you for days!" she fairly cried. "Let me get away from these evil clowns." The tinkling horns faded. "Sorry. Some continental confection. Winterfest type of thing."

"At least one of us is having fun," I replied.

"Listen," she began urgently, "I've got a letter sent to me from an employee of Chase Manhattan Bank. Not a friend."

"How did you get it, then?" I asked, and immediately regretted doing so. Nina summoned up her indignation.

"Sometimes those of us with reputations for tough reporting get unsolicited rewards out of the blue," she snapped. "Do you know a man named Tsaldaris?"

"No clue." I jotted the name down on a scrap of paper.

"He's the second in command of a political party in Uzbekistan that's supported by the U.S. They get millions and millions in aid from us. Tsaldaris is half-Uzbeki, half-Greek. He also is the guy who's been stamping the papers of oil companies that get the drilling rights in Uzbekistan—and he's got contacts with some guys at a company called Perun. You know what that means?"

"The Essex Group loves him," I guessed, and I thought again of Joffre's chiding Cross for his "thug tactics."

"You better believe it. This letter proves that Tsaldaris just deposited a half-million dollars into a personal account at Chase. This is a public servant of a bankrupt country living off of American foreign aid."

"You don't think *he* got U.S. aid money," I said.

"No, I think this looks like what it is: a kickback. An obscene kickback. They didn't even launder it well! And if this got out, it would make it extremely difficult for the administration to go back to Congress and ask for more money for any of these oil-rich countries."

"And Jaures knew about this?" I asked.

"Oh, yeah. This story was going to be bigger than he ever expected. Can you imagine how many others were going to go down with Cross? There's nothing these international dicks wouldn't do to protect their investment."

Impetuous, stupid, brave Jaures. For that matter, impetuous, stupid *me*. I had done everything but challenge Cross to a duel in Brussels. Sweet spot, indeed! An angle on oil! My father was right—I was out of my mind.

12

The Art of Eating

Jack made dinner that night, to the infinite surprise of Mathilde. She had an onion in hand when he strode into the kitchen, plucked it out of her hand, and slightly bowed his head. "*Per favore*," he said, probably the only Italian he knew. Mathilde was utterly charmed, of course. She placed her newly freed hand at her neck and exclaimed, "Oh!"

Unlike most American kitchens, Mathilde's was stocked only with the food she thought she might consume that evening. She had glistening fresh pink rabbit meat, which Jack happily scraped off the bones and into a heap, tossing it into a pan spitting with olive oil. A handful of ground pepper, a toss of coarse French salt, a dousing with the rough red wine Mathilde had procured from a family down the street who made their own from grapes they grew in Puglia. This didn't look all that hard to *me*, but Mathilde seemed mightily impressed. Jack threw in a few dried figs he excavated from her cupboard, and Mathilde was off to fetch a very old bottle of wine that she had obviously been saving for a special occasion.

"Peasant food," Jack shrugged nonchalantly as he served up

three plates of braised rabbit with slabs of pan-fried polenta. I rolled my eyes.

"This is not peasant *wine*," Mathilde said sternly, looking at us over the rim of her glasses. We both nearly dropped our glasses.

"You speak English," I said.

"Certainly," Mathilde replied. She had the barest trill of an accent. "I *prefer* to speak Italian."

She uncorked a velvety Barolo, made by a very close friend, she said. He was dead now, an enormous loss to the winemaking world. Mathilde swirled the bright garnet liquid in her glass lovingly. The cleanness lingered on my tongue. "Intimate and discreet," Mathilde said with a little sadness.

"So you are beginning a war," she said abruptly. "I wish you luck, and I wish you fortitude." She raised her glass.

"I wasn't thinking of it that way," Jack said.

"You should. Everyone knows about the Essex Group. They are the most powerful in the world." Mathilde refilled his glass. "What do you intend to do?"

Jack looked over and gestured to me as if he was introducing me at the Vienna Ball.

"Well," I began slowly, "we're still insiders. There's a lot we could do."

Mathilde looked doubtful. "You should hurry, then," she said. "If you don't, these people have ways of finding out if you have turned on them."

Jack and I exchanged glances, which is how I know I was not the only one of us to visibly shiver at this.

The Ida Tarbell blog, evidently growing exponentially in readership (OVER 5,000 HITS SERVED EACH DAY! trilled the banner at the top of the screen), had posted a doozy:

Hey, hey, boys and girls! This is the latest from the greatest: The Mulch Committee—yes, that Special Club filled with Special People—is a farce.

The key here is the blowhard now assigned as counsel to the Mulch Committee. This political hack replaces a fine, honorable and anonymous woman who questioned the validity of the "official" explanation of John Jaures's death.

The hack appears to have been recruited by Crispin Mulch, who you might also know as the president of the Overseas Writers Association, under whose aegis the committee functions. Guess what? He did not choose alone; the Secretary of State was also a party in the decision. The hack has legendary status as an insider's insider. He is ideally situated to effect a politically salutary outcome, and he did so. "Terrorists" killed our John Jaures! How handy! Keep scaring the people, so you can keep winning elections, and kill an investigative journalist or two along the way to frighten the bejesus out of the po-faced wankers who masquerade as the press corps.

Whether Mulch and his pod people were complicit in this from the beginning is a question, except that they've already said it was "terrorists" so why do they need a fall guy?

I wanted to scream. One, however, does not indecorously erupt after a beautiful meal. Instead, I called Nina Scott Lee, who had no such qualms. I was grimly pleased. Nina, of course, had expected this turn of events. It held with what she already believed about journalists like Crispin Mulch—that there was no way they would ever compromise their status in the journalistic hierarchy. She dismissively deemed this "journalism-as-usual," and asked me, "What do you think of Ida Tarbell's blog?"

"I read it every day," I said.

"It's catchy," she agreed. "So you know this woman Mathilde Spiagare that you're staying with in Canegrate?"

"How did you know—" I began, and Nina laughed.

"I talked to Jack when he was on his way, remember? So you know who she is?"

"A friend of my ex-boyfriend's deceased mother," I said. "And how do you know her last name?"

"She's served on the staff at every major Italian embassy. She has all the connections." Nina let out a low whistle. "Nice playmate you go there. Your ex has got it going on."

"He's all that and married," I said.

"Eh, it happens. Listen," Nina's voice closed over the receiver, "you should really talk to her. She could be useful to us later on."

After hanging up with Nina, I slowly walked into the sitting room, where the gray lady in question sat, reading. Jack, from the dining table, lifted his eyebrows, and I shrugged.

"Mathilde, what else do I need to know?" I asked her. Jack coughed, probably wondering if some mystery of femininity was about to be imparted right in front of him. Mathilde slowly removed her reading glasses. There was no doubting my tone.

"Before you do anything, you need to understand who these people are, and why they do what they do," she said quietly. "The century ended in a global disorder without an obvious mechanism for either ending it or keeping it under control. There is no international system or structure, except a democratization of the means of destruction. The skirmishes of the last few years, no matter what the billing is on cable television, remain skirmishes. You haven't seen *war*. But war, anyway, is an asterisk. In a hundred years, no one is going to remember a bombing campaign in Afghanistan or an invasion of Iraq. They will remember the effects of these financial deals. That is what will be studied, because that is what will have had real impact worldwide.

"You need to block out everything you see in the media," Mathilde continued. "You need to recognize that the rules of the traditional game of international diplomacy have changed. The rise of the global industrial capitalist economy brought about different stakes."

She was right. These were the very big boys I was tangling with, and I needed to rise to the occasion. Mathilde smiled warmly. She reached over and patted me on the cheek, as I would imagine a kindly aunt would have done.

I am not exceedingly clever. I did not instantly understand everything Mathilde was telling me. But one very important component came through clearly: There was no way I could go after the entire entity known as the Essex Group. It was too vast and too ingrained in multiple governments ever to be knocked around. I would have to focus on one area: the part that Philip Cross headed up, and that Donovan worked for.

Cross, like the rest of the Essex boys, had two types of currency: money and influence. I needed to offer him a big prize.

What did Cross want: influence—and more money, presumably.

Where did Cross want it: in oil.

And what the hell did I know about oil? Not much, but I knew someone who did.

Donovan—

So sorry, I'm fine, very eager to chat. I'll ring you up as soon as I finish up some other business. And don't you owe me dinner?

—Kate

There. I pushed SEND and thought to myself, "Come to Jesus, baby, this is when you decide who you are going to be."

Mathilde drove us to the local stop on the commuter train. We would take that straight into Milan, and hop a Eurostar to Brussels from there. My luggage, presumably, remained in my hotel room there—an empty hotel room that was costing more or less three hundred dollars a day, according to exchange rate fluctuations. Jack nearly choked when he added up the "wasted" expense, even if ultimately it was billed to the Essex Group. I still wore a sock-brace over my right foot, which I'd be living with for six more weeks.

On the platform Mathilde sized us up with her flinty eyes and with a nod wished us *"buona fortuna."* She left us in the rain, waiting as the two-level silver commuter train screeched to a stop.

Jack gave me a little smile. Our few belongings were crammed into his leather bag, which seemed to have an endless capacity to expand. His father had carried it throughout college, and the years were beaten into it. Jack nudged me into the car just as the doors clattered shut behind him. The other passengers' faces were buried in their newspapers of various languages, as the train accelerated past the outer layers of Milan's suburbs, strung out like jagged teeth.

It was eight in the morning, the forty-second day after Jaures's murder. I leaned my head against the window and wished I could call my parents. They used to bounce strategies around the dinner table, whenever we all managed to eat at the same time, that is. But they had no imagination, having lost what little they had in law school. The grappling I had to do now would be a lot for their brains to wrap around.

Jack's cell phone rang. He checked the incoming number and, with a sigh, handed the phone to me. It was Lili. I was so happy to hear her voice that I almost missed what she said.

"Can you get to Dijon?" she was asking me.

"We're on our way to Brussels," I said.

"Get off at the next stop. Switch trains. Charter a flight. Whatever you have to do to get here. I'm at the Château de Gilly, the place Jaures mentions in his notes."

"What are you doing *there*?" My voice was sharp enough to prompt a questioning glance from Jack. My best friend was at the very place where Cross's scheme began.

"I'm at a wine conference. And, Kate," her voice dropped to a whisper, "I'm looking at Philip Cross *right now*. He just walked in the door."

"What is *he* doing there?" I practically shouted. Several passengers looked up from their newspapers, startled.

"I don't know, but I think you need to come."

It was the longest fifteen hours of our lives. First the commuter train was delayed because of a flood on the tracks. Then, we got off on the wrong stop. ("But it *said 'stazione'*!" Jack exclaimed, stomping around what was, indeed, the tunnel to a train station, just the wrong train station.) We had to pick our way through the dirty Milan metro system, crammed with impatient businessmen and squat old ladies and Africans in worn sweaters carrying plastic bags of cheap toys for sale. And when we were at last deposited outside the formidable Stazione Centrale, the right train station, the grounds were oddly quiet. As we walked into the station a young boy leaned against his moped and called out something—in Italian, of course, so neither of us understood. It was only when we reached the ticket counter that we realized what the kid had said: *Sciopero.* Strike.

"What does this mean?" Jack demanded, his face flushing an unbecoming shade of purple. The agent safely behind the Plexiglas information kiosk regarded Jack as if he were a slow child.

"That there are no trains."

"Until when?" Jack's fingers clenched the edge of the counter.

"We do not know," the man replied, shrugging. "It is a strike. One day, maybe three."

"How are we supposed to get anywhere?" Jack asked. I put my hand on his to stop him from tearing out his hair.

"This is why the strikes are announced in advance," the man said, "so you make other plans."

"Announced in advance," repeated Jack. "What kind of a country is this?"

"We'll catch a flight," I quickly told him.

"There is a strike there, too," the man said.

"All the airlines?" I tried to clarify.

"I do not know. Many of the airlines."

"But if the strikes are announced in advance," Jack began, looking like he dearly wished to rip through the Plexiglas, "don't you know which airlines are striking?"

"You go to Linate and find out." The man was through with us. He nodded and turned his back to prove it.

Jack decided to rent a car instead.

"How long could it take us?" he asked me as we waited for our car. "We're practically *in* Switzerland. France isn't too far. It's like Washington to New York. Switzerland can't be bigger than New Jersey. This can't take too much time."

But it could. When you have to get out of the tangle that is the Milan street system, with its no-entry areas and one-way alleys and traffic jams behind trams, and then struggle with the ring roads ("Follow the *Tangenziale* sign! *Ovest!*" I cried, although, actually I had no clue what I was yelling about) before actually hitting the highway, you can bury about two and a half hours. And, for the record, France is a lot farther from Milan than you might think.

Nine hours later, we careened down a narrow road that led into the village of Vougeot, which was shuttered and still for the night. Even the hulking château was discreet in the darkness, only a few dim lights leading the way.

The lone man at the château's front desk, yawning, was expecting us. Lili had made a reservation, and he was very sorry to inform us that, due to the limited number of rooms, he could offer us only one, not two.

We said nothing. He could have offered us space in the moat, and we would have taken it. We crept up the winding staircase that creaked with every step. We were too tired to care that the staff had put us in a magnificent suite, hung with crimson silk and sporting a bed that was quite possibly larger than my apartment. Jack was so exhausted, his hands cramped from gripping the steering wheel, that he didn't even notice, posted on the back of the carved wood door, the price of the room: six hundred euros a night. He dropped his bag, and we both collapsed on the bed.

And after all that, we missed Cross. Lili woke us up at seven the next morning to gingerly inform us that Cross had already departed. We were too catatonic to react. Now we were stuck for a six-hundred-euro bill, not to mention the little silver rental car parked in the gravel lot below, and for what?

"Well, we're in France," I tried, but Jack could only growl. We had been on a wild drive from hell, all for nothing, and now he had Mandy to call and tickets to arrange. He picked up his cell phone, glaring blackly around the pretty room, which was my cue to give him some space. We hadn't logged in all that time together on the backroads of campaigns for nothing.

I joined Lili for breakfast in the vaulted dining room. The place breathed history. The chairs were high-backed and em- broidered, and the table was set with heavy silver. Lili smiled weakly when she saw me.

"I didn't know what to do," she said as I sat down next to her. "I didn't want to talk to him. I thought I'd say too much."

"You were right," I said.

"I watched him, though. I spent almost the whole night in the parlor. I drank a lot of cognac."

"You took one for the team," I said.

"He had dinner with two other men—Americans, I think," Lili continued, handing me a basket of croissants. "Older gentle- men. It didn't go well. One of them left the table before dessert."

I told her Jack was getting ready to check out, that we were heading back to Paris.

"Don't go yet," she said, smiling. "Laurent knows the assis- tant manager here. He's arranged to let you see the guest records for the Essex party."

"Who's Laurent?" I asked absent-mindedly pulling apart a pastry in a rain of flakes.

"The jerk from Beaune," she said.

The man who broke her heart! Before I could even ask her why, Lili blushed and said, "What can I tell you? He knows wine and food."

"Everyone in your business knows food and wine," I reminded her.

"He's sexy," she said helplessly.

My best chum's bad sleeping policy aside, getting the list went a long way toward placating Jack. He greeted tall, gangly Laurent like an old pal, and even suggested we stay for lunch. After all, he argued, we were in the heart of Burgundy; we should partake in a little escargot or a bit of Bresse chicken. (The phone call with Mandy must have gone very well, I thought.) And our one-hundred-forty-euro lunch tab made the assistant manager downright amiable about opening up his guest files. He printed out the list of Americans who stayed at the château during the Essex extravaganza and gave it to us, sealed in a dark blue envelope.

Jack let out a low whistle as we read through the pages. There were no less than six congressional staffers on that list whom we knew—one of them very well, having been recruited by her for the Northern Virginia chapter of the Junior League.

"You want to check in with her?" Jack asked.

"Jack, I heard the oddest thing," Lili interrupted, while caressing Laurent's fingers. "Are you really engaged to a Vegas showgirl named Mandy?"

Laurent burst into a cheer and slapped Jack on the back.

"Mandy. Amanda, that is," Jack corrected himself. "I call her Mandy, though. Mandy."

"With an 'i' or a 'y'?" I couldn't resist asking.

"She's not a stripper, Kate," Jack said. "And why don't you tell Lili about your Harry Potter and his Car with a Name."

Typical. Not a single guy passed through my life without being subject to Jack's withering commentary. Years ago, when things were serious with me and the most handsome man in the world, Jack had really been in fine form.

Lili, however, wasn't so easily distracted. "How old is she?"

"A shooowgirl!" Laurent raised his glass.

"She also rode the elephant in the circus," I piped.

"Don't you have a phone call to make?" Jack snapped. Laughing, because I knew Jack was also Lili's friend, and she wasn't about to let the bit go, I pushed back from the table to head upstairs to the suite. I could hear Lili as I left: "She's twenty-five? Oh, an eight-year difference is *nothing*. She was wearing kneesocks when you graduated from college. It's nothing."

The mysterious force that is a hotel staff had built a fire in the stone hearth in our room while we were at lunch. I gingerly rested my right foot on the vibrantly striped cushion of a Louis XVI chair, and reached for the phone. It was very early in Washington, of course, but the congressional aide I was calling happened to work for defense appropriations. Those folks usually cruised in to their offices at the crack of dawn.

The staffer, who was just a few years older than me, was a little startled to hear my voice. It wasn't as if political consultants poked into committees very often. I told her where I was. "A gorgeous, amazing place," I gushed. "You should visit sometime."

"I did," she said. "It *is* amazing."

"When were you here?" I asked casually.

"Oh, God, I don't know. A few months ago. It was only for a couple nights. Incredible food. Check out the Armagnac selection." She paused. "So, you're calling me all the way from the *French* countryside. What's going on?"

"How much did Essex offer you?" I asked.

Of course she protested and pretended to be outraged. My ace in the hole, though, was that her ambition, as far as I knew, never was to be rich. She was part of the small but earnest legion on Capitol Hill who were truly proud to work for their country. She needed to mount some kind of denial, though. She had no idea what I was after, or whether I wanted to use what would have been an illegal offer to bury her. I let her stew for a bit, and then I reassured her.

"I'm only trying to find out what Essex was doing," I said. "You may not know this, but a reporter was about to write about the whole thing."

"Oh, *no*."

"Don't worry," I said dryly. "He's dead now."

"Oh my God. Who was it?"

Nina Scott Lee was right: memories *were* short when it came to the death of a journalist. As murders do not happen very often in political circles, my brief reminder of Jaures and his demise appropriately appalled the staffer. She was in the Junior League. Charitable thinking was part of her character.

"I took the trip because I'd never been to France," she told me miserably. "What could a few days hurt?"

"But it was in the middle of appropriations," I reminded her. "That's your busiest time."

She paused a moment. I could hear the echo of the transatlantic connection. "The chairman asked that I go," she said.

"Why didn't he come? Wasn't he invited?"

"I'm sure he was," she told me. "But if you're the chairman of defense appropriations, do you want to be seen at a French château with a bunch of Russian weapons guys and the Essex Group? Not hardly. He sent me and a few others."

"He knew what was going on," I said.

"Check his campaign contributions," she said. "Essex is in here all the time. I'm sure they've made it worth his while."

Essex wanted the hidden line item for Perun. And the staffers gathered at the Château de Gilly gala were pleased when none other than Philip Cross spoke with them individually about their futures.

"He told me I could walk off the Hill and into the Essex Group and make three hundred thousand, right off," she said. "He even gave me a potential start date."

"And you said?"

"I said, 'thanks.'"

We had him. I hung up the phone and, feeling something between triumph and anxiety, I limped out of the room to tell Jack.

13

Ready, Aim, Fire

I don't always trust my eyes. My sight is downright terrible. I've worn glasses since the age of five, a devastating thing for a kid. Boys really *don't* make passes at girls who wear glasses. My mother urged me to eat carrots; the more carrots I ingested, the better my eyes would get. So I ate carrot after carrot, and my eyes stayed exactly the same. One glorious day, at the age of thirteen, I tossed the glasses aside for contacts. On an even more glorious day at the age of thirty, I tossed aside the carrots. My eyes had never improved, and I felt betrayed. I remain firmly anticarrot to this day. My lousy nearsightedness, I've come to accept.

Corrective lenses are terrific, but sometimes these can cloud up. So, as I made my way back to the vaulted dining room (I could hear Jack and Laurent still roaring through the six-course lunch), I happened to gaze out the glazed windows at the magnificent formal gardens below. And I thought I saw the strangest sight, striding down the manicured paths, with what looked to be a shotgun slung over his shoulder. I blinked hard to clear my eyes, because the rangy man looked exactly like my father's rainmaker, Joe Joffre.

I walked as quickly as I could to the front desk. The young assistant manager was standing there, none too pleased to see me approach. He must have thought he was finished with me. "Is there a Mr. Joffre registered here?" I asked him. The man regarded me with a grim smile and said nothing. That was all I needed.

I hobbled over to the table, where my friends were loudly plowing their way through a thick cassoulet and swishing wine in their glasses. I leaned over to Lili and asked her to come with me.

"What's going on?" Jack stopped, his fork in midair.

"A little skeet shooting," I told him as Lili whispered a few words in French to Laurent.

"We're going to Brussels!" Jack called after me. "And what about your ankle?"

I wasn't really going to shoot, of course. I wouldn't have been much good like this. In her sweet manner, Lili asked for directions to the shooting grounds. She didn't remember, exactly, what Cross's dining companions had looked like, but the more I thought about it, why else would Joe Joffre be in a place like this? This was a man who made a meal out of the mixed nuts in a hotel salon. And he *had* mentioned an upcoming "round two."

It was a long walk to the gravel strip where clay pigeons were launched into the air. My ankle was very sore by the time we reached the small cluster of men in cinnamon-colored pants and padded shooting vests. There shouting "Pull!" was indeed Joe Joffre.

I waited until he fired. The pigeon split into fragments, and Joffre grinned at the sight.

"Nice one," I said, and Joffre craned his neck toward me.

"Young Boothe!" he boomed. "You shoot?"

"I do, but not today." I pointed to my braced-up ankle. I introduced Lili to him.

"Yes, hello." Joffre was polite. Then he focused again on the sky. "Pull!"

He missed, and he cursed. His French support crew snickered.

"Nice place," I said. "You eaten here yet? The restaurant is supposed to be amazing."

"It is," Joffre said.

"What brings you to France?" Lili asked.

"A little business." Joffre winked at me.

"How did it go?" I asked.

Joffre lifted his gun. "Pull!"

He missed again. The acrid smell of gun smoke filled the air. "I didn't know political consulting took you to Europe," he said. "Quite a surprise to see you in Brussels, and now here."

"My work with the Essex Group takes me to Europe," I said.

Joffre put down his gun. "Yes. I had another meeting with your guy."

"Philip Cross is hardly my 'guy'," I said.

"Sonofabitch," Joffre said. It was all I needed. A second multinational meeting gone bad, evidently.

"I *thought* I saw you at dinner last night," Lili said sweetly. "If I'd known you were friends with Kate, I'd have said hello."

"We're friends, are we?" Joffre was amused.

"We could be," I said. "Want to have a drink after you're through?" I didn't say this flirtatiously; I was quite matter-of-fact, and Joffre noticed.

"What's on your mind?" he asked, lifting the gun again.

"Something that could serve both of us well," I said. A clay pigeon shot into the air, and this time Joffre brought it down neatly.

"All right," he said. "I like a good scotch after shooting."

I was dancing onto delicate terrain. Joffre was supremely important to my family's business, so I probably should have called my father first. But a little voice that said, "Don't do anything until you've lined up everything" kept nagging at me.

I thought about the lengths the Essex Group, lead by Philip Cross, had gone to lock up an oil deal in Russia and, evidently, the former Soviet republics. I knew nothing about Russian oil deals other than that the details always seemed a little shaky and they were riddled with gangsters. I thought about all the other oil holdings the Essex Group had, mostly with Saudi Arabia.

The château had a business center. I logged on to one of the computers for some hasty research. The royal family of Saud owns all the land in Saudi Arabia. Essex Group members had the rights to the Saudi oil and set about taking care of each other. A cousin might be named as receiving a half-cent for every gallon pumped; considering that there are thirty-three gallons to a barrel, and hundreds of thousands of barrels pumped every day, that adds up nicely.

I continued to develop my primer. (What *did* we do before the Internet, anyway?) Only governments are allowed to stockpile crude oil. If you wish to become a player in the industry, you have to refine it. Therefore, if you want to make a deal you have to have a buyer that is a refinery, and you have to go to an OPEC nation. And if you are prudent about this, you realize that the lighter and sweeter the oil, the less refining it needs to become high octane (ergo, more profit). Russia's dark, sludgy mud would be very expensive to refine. Saudi Arabia's crude oil, however, is ideal.

And Saudi Arabia has very tough rules concerning its oil. Aramco, the governing body of Saudi oil, has to approve of any deal made, and the deals must be with a refinery.

Jack poked his head into the business center. "Joffre's waiting for us," he said. "Come on, gimpy." My partner offered his arm to me.

I rattled off what was going through my head: We didn't know where the Russian deal was at, the deal that Jaures evidently had died for, but we could come up with our own deal. What if Essex got its oil deal, and the best, sweetest, lightest oil at that? Oil that needed very little refining, which made it that much more profitable to the company?

"And what if we offered Cross a deal," I said, my blood beginning to race. "What if we found one and presented it to him, all shiny and irresistible?"

"I don't get it," Jack said. His cell phone was ringing again. Jack checked the number and rolled his eyes. "You need to replace your cell phone." He handed his to me.

"What's up?" It was Nina Scott Lee. Just the girl I needed.

"What happens if a Saudi oil deal is cut without Aramco knowing about it?" I asked softly so that my voice didn't bounce off the château's cream-white stone walls.

Nina considered this. "It happens all the time. There's always a Saudi prince with more oil and greed than brains who's looking to dredge up an extra fifty thousand or hundred thousand barrels a day."

"And what happens if they're caught?"

"Not much to the prince," Nina said.

"But what about the Essex Group?"

"Seriously, seriously screwed. Aramco would cut off all their other deals, go after them, things like that—" Nina stopped. I could hear her taking a drag off a cigarette. "Oh. *Interesting.*"

Jack was staring at me, both concerned and confused. "What are you doing? What are you doing?" he kept asking as we walked closer and closer to the salon, where Joffre sat, scotch in hand.

I clicked off the cell phone and gave Joffre a wide smile.

"How's the effort to get the pipeline going?" I asked him.

Joffre shook his head. "It's going to be a no-bid contract through the Defense Department."

Jack pulled out a chair for me—a first for him, but impressively done at exactly the right time—and asked the waiter, who had just approached, for two glasses of an artisanal burgundy. Part of his new knowledge of such a thing was gleaned from Laurent, I supposed. I didn't mention to my partner that this was wasted on Joffre.

"What are your chances?" I asked.

"Not good, I was told." Joffre drank long and hard from his tumbler. "Someone else wants it. Your client, as a matter of fact. And he's got more . . . friends . . . there than I do."

"Well, I'd like to talk with you about that," I said. "What would pull in more money: this pipeline of yours, or an oil deal with the Saudis?"

Joffre gave a little shrug. "That's kind of a wash, depending on the amount of oil. An oil deal is a *safer* bet than the pipeline."

"Easier money," Jack suggested.

"One might say that, but it's more boring." Joffre kicked his heels onto the embroidered chair in front of him. Out of the corner of my eye, I saw our waiter wince. Joffre's shoes were spattered with mud and clusters of gravel.

I leaned forward, already guessing the answer to what I was about to ask Joffre. "What do you think of the Essex Group?"

"Well, now, Boothe, am I talking to the savvy daughter of my lawyers, or am I talking to the little bastard doing spin control for those assholes?"

I hadn't quite expected that reply. "You had dinner with Cross here last night and he told you to back off the pipeline."

"And not very politely," Joffre said, and Jack couldn't help laughing.

"Sorry," Jack said. "Just imagining how he did it."

"What if I could get you the pipeline deal," I began, as Jack slid me a glance that declared he, in addition to my father, thought I had lost my mind. "What if I could, and do a little quid pro quo for your buddies at Essex at the same time."

Joffre raised his glass to his lips. He did not look the faintest bit surprised. I was dangling an intriguing option before him that he couldn't possibly have imagined: He could get his coveted deal and screw over a rival at the same time. What cowboy wouldn't love *that*?

"What's your problem with Essex?" Joffre asked finally. "They must be paying you well for your time."

Jack fixed a level gaze on Joffre and said, simply, "They killed our friend." This was the first time I had heard him say it, and the words made my throat catch.

"Well, now, that's a pretty serious charge," Joffre said. He waved to the waiter for another scotch. I saw the bottle that the waiter brought over: forty-year-old Bowmore.

"Would I propose this kind of thing if I didn't truly believe that?" I asked him.

"Boothe, I have no idea. I don't know you." Joffre smacked his lips as he set down the tumbler. "But I like your style. You're crazy."

I never quite considered myself crazy, but if that sealed up Joffre's interest, I'd go along with it.

"We'll need some funding," I said. "Say, a million dollars."

Jack coughed into his glass. But I knew that lobbying firms regularly shelled out a lot more than a million dollars to get a deal like the one Joffre wanted. A million bucks was nothing for a multibillion-dollar pipeline. And the chance, of course, to kick Cross in the teeth.

"What're you planning to do with it?" Joffre asked slowly.

"I'm going to set up an under-the-table oil deal," I told him, "and I'm going to offer it to Cross."

Jack held his breath—I could tell because his face went completely still. I couldn't move, either. What the hell. It was time to set *my* rules.

"You think you can pull that off?" Joffre demanded.

"As a matter of fact," I nodded, "it will be irresistible."

Joffre put down his glass—the waiter winced again as he ignored the coaster and set it directly on the ancient carved wood table next to his chair—and looked me up and down like he was evaluating merchandise.

"All right," he said. And that was that. He stood up, said something about his "people" getting the money to us, and walked out of the salon, chuckling to himself.

"What—what just happened here?" Jack asked me. I smiled at him with what I hoped was bravado, thinking, "I really hope Joffre doesn't tell my parents about this." And then we both realized that Joffre had stuck us with the hundred-euro bar tab.

We would bill it to the Essex Group, of course.

14

How'd You Like to Buy a Bridge?

By virtue of the fact that I am a girl, Jack landed the job of finding and securing our rogue oil baron. Saudi men weren't about to deal with me. He planned to start this in Washington, but both Laurent and Lili suggested Paris instead.

"Trust me on this," Lili said. "I know the places they hang out. You can't roll a nickel through some of these bars without hitting a dozen of them."

Jack had the correct clothes and the right kind of air. He would be able to pull this off. My partner tried to seem unflustered by his share of our task ahead. "I am sure this means many hours of hanging out with gorgeous women and guzzling champagne," he said solemnly before he left. "I will not fail you."

But Arab princes, played for dupes, were not known for their patience. This was a nasty part of the economic world we were waltzing into, and Jack carried enormous risk as he peeled out of the long gravel driveway. I watched the silver car disappear into the Burgundy countryside, and my hand moved to the stitches on my forehead. It was best not to dwell on this too much.

My part of the plan was decided by some quick research on Jack's part. If we were going to tempt Cross with an oil deal, we needed to create something that looked like one. Before Joffre departed the turreted confines of the Château de Gilly, he tossed out a reminder, via a scrawled note: "You need to bribe a refinery." How in the world did one find a rogue refinery?

It seemed to me logical that we'd find one in a nation that hadn't established a firm economy, where the rules would be more pliable. Accordingly, Jack thought we needed a refinery in Eastern Europe, preferably one that wasn't doing too well. "There ought to be a lot of those," he said before he plugged his request through an Internet search.

He was right. It didn't take long to come up with a list of refineries in various countries. I scanned the paper he had handed me, and found the usual suspects: Poland, Czech Republic, Slovakia, the rusting remnants of an old society. And there was one not far from the capital of Romania.

"What do you think?" I asked.

"I think you should make a call to Rome before the new Italian ambassador leaves for his post," Jack said.

In launching our little plan, I would have preferred to go straight to Rome, the city I adored. But first I had to collect my things in Brussels, and do a little more business there. We all agreed that it was of utmost importance to hustle back to Washington and resume the fine art of sucking up to our biggest client. I had been out of the loop long enough to raise suspicions.

I did sigh, though, as a taxi circled through Brussels, on the way to the bank recommended by Joffre. I would have said

Rome was perfect for this. The banks there had a reputation of being a bit loosey-goosey, kind of like the rest of the city. A common Roman tactic: taking a piece of nineteenth-century paper, printing it with an engraving that appears old, and then selling it to unsuspecting tourists as an eighteenth-century artifact. There was the time I tried to buy a cornelian ring, carved with the face of a soldier. The jewelry shop owner told me it was two thousand euros because "it is very old, from the Etruscans." The Etruscans left us shards of pottery, not rings, but when I pointed this out to the owner he did not excuse himself. He smoothly brought out a different ring "made from a coin used in the time of Julius Caesar" for me to examine. Here in Brussels, rules might be bent, too, but not nearly in a way that was so much fun.

I marched up the stone steps of the imposing bank, Joffre's letter of authorization for a transfer folded in a yellow-colored envelope safely in my purse. Despite Joffre's recommendation, I still would have thought that the promise of a wired deposit of a million dollars, along with a letter for an additional, unnamed sum, would have brought a rush of inquiries. But the director set up the account himself, his eyes barely flickering, and asked only one question: "Would you be interested in any of our off-shore options?"

This was his first, out-of-the-box offer? I tried hard not to burst out laughing, and shook my head. No sense barely skirting any more legalities than was necessary.

"We also have an office in Campione," he said. His narrow tongue darted across his teeth.

I had heard of Andorra, Lichtenstein, and I'd even visited, for three incredibly tedious days, Luxembourg. But Campione had escaped me—and I got good grades in geography. What I said to the director, though, was a vague, "Oh, really?"

"Many of our valued, exclusive clients prefer to have their accounts placed where funds are easily deposited, easily removed. This is quite discreet."

"I think that's a splendid idea," I told the director.

"Some there, some here." The little man gave me a cozy smile.

I almost rolled my eyes, until Joffre came rushing back through my mind: If you're going to take the risk, you have to educate yourself very quickly to get taken seriously in some corners of the world. Evidently, a million dollars and Campione put me on a certain level. The director sure seemed to think so. He escorted me to the door of the bank, with every step assuring me of his institution's discretion.

The air was cold and damp, even in early March. The bells of a cathedral—God only knew which one—rang out, clanging, as I returned to the hotel at last. The staff did not flicker so much as an eyelash. They handed me my suitcase, neatly repacked and collecting dust in storage, and then a fax from Jack. I waited until I was sitting at the bar, nursing a glass of champagne, to read it.

9:02 p.m.
Kate,

Okay, I'm at the Hotel Costes. Nice room. The bar makes a good cocktail, the restaurant has a decent tuna tartare but I'm paying for the scenery—if there is a God, he's a Frenchman, because he made these girls *gorgeous*. A lot of Arab-looking guys around, not too friendly, though. I am a guy.

Gotta go back down now—just came up to send you this; I'm here, it's good. Met up with a creepy p.r. guy Lili knows—he's in, get this, the music business but dabbles with these guys, hooking them up with music deals and who knows what else. He could definitely be had for a price. I had to hand over about five grand just for the promise of an introduction to a prince with oil rights. Jean-Claude (that's his name) says this is cutting through about six layers of people and that I should pay him more; ends up he wants a half-cent on every gallon. I told him, why not?

—Jack

Oh, sure, why not make a promise on a deal that didn't exist. I tried to push down the little flutter of panic. I had my own end to hold up now, and an unsteady voice was not going to help.

I planned to call Roberto from the airport. I wavered between determination and embarrassment (who enjoys calling their ex, really?). In the softly lit, golden first-class lounge, I poured myself another glass of champagne before I could do it.

"Where are you?" was Roberto's first question.

"I'm heading home," I said. "I have a lot of business to do."

I did not ask him about his wife, and he did not mention her. He did say he was leaving for Bucharest in two days, and I assumed she'd go with him. He did ask me, politely, about Jack, and seemed surprised to hear that he was in Paris.

"I'm still working for the Essex Group," I told him. Roberto considered this, and I could almost see him giving it the half-shrug that Italians must learn in the womb. I thought I had stopped breathing. So much depended on him and his good graces—or, at least, his feelings of abject guilt. Dear God, I thought as I crossed my fingers on my right hand, *please*.

I came straight out with it and told him what I needed: an oil refinery, preferably a certain one near Bucharest that had been virtually defunct for the past few years. I let the words hang in the air, thick with cigarette smoke in the airport lounge, and braced for the flurry of questions which I was sure was coming. But all Roberto said was, "You'll need a letter of revolving credit, too."

"For what?" I couldn't stop myself.

"What kind of cash do you have now?" he asked.

"A million—in Campione."

Roberto acknowledged this but advised, "You'll need the promise of more."

He couldn't have known exactly what I was up to, only that I had never before expressed an interest to him in oil refineries. This was exceedingly off-topic for me.

"I'll get it," I said.

Then the dashing new ambassador to Romania said, "Please be careful, Kate." And he hung up, just as my flight to Washington was called.

Yes, be careful, now that Jack was making promises that came easy when a deal wasn't real. I pulled out my ticket to show the smiling flight attendant and I admitted to myself, for a fluttering moment, that we were out of our league. These people, jostling for position in the greatest of great industries, where *oil* meant *mastery*, suspended the norms of civil society. Luckily, I suppose, in this world, honesty is valued less than, say, intelligence. I pushed my bag into the overhead compartment and thought, let social Darwinism work for us.

15

A Fine Routine

Washington was almost blooming. The daffodils had pushed up through the thawed soil, and the trees had begun to pop with tiny green leaves. I hardly noticed. My legs were knotted from sitting, squished, for eight hours, and my stomach felt queasy from the bad airline food. I went directly to the office from the airport, and I suppose I was fortunate that my assistant even recognized me. I had been gone a lot longer than expected.

She handed me a stack of letters, explaining, "I've sorted all the mail into fifteen, ten-inch stacks, from most to least important. Here's round one." I barely listened, so many thoughts of what I needed to do next were ripping through my mind: follow up with Roberto; touch base with Donovan; give Mulch a call. I certainly didn't hear my assistant if she warned me about what was waiting in Jack's office.

"Hello," a wispy voice said as I walked by. I stopped and leaned back in the doorway. Sitting in Jack's big chair was a very small young woman. Her hair, eyes, lips, and complexion were all the wash of unbleached wool, and she wore a long gray sweater and a short denim skirt. "I'm Mandy. Jack's fiancée."

I stared, quite rudely, I suppose, before regaining my manners. "Kate, Jack's partner." She said nothing. "So—you're a wine angel." It was all I could come up with.

"Yes."

"And you used to be in the circus." I tried to cajole her into conversation.

"Yes."

How in the world had Jack fallen for this girl? The women he dated had *tongues*, for God's sake, and usually wore cardigan sets. Zipping up and down a tower of wine seemed like a far-out job for someone so bland. Yes, that's exactly what she was.

"Well," I said, "I'll be in my office, if you need anything."

Blandy—the blandest bland who ever blanded—said, "Oh."

I backtracked to my assistant, who had been trying very hard to catch every word from her desk.

"Does Jack know about this?" I whispered.

"Not ye-et," my assistant sang out. "She said it was a surprise."

I'll bet, I chuckled to myself as I headed to my office, but first I couldn't resist asking Mandy where she was staying.

"At Jack's," she said. "I've been organizing his cupboards."

That was even better. Mess up the cupboards of a man who fancied himself a gourmet chef, who had every spice and oil exactly where he wanted them. For the first time in a while, I smiled broadly, and for real.

Like me, my grandfather was a big one for jotting lists. He wrote them up when he took a case, made a hire outside of the family, and even—legend had it—when my father wanted to marry my mother. (It was said to read: "Pro—she's a lawyer.

Con—she throws a better fastball than you.") I broke out the pen and paper myself for my last list.

First up: Philip Cross. My ignomious exit from Brussels required some damage control.

I called six wine stores before I found a bottle of 1982 La-Tour. Jack would kill me when he found out what I paid, but there was no other way to get back in Cross's good graces more elegantly or quickly. I dictated the message card: "I understand now." That's right—the girl's pique was over, and the lesson was learned. We were in a war, all right, and I wanted to have a very nice career.

My assistant informed me that Crispin Mulch had invited me to be his guest at the White House Correspondents' Dinner, an annual tribal ritual (or circle jerk, as Ida Tarbell called it on her blog) that had very little to do with being a correspondent covering the White House but quite a lot about luring the right power players to your liquor-soused table. I accepted, and with alacrity. Another item on my list: Reestablish contact with Mulch.

And then, there was Donovan. I didn't know exactly what to do with him yet. He seemed so nice. When I called him, he absolutely insisted on dinner. "You're back at last, and I want to look at you," he said. He seemed genuinely pleased to hear my voice. I knew my limits, though. I was still jet-lagged, and if I had a full meal, I would probably fall asleep in the soup. Ever the gentleman, Donovan instead offered up port and stilton at his place. "Don't worry about anything," he said. "I'll take care of you."

I was touched. I knew Jack would have rolled his eyes and gagged if he had heard. How bad could Donovan Lawrence be, a guy who had the name of two saints? I rubbed my eyes and hoped I wasn't being naive, just optimistic.

"Besides, love, you're going to need all your energy," Donovan added. "They're trying to be very nonchalant over here, but the halls are afire with what that blog came up with today."

"What blog?" I innocently asked, although I knew exactly which one.

Ida Tarbell, of course.

Grab those pens, kids, because if the company you keep says a lot about you, get ready to hear who a top doggie over at the Evil Empire is breaking bread with: a nasty feller from that cesspool known as Uzbekistan. Our Good-Time Phil (hey, the boys and girls over on the armed services committee had a swell time at the soiree in France) is palsy-walsy with an arms dealer—yep, one of those guys who ships anything anywhere, even places where no one else will, for the right price. And this playmate himself hangs with a baddie by the name of Tsaldaris. More on him when I'm not checking to see how I look in orange.

I'm not saying Good-Time Phil is dabbling in the murky world of illegal arms sales, but he knows the people. It's not much of a stretch from them to, say, the ones who will knock someone off for the right price. Now what is that excuse for a "blue-ribbon investigative committee" going to do about *this* tidbit?

This was *better* than a super-expensive mea culpa. Oh, I knew I had been reduced to a mere number on the Essex books, just like Jaures—he hadn't counted as an intrepid, brave young man with terrible taste in suits and a preference for

watery Pennsylvania beer. He was a single digit in a green column, at the bottom of which was the grand sum of Progress.
And if for one minute those old boys thought I stood in the way
of Progress as they knew it, they would not hesitate to dis-
pense with me as easily as if they eliminated Jaures. Loyalty,
after all, was paramount.

I picked up the phone. I would prove my loyalty, all right,
and in the most public way possible.

One of the more hideous wastes of airtime belonged to a man
who looked literally like death. His eyes were sunken deep in
the droopy folds of his wrinkled cheeks, his mouth a permanent
frown, his skin ashen, and his gray hair swept back to reveal
every contour of his skull. The general public paid no attention
to him, but his talk show did extremely well in the hothouse atmosphere of Washington. My own feeling is that his colleagues
in journalism and the toadies in politics watched him because
they were afraid of him. He once boasted to a senator at a cocktail party, "You'll never know how powerful I *really* am."

Naturally, I was going to appear on his show to mount my
defense of Philip Cross. The host would be sympathetic to the
plight of Cross—they often attended basketball games and
even church services together, according to Celerie, who was
smug. "I'm glad you're *finally* taking *my* advice and going on
TV about this," she said over the phone.

The studio was very cold. Who said hell was hot, I wondered
while I dropped the microphone down my suit jacket. I was on
with a nervous young man who ran one of the better known political blogs in town. He had floppy brown hair and wore a
striped shirt, which was sure to strobe through the camera lens.

The show was live-on-tape, so we would not stop for any misstatements or flubs. The host stared at his notecards and then, as the stage manager gave the count, took a long sip from his coffee mug. I thought I smelled whiskey in it.

We plunged right in. I went out of the gate with a camera-pleasing grin.

"First of all, these are ridiculous charges made up by some-one hiding behind the blogosphere. This so-called Ida Tarbell isn't a responsible journalist, and this blog is certainly not jour-nalism. I think you will agree with me."

"I do indeed." The host nodded his frightening head.

"Well, wait a minute—" the young blogger tried to interject.

"All Philip Cross has done, besides work hard for his country, sponsor a math camp for gifted students, and volunteer his time for a children's hospital, is earn a paycheck at a company that a lot of anonymous people like to snipe about," I said. "I think I know a lot about the usefulness of scapegoats, and to a lot of bloggers, the Essex Group is a useful target to hang blame on."

"I would hardly say that a company staffed by former politi-cians, that rakes in billions in government contracts around the world—no-bid contracts, by the way, the kind that any com-pany would like to get—is a scapegoat," the young man said, licking his lips several times. "It's not as if a twelve-billion-dollar company can be considered an underdog."

"Goats, dogs, what is this? A zoo?" the host sniped.

The young man turned to me. "Frankly, I'm surprised that you, of all people, are defending this company, which has highly questionable business practices. John Jaures, the journalist who was murdered in Paris, was a friend of yours, if I'm not mistaken."

I was impressed. My fellow guest was tougher than I thought. But he gave me the opening I had been waiting for.

"Yes, I am proud to have counted John Jaures as my close friend," I said. "And this is exactly my point: If I thought, for one moment, that Philip Cross and the Essex Group were truly responsible for what these bloggers are accusing them of, would I, as a close personal friend of John Jaures, be sitting here on national television, defending them?"

"Excellent point," the host said, but just before the segment was over, the young man looked at me and answered my rhetorical question: "It would make you a bitch."

"Cut, cut, cut, cut, cut!" screamed the host. "That last line is *cut*!"

I nodded my thanks and unclipped the microphone. The young man glared at me.

"You should be ashamed of what you're doing," he hissed.

I said nothing as I walked away. But even though I knew I had to do it in order to pull off my scheme, so that no one from Philip Cross to Crispin Mulch would think me errant, I did feel ashamed. It was almost as if I had betrayed Jaures. But I said what I said in order to avenge him.

The next day at work was really rotten. First, I broke a heel on my favorite pair of shoes by tripping on a steel grate, dumping coffee all over myself in the process. I looked like a disaster when I walked into my office and saw sitting at my desk, in a snug pink sweater, proper gray skirt, and the Hermès scarf that my mother gave me one Christmas just to irritate me (which I had hidden in my desk drawer), none other than Blandy herself. And not so bland anymore—she had her hair pulled back in an newly ultrablond twist, and a layer of dark-blue shadow was brushed across her eyelids.

"Oh, hello," she said. And then, to my annoyance, she did not bother to get up from my chair. Now I was the one who was speechless.

"Can you . . ." I motioned for her to move, for lack of words. Mandy grimaced a mincing smile and slowly vacated the chair. "Thank you."

"Have you talked to Jack?" she asked as she pulled herself by me. Her small-boned hand clutched the silk knot of the scarf.

"No." I threw my satchel into a corner. Let her have the damned scarf. Although now, I thought I might like to have it, after all. I kept this to myself for once. Jack could retrieve it from her when he got back from gallivanting around Paris.

All morning long, the blogging world exploded with invective from people who felt I had sold out. "Hard to believe this is the same girl who was on the right side of the Gold affair," growled one. "What Kool-Aid is she drinking?" and "Kate Boothe is *gone* and a pod person has replaced her!" were two others.

I got e-mails from shocked former allies, one of them an alternative journalist in Chicago who wondered, "What the hell happens to you people when you stay too long in Washington? What happened to the girl who once told the White House to go screw itself?" Another was a rock star who went to jail for writing subversive songs in a time of national crisis. All he could write was, "Wow, Kate, I don't know what to say to you anymore."

The worst, though, came from Jaures's younger sister. She

actually called me at the office and shouted, "Next time you decide to insult the memory of my brother on national television,
please don't say you were his friend. You saw his notes. My
mom even sent more to your stupid partner. You were not his
friend, because his *friend* would never be so disloyal."

She might as well have kicked me in the stomach. I closed
my office door and spent the next hour at my desk fighting
back tears, wondering how much I had to lose before I started
winning.

Donovan lived in a cul-de-sac of brick colonials and wooden
saltboxes. His was a magnificent colonial with a flagstone walkway leading to a wraparound porch. He was still in his suit
pants and oxford shirt when he opened the door.

"Just stilton and port," he said as I walked in. On the right,
there was a formal dining room, painted deep red, and on the
left, a sitting room with a Staffordshire porcelain collection displayed. Donovan had already set out a silver tray with the
cheese and two delicate glasses filled with ruby liquid. He
waited until I sat down on the cushion-laden sofa, and then
raised a glass to toast me.

"You were marvelous," he said. "Really, truly. Everyone
thought so. Old Cross looked like a proud papa. Even Celerie
was impressed." He clinked his glass against mine.

"You're kidding," I replied. "Even Celerie."

"You've done the impossible," Donovan laughed. He sipped
the port and then patted his lap. "Give me your feet. You poor
girl. You have been through a lot."

He tenderly rubbed my battered ankle, which had improved
considerably but still ached. Donovan bent his head, his sandy

hair falling across his forehead, while he went to work on my feet. I very nearly melted. For a fleeting moment, nothing mattered except the crunch-crunch-stroke of tension-releasing motions working through my ligaments. I groaned, and Donovan laughed again.

"You needed this," he observed. "So, how is Jack?"

"Out of town," I murmured. "Out of town, and engaged."

"Good for him," Donovan said, his thumb on my arch.

"How come you aren't married?" I squinted at him.

"Who says I'm not?" He winked at me. "I travel too much. I spend half the year on the road, in and out of places like Dubai and Saudi Arabia. Not a family-friendly schedule."

I thought about this, but not for too long. "You must meet some interesting people," I said, and then added, "an oil baron or two."

Donovan nodded, still focused on the task of my ankle. "Quite a few, yes."

He did not ask me about the dinner at Comme Chez Soi, and he did not inquire as to my inexplicable absence of a week. Donovan only said, "It's good to have you back, Kate."

16

The Magicians

Jack returned from Paris, having had his fill of the ferociously chic Hotel Costes and endless cocktails with questionable types. He came to the office straight from the airport, shouting, "Kate! Kate!" as he walked through the door, and Mandy came careening out of his office to throw her skinny arms around him. Jack nearly fell back against our assistant's desk, much to her amusement.

"I've been here for days! I wanted to surprise you!" Mandy exclaimed, nibbling his neck.

"Wow. Yes. Well. You did. I'm surprised." Jack grappled with her clinging fingers. He looked very confused, and Mandy suddenly appeared as if she might cry. "A *nice* surprise." Jack hated to see girls burst into tears. "I really like your hair."

Mandy beamed. Jack's compliment was enough to hold her while he and I convened in the kitchen. Jack was tired, but not so out of it that he couldn't whisper to me, "Thanks for the head's up."

"She's your fiancée," I retorted. "I figured you two were in contact."

My partner glared and poured himself a cup of coffee.

Jack had found an excellent candidate for our rogue prince. He was the tender age of thirty and deeply concerned about the paltry forty-thousand-a-month stipend he received from his family; after all, it cost a million annually to dock his "small" yacht on the French Riviera, and he had other expenses, too, like the apartment in London, the excursions to Bangkok, the private jet. He made ends meet by entertaining offers like the one Jack was dangling before him. He had oil rights, which meant he had options. And, he was coming to Washington later in the week.

I wondered if Donovan knew him. But what I mentioned to my partner was Roberto's advice about obtaining the promise of more than a million dollars. Jack shook his head slowly.

"Where are we going to dig up that?" he asked.

"I'm not sure yet," I said.

Jack shook his head again. "We do need to keep to a minimum the number of people we are screwing over." And on that note he headed to his office and to the arms of his delighted fiancée.

We had other clients, of course, because elections happen constantly. One of our state senate candidates in Georgia called up, very upset, because his signs were disappearing. No sooner had he pounded the stakes into the flat lawns of the suburbs than they would vanish. He told me he had figured out the mystery: "I was sitting at a Waffle House with my wife, and a man came up to me and asked if I was Rick James—I was wearing one of my 'Vote for Rick James' T-shirts. He said he saw one of my signs at his son's fraternity house in Tennessee!"

He wanted the estate of late singer Rick James to reimburse him seven hundred dollars for the missing signs. I told him we had other, more effective, courses of action. I called the local television stations, knowing that the assignment directors would love a story like this one. My candidate was happy— more exposure for him—and the local journalists were happy— nothing like a zippy little *bon mot* to chew on. Our numbers would probably spike a few percentage points after this.

And then, the realization dawned, finally: I am an illusionist. Jack is always going on about how the two of us deal with the art, not the science, of creating an appearance of substance. Building the picture frame is the necessary step and, after that, most people happily project onto the blank canvas their own desires and expectations. Likewise, we didn't have to come up with the promise of more money. We needed to project the *appearance* of a guarantee of more.

I needed to track down Joe Morgan. I had no idea where he was, if he was even still overseas, but I did have his cell-phone number.

There was mysterious clanging in the background, like a hammer hitting a rock, when he answered. I told him what I needed and why, in the barest terms, and asked him to help me.

"Jesus Christ, you're out of your mind," he said. The old refrain, again.

"You must know someone," I cajoled.

"Do you know what these guys will do to you if they find out? You will lose your home, your family, your life. Jesus Christ. Je-sus Christ!" Morgan, from wherever he was, groaned. "Are you stupid?"

"We're not going to *use* the money. We need something on letterhead. That's all."

"That's all!" Morgan ejaculated. "It is still illegal."

"I thought you said you didn't see a light at the end of this tunnel," I said. "I'm offering you a match."

"You stupid, stupid girl," Morgan roared. "You want to know about the message I intercepted yesterday, going to the secretary of state? It's from the special investigator assigned to the Jaures case by the FBI. Want to know what it says? Here. Let me read it: 'Following from highly placed contact, crime not planned or committed in Paris but possibly on orders and through an agent of the SAS.' What do you think of that?"

"That I don't believe it," I retorted. "Special Air Services? The British? Forget it."

"That means a cover-up is happening," Morgan said. "We'll never know who really killed Jaures because some people have decided we don't need to know."

I was silent for a full moment. "*I* can screw them over, Morgan. Please, trust me on this." Perhaps my voice wasn't strong enough, or he could tell that my legs suddenly gave out, because Morgan promptly hung up on me.

Fortunately for me, he must have reconsidered, because he called back about an hour later and asked, "Where are you?"

"At my office."

"Go to the bar at the Hay-Adams."

Jack went, and an hour later called me to say that a document had been delivered to him: a letter from the Bank of Shanghai that guaranteed a revolving line of credit of one hundred fifty million dollars, signed by one Bing Win.

"I called to check—he answered the phone himself," Jack said. "He told me never to call him again, but it *was* a man named Bing Win who answered. There you go."

There you go, indeed. Morgan had promised Bing Win that

I would pay tuition for his daughter for two years at Harvard. A random offer, but Morgan would know if this gesture was the accepted quid pro quo. It did give Bing Win a cover. We dipped into the Joffre fund. And I thought that this really wasn't that different than a campaign. How many times had I seen campaigns use "walking around money"—sums passed out to different groups by campaign staff to get people to the polls—or dangle the promise of a sizzling government contract in exchange for bankrolling that last-minute television commercial. It was all the same, just on a different scale.

I met with the prince in the private dining room of a wood-paneled club. I had never been there before—it cost too much to join, and women were not allowed unless they were guests of members. As I approached Jack's table, he was already well into his evening, chuckling jovially with a slight, angular man whose round face was wreathed with smiles. He was also jabbing Jack in the ribs with a sharp elbow.

"Ah-ha! My fiancée, Kate." Jack sprang to his feet and pulled out a chair for me. I flicked a glance at him. The title "fiancée" seemed to roll off his tongue easily enough, and then I realized the cold, dull fact that "business partner" would have sounded absurd to the prince; he probably would have taken it in a much more salacious way, as none in his tribe had any use for a woman in business. Well, there was nothing I could do about that now. I smiled (demurely, I hoped) and snuggled up to my "fiancé" at the candlelit table.

The prince ignored me, although he made a show of ordering a bottle of wine. It was an old vintage, and a choice that made the sommelier flush and tremble with excitement as he rushed off to the cellar to fetch it. The prince, of course, acted as non-chalant as a man who had just requested a can of Iron City beer.

"His Royal Highness," Jack said with exaggerated vowels, evidently an "inside" joke he had with the aforementioned, as his pronunciation prompted the prince to once again erupt into laughter, "has invited me to visit him in Dubai."

"Really," I said. "Is your palace there?"

"I have a small house," the prince replied with the lightest of accents—he had gone to college in Los Angeles.

"The palace is in Riyadh," Jack informed me. "His family's pad."

"Dubai is for business," the prince said, and he and Jack laughed again. Really, this fraternity-brother act was becoming a bit much.

The sommelier brought over the bottle of wine, carefully wiped free of dust, and presented it as if it were a bar of gold. The prince cast a cursory glance at it—"Yes, yes"—and with a solemn nod, the sommelier whipped out a corkscrew. He poured a little into his tasting glass, swirling the liquid and lifting it to his lips reverently. It was quite a display, especially as he closed his eyes and swallowed. Nectar of the gods. The prince didn't even try it. He nodded for the sommelier to pour for Jack and me. The elegant old man did so. Then the prince did something outrageous. He wrinkled his nose as the sommelier poured his wine and reached over for the bottle of sparkling mineral water on the table and *poured it into his wineglass*. He tasted it, looked at the ashen-faced sommelier and said, "Much better."

The poor steward literally swooned. The prince turned to me and offered me the mineral water. I covered my glass protectively with my hand.

"Oh, come on, Kate," Jack said. "His majesty says this is better."

The prince smiled nastily. I suddenly realized he was challenging us. What a miserable jerk. Maybe Jack had to play along to curry his favor, but how many times in the last couple years had I heard him say, "In these times, when we don't know what will happen from day to day, there's no excuse for drinking bad wine?" But what was I supposed to do now: Be the obnoxious Western woman and defy his masculine honor in front of the man who might hold the key to our ultimate success? I winced, and then held out my glass to the prince, who befouled it and grinned.

"So, where were you saying we should go in London?" Jack asked the prince.

"Monty's," the prince replied, his goatee rising up and down. "There are many private clubs. That is only one, but I have found it to be very . . . helpful."

"Helpful in what way?" I asked.

"Socially." The prince was almost friendly. And why wouldn't he be, as I was kowtowing to him, drinking his awful ruination.

"Quite a life you lead," Jack observed.

"Yes, well, there are those who disagree with you," the prince said. "I call those people jealous." He looked at Jack, and they laughed.

Oh, yes, it was all very funny, as the people who were angry with royalty like this man also happened to express that frustration through violence. I knew that Jack laughed because he wanted to establish camaraderie; the fact that the prince laughed drained me. Here we were, attempting to hurt a company that was lacking in moral consciousness, and we were doing so with a man who was missing the same vital part. It was entirely possible he would get slapped, too, metaphorically. We could only be so lucky.

Jack was to fly off with the prince to parts unknown. Mandy was disconsolate at his exit, but spent the rest of the day in his office, leafing through real estate magazines, stopping in my doorway every so often to inquire, button-eyed, if I thought Jack would prefer a colonial in Virginia or Maryland. I could only smile tightly.

I did have other concerns. The hard fact was that the refinery had to be locked in immediately, especially when dealing with a greedy rogue prince. And while I believed Roberto would do what he could, I did not trust the speed with which he would do it. He was an ambassador now, and married, and had responsibilities to people other than me.

It was Nina Scott Lee who went to Bucharest to follow up. She made sure to inform me that this was a bit of a sacrifice on her part. She had been there before and hated it. "Paris of the East!" she snorted. "Neglected except by snow and roaming, random dogs. This country is a place where mass tourism means you, a horse and cart, and a handful of farmers."

Nina threaded her way through clunky communist-era apartment buildings and neo-Roman wrecks, pounding through pothole after pothole and past prostitutes, beggars, men in dirty suit jackets, all of them wandering about with cigarettes in their mouths or clenched between their fingers. From Bucharest's wilted Hotel Inter-Continental, which, Nina grumbled, looked like a concrete radiator turned on its side, she left a message at the Italian embassy. Presently, the hotel concierge handed her an envelope that contained a terse note written on Roberto's personal stationary. "You have your refinery," was all he wrote, other than to ask where to forward the documentation.

"That kind of thing takes a lot of diplomatic smoothing-over. At a big personal risk for the ambassador involved. Just so you know," Nina told me.

I am not a very reflective person. I don't particularly enjoy pulling out the threads of emotions. Onward and upward, I say; never look back. But I also had not fallen in love with Roberto just because he was handsome, so I felt a twinge of regret now at doubting his capabilities.

A college professor of mine once told us the story about the ring of Gyges. Gyges was a shepherd who discovered a skeleton wearing a ring. When Gyges put on the ring, he became invisible. Gyges, then, had a choice: Did he use his invisibility for good or for evil? In the end, Gyges did awful things—he seduced a queen and murdered a king. The story was used by Socrates to pose a question to one of his students: Would any man (or woman) resist the temptation of evil if he knew his acts would not be witnessed? Socrates argued that people *were* good, even without enforcement. Roberto, for instance, didn't need me checking up on him: He was a good man and, therefore, would act accordingly. But what about Cross? Was he a Gyges? Everything I knew about him said he was. The odds on my faith in humanity were running exactly even.

17

My Party Is Better Than Yours

1:03 a.m.

Kate! You won't believe the plane ride. Three of us, in-cluding the prince, and twenty—TWENTY—girls, all of them gorgeous, supermodels, blonde, leggy, and naked. I am not joking. They said they wanted caviar; the prince said if they wanted it, they had to take off their clothes. And they did. Do you believe this? I didn't believe it—I still don't—and I was there! We drank Cristal (no water added) and ate caviar and watched these girls do things . . .

I stared at the computer screen, my eyes a bit bleary, and wondered whether there was a male friend to whom Jack might better have spilled all this, because I sure didn't want to know about it. This was what oil could buy—along with na-tional strategies, global politics, and power.

. . . the prince showed me his F-15 today. His dad bought it for him, and he keeps it in Dubai. And by the way, his house here, the one he called small? It's got fifty-five rooms!

The prince is really proud of his F-15 but kind of bummed because he says his dad won't let him have stinger missiles to put on it. Any way we can land ourselves a couple of those? Might help him out, he'll help us out. You know?

Jack

I blinked several times now. One plane ride with twenty call girls and Jack had completely lost touch with reality. We were doing an oil deal, not an arms sale on the side, just for "kicks." I wrote him back, saying as much.

I had a message from Roberto—"You'll need a hundred thousand dollars for the refinery; it was the best I could do"—and a confirmation call from Mulch about the White House Correspondents' Dinner. I made a note to myself to bring my red ball gown to the dry cleaners.

Once upon a time, there was a creature known as a muckraker, who untied the most complicated, dirty, dangerous stories of the day: octopus scandals like the ones involving Standard Oil or the railroads or coal, all of which seemed to have an arm in every facet of American life. Who among the press had the patience to do that these days? And for those souls that did, who among them had a boss with the patience to tolerate them? Shareholders never care much for investigative work, and nowadays it is much more rewarding for journalists to master a few well-timed quips (which might even vault them to their own sandbox television show) than the techniques of the tedious chipping away of falsehoods and duplicities that muckraking required. No muckraker would have attended a self-congratulatory fest like the Correspondents' Dinner. I bet Ida Tarbell wasn't going to be there.

But I would be, whooping it up with the princelings and the showmen who trotted into the White House press room, a place that plenty of journalists would give their eyeteeth to enter, and wasted their moments during televised presidential press conferences by asking, doe-eyed, "Mr. President, how has religion played a part in your decision making?" None of them were worth Jaures's half-weight in salt.

I felt very alone without Jack, or even Lili, in town with me. The latest celebrity trial was splashed over the twenty-four-hour cable networks, Congress was consumed by hearings about the proliferation of swearing among America's children, and I was worried about my dry-cleaning schedule.

Then again, the Roman emperors had games at the Colosseum to distract the populace while the empire fell and burned.

The White House Correspondents' Dinner occurred on a mild night that year. I knew the routine—the flabby vegetables and chewy chicken doused with sauce, served in the ballroom of the Washington Hilton, the more or less dull speech delivered by the president (they always attended, always grudgingly), the milling around from table to table of journalists and their decorative guests, strategically chatting and schmoozing. The whole thing lasted about three hours, and I had to smile over the sad little asparagus bundle set in front of me. The Ida Tarbell blog had nailed it earlier that day:

The letter from the White House Correspondents' Association president about the remodeling of the WH briefing room tends to prove that the whole most-anticipated-social-event-of-the-year aspect of the WHCA dinner is pretty much a combination of dumb luck and lack of other options. I am reminded that much of the WHC's lot is dull, and that committees are the underemployed's method for killing time between scandals. (Drinking also works.)

We were all just marking time, anyway. Up the hill from the Washington Hilton was a mansion that used to be the Russian embassy. Now, it was the location of *the* after-party to attend. Very few of the dinner guests ever gained admittance to the party. It was on an entirely different level. If you worked for, say, the *New York Times*, which recently had made a point not to buy a table at the actual dinner event (the bureau chief deemed it "unnecessary"), then you tried to wrangle an invite to the after-party at the Russian embassy. There, you could share a smoke with big-time actors who believed they had something significant to say, with politicians who really wanted to be actors, and with journalists whose ambition was to call them all "friends."

A wealthy media mogul hosted the event. *This* guy knew how to do it up right, I heard, and because I was a prized guest for Crispin Mulch, the latter was delighted to inform me that he had procured for me one of the hard-to-get invitations. At around eleven o'clock, Mulch looked at me and said, "Shall we, my dear?" And, like a progressive drinking party on steroids, we joined the crowd of already-tipsy event goers pushing toward the mansion gates.

At the Russian embassy we walked into a vaulted ballroom full of black-clad waiters bearing silver trays of champagne; a fountain of liquid chocolate, coating strawberries and orange slices; a slab of ice, stocked with mountains of caviar, and jagged with bottles of vodka. A doll-like cigarette girl, her lips painted into a red bow, carried a selection of cigars. I was so taken aback by this garish affair that I was literally body-checked by a striking woman ("Watch out!" she snarled) who happened to be the political anchor for a top-rated show, and collided into a young man who, to my dismay, turned out to be my blogging nemesis from the talk show.

"How is your personal ring of hell these days?" he quipped.

I did not answer. Anything I said would just be written about, anyway.

The rooms of the mansion—and the terrace, too, as far as I could see—sweated and slithered and puffed with the very people who would tell me, quite sincerely, how very sorry they were that John Jaures was no longer among them, and with their very next breath, would approach none other than Philip Cross, who was holding court in an Hermès tuxedo and brandishing a Cohiba, to brown-nose him. Cross saw me, too, and lifted his martini glass in my direction.

Cross managed to make his way to me. "I haven't had a moment to say well done."

"It's my job," I said.

"We might have to renegotiate your contract," Cross said. "There might be more we want you and Jack to take part in."

"We'd be happy to entertain the thought," I replied, and with a nod, Cross left me for the sycophantic arms of the Treasury secretary.

"Are you having a good time, my dear?" Mulch sidled over, bearing miniature crème brulées. He offered one to me, and I looked at him thoughtfully.

"You know, Crispin," I said as I cracked the harsh scars of burnt sugar with a spoon. "I've been considering turning over

John Jaures's notes to you. I think you are just the person to run with the story he had."

Mulch's eyes brightened with a greedy gleam. He tried not to appear too eager.

"That's up to you, my dear, but you know I'll do the right thing with them," he said. "Just as I have with the committee."

"Exactly," I said, and I felt proud for having prepped him so well to be spoon-fed later.

And what did Jack do while I was sucking up to the devil's minions? Jack spent a day racing cars. The prince really liked cars and, after learning that Jack owned an Alfa Romeo, wanted Jack's opinion of his fleet. So the main highway out of Dubai was shut down by police for four hours while Jack and the prince and two of his cousins zipped up and down the concrete stretch. "Got to tell you," Jack said, his voice still trembling with excitement, "out of the eight cars, I really liked the Ferrari best. The Lamborghini was faster, but tougher to handle. The Diablo"—he let out a low, appreciative whistle—"that is a hell of a car. A *hell* of a car. I'll tell you, though, the Ferrari was amazing. It's an F1. Only ten or twenty were ever made. Can you believe it? Ever made! And I drove one!"

"That's nice, dear," I said to him. It was six in the morning in Washington, an hour I never liked to be awake for. "Did you know Mandy is still here?"

"She is?" he sounded surprised.

"Yes. And she still has my scarf. Which I plan to have you return to me."

"What am I going to do?" he actually sounded a bit anguished.

"Oh, for God's sake, Jack!" I wanted to strangle him. "Finish the deal!"

* * *

I am not sure exactly how my father found out; perhaps he called Joe Joffre's office and the secretary there slipped a mention of "the business with your daughter." Whenever you are trying to cover up something or lying, the worst thing is to get caught up in the particulars of what went wrong.

"What the hell are you doing?" my father's voice, stripped of emotion, cold and unrelenting, was usually enough to cause me to dissolve into tears. It came through loud and clear on my cell phone.

"This isn't a good time to talk, Dad." I was walking from the parking lot on my way to the office. It was difficult to keep my voice steady.

"I'm sorry about that, Kate, but this is our biggest client and I would like to know what's going on."

For one who's usually so glib, I found myself at a loss. My father who, unlike my mother, never called me "Katherine" when he was angry, who encouragingly pushed me along in college when I insisted on film studies as a minor, who cheered me on when I opened my own business—my dear, darling dad now felt that I had betrayed him. I had gone behind his back with his rainmaker, and I couldn't even offer a word of explanation.

"This is very disappointing," my father said, slowly and finally. "Don't you have anything to tell me?"

"Dad, I do," I said in a whisper, "but I can't—I can't tell you yet."

"Are you asking me to simply trust you?" he asked.

"I guess I am."

I seized this escape clause with relief, but, my father said in sadness and frustration, "That's not good enough, Kate. Not as your father, not as a partner in this law firm, not as the man who put you through school. Now, for the last time, *what is going on?*"

My throat closed up, and I wished that I could tell him. From a thousand miles away, I could hear my father's sigh. His disappointment was almost palpable.

"I'm going to hang up," he said at last, "and wait for you to call me back."

I couldn't, not yet. Suddenly I realized the distinct possibility that in trying to bring down Philip Cross, Jack and I stood an excellent chance of bringing ourselves down with him. If we weren't clean and elegant about this, who—client, friends, family—would ever trust us again?

I was feeling more than a little sullen when, about a half a block away from the office, I saw my assistant standing in front of the building. Her mouth was agape. Mandy was in front of her. I strode over quickly to see what was wrong, thinking the worst: Jack might be hurt—Jack was kidnapped! But my assistant uncurled her fingers to reveal a set of keys.

"Um," she said. It was all she could manage. I wanted to shake her, and then she pointed.

Across the street, a flatbed truck was unloading a fiery red Ferrari.

"It's Jack's," my assistant finally said. "I signed for it, but it's Jack's. That's what the paper says. He has twenty-one days to register it."

"Really." My voice was flat, but only because my brain would not accept this information; my temper was rising fast.

"Is it really Jack's? Really?" Mandy chirped excitedly.

"He'll have to take you out in it," I said, and her eyes lit up.

I stormed into the office, seized the phone, and punched in his cell phone number, and, damn it, he had better answer no matter what time it was in Dubai, where he evidently was blowing frivolously through our cache. His tired voice had barely bounced across the satellites when I screamed, *"Why is there a Ferrari in front of our office?"*

"There's a—what? Oh my God. No way."

"I can't believe you bought this," I said coldly.

"Kate, I didn't. Oh my God. The prince, he asked for my address. I didn't want to give him my home address so I gave him the office. He'd asked me which car I liked best, and I said the Ferrari. Wow! Is it the F1?" Jack recovered from his shock rapidly.

"I didn't see anything about an F1. I think it's just a regular old Ferrari."

"There's no such thing as a regular old Ferrari," Jack corrected, and then he let out a whoop. "Too much! I can't decide if these guys are dangerous or if they're cool."

"Corrupt is more like it," I reminded him. For if they were not, they would not even consider the deal Jack was pretending to offer.

"Damn it, damn it, damn it." Jack let out a cathartic sigh. "At least keep it there long enough for me to see it."

"Then wrap things up soon and get back here," I said.

"That's just it," Jack said. "I think that's why he gave me the car. Why else would he do it?"

And so it had happened. The prince agreed to pump two hundred thousand barrels of oil a day for us. A barrel of oil was worth about fifty dollars. My mind swooned when I scratched out the math. Too bad it wasn't a real deal, one that we could keep. A more lucid moment later, I reminded myself that the real thing would have required a lot more money to grease the necessary people, and there would have been the small matter of such an arrangement being in flagrant violation of Aramco rules, a situation that would put us in a much more dangerous position than our real goal of ticking off the Essex Group. Yes, there *was* that.

First I called Joe Joffre to give him the update: We were a giant step closer to his natural-gas pipeline. And then I called the offices of the Essex Group to track down Donovan.

18
All at One Aim

I told Donovan to shift into business gear, that what I was about to lay out for him had nothing to do with a social chat or a romantic interlude. Donovan understood, but then, he is British.

"How about a jog, then?" he asked. "Your ankle is better, right? And the weather is perfect for it."

I've never been keen on running with people. My high school cross-country team was one thing, the thirty thousand people in the New York City Marathon was another. A running partner had never been my style, especially for a business meeting. Nevertheless, Donovan and I went running, and at the first pink streak of morning light that Saturday. It was a marvelous way to ruin a potentially lovely weekend.

He met me at the park benches in Old Towne Alexandria and suggested the tow path from there to Mount Vernon and back again.

"But that's twenty miles," I said.

"We'll stop if you get tired." He was jumping up and down in tiny striped shorts and a T-shirt that said WHEN THE RAPTURE COMES, CAN I HAVE YOUR CAR?

"You're a funky guy, Donovan," I said. "I never would've guessed it."

The air was light and misting, and we were seven miles in before Donovan asked what I wanted to meet about. My ankle felt fine—we weren't running very fast—but I was having a tough time talking and breathing. It had been a long time since I'd logged twenty miles.

"Well . . . I've got . . . a proposal," I panted. Donovan, flush and practically running circles, said, "Love, let's stop and stretch. What do you think?"

I am a traditional runner, ergo, I hated stretching. This is why Jack dragged me to yoga when he could. But because I was desperate for a breather, I agreed. We were near the river; I could hear the water rushing by. Donovan squatted down on his left knee to stretch his right groin and hamstring. I did the same, and promptly felt something in my groin pull and snap. I fell over, groaning.

"You're really bad off," Donovan said.

"Who's going to believe I got a groin injury while *running*?" I wailed.

Donovan propped my arm around his sweaty shoulder—he must have felt guilty—and helped me walk a few blocks. So while I limped, once again, and gasped and otherwise operated under diminishing charms, I drew out my case for him. Luckily the pain kept me from having any anxiety about lying convincingly.

"A client with an oil deal in exchange for the pipeline?" Donovan repeated. "What's the catch?"

I thought fast. I told him my client had spent some of his childhood in Afghanistan. His parents were missionaries who had gone there to teach children how to read. The more I talked, the more I liked the story I was fabricating.

"He knows it's risky, but he really wants to give something back. He loves the Afghan people—he was friends with the late mujahedeen, Abdul Haq."

"Sure, sure." Donovan recognized the name. I could walk on my own now, so I pulled my arm off him in order to look him in the eye while I talked.

"He's got a lot of businesses. One of them is with an NGO there. He imports rugs and earrings and other items made by Afghan women."

"That's remarkable," Donovan said.

"So he really wants the pipeline contract, and he's willing to do what he has to do to get it."

I didn't feel bad at all as I spun this out. It was for a good reason.

"What do you want to do? You should bring it to Cross, you know," Donovan said.

"Will you help me?" I asked.

"Of course, my little cripple. Whatever you need."

The only way I would ever be invited to a state dinner would be if I landed a presidential campaign and my guy won. There was to be one the following Thursday night to honor the prime minister of Great Britain, an event everyone wanted to attend because it promised lots of glamour; English actresses, Booker Prize winners, glitter like that, as opposed to, oh, say, a state dinner for the president of Bulgaria. There was none better than one thrown for the British.

Cross would be there. "Naturally," Celerie informed me

while handing over the latest contract, which bumped our retainer up another twenty grand a month. "They're old British stock. They came over on the Mayflower."

"Indentured servants," Donovan cracked as he walked by us in the hall. Celerie gasped a denial, but Donovan kept moving with a grin. He wasn't invited to the dinner. As he explained it to me, he was staff, not gentry.

I had a good idea of how to find out where Cross would be afterward, though. I asked Celerie. "I'm sure you know," I said. "You're his confidante."

"Oh, he likes to go from the White House to the bar at the Hay-Adams," Celerie said happily. "He likes to smoke a cigar with the boys."

So that was where I made certain to post myself the next Thursday. I had an unlit cigar in my hand and a half-consumed glass of cognac on the table in front of me. Sure enough, Cross entered, guffawing at a comment by the editor of the *Washington Post*. He saw me, and came over.

"Trim your cigar?" Cross asked me. That line was a first for me, but I assented. Normally I am not a girl who smokes cigars—an affectation that can curry favor in this world, where women in black miniskirts who pretend to enjoy stogies can vault into the stratosphere, mostly as glorified pets—but I could make it through half of one.

"How was the state dinner?" I asked.

"Dull," Cross said. "So, when are you going to dump that partner of yours and come aboard with us?"

Cross *was* good, I'd give him that. "You did just sign us to a whole new contract," I reminded him. "I'd hate to waste your money."

"The two of you are exactly the team to have on board."

"I do have a proposal for you, though," I said, exhaling and desperately trying not to cough.

"What is it?" Cross puffed.

"I'd rather not discuss it here," I demurred, and Cross nodded.

"In that case, come on by the office, won't you? Call my assistant, set it up for tomorrow." He was very friendly. It could have been the Cohiba, or maybe the alcohol, or perhaps the White House chief of staff who had swiveled his way over to us at that moment. Whatever it was, it worked. I swept up my silk skirt to make the quickest possible exit.

I asked for a meeting the very next day. The rest of the Washington uber-elite was staggering into work, shaggy with hangovers, but the only substance bothering me was the thick aftertaste of the cigar. I tried slamming cup after cup of espresso made from Jack's fancy machine, to no avail.

I was given twenty minutes with Cross in the late afternoon. I felt proactive, so I stopped in Jack's office before I left. Mandy was sitting there, as she always did, leafing through a bridal magazine as big as a doorstop.

"What do you think, Kate," she began. "Cream or white?"

"Whatever shade best suits you," I replied. "I have a very important meeting today. I'd love to wear my scarf."

Mandy reddened and narrowed her eyes, but she reached into Jack's desk and pulled out the Hermès scarf in question. "Thank you," I sang, and without waiting for Mandy's reaction, I tied the ends around my neck, and left.

Two sides of Cross's office were glass; I could see tiny yellow-green leaves sprouting from branches on the trees four floors below. It would not be long before tulips and daffodils bloomed, the legacy of a beautification project from the sixties, and allergy season would begin, one problem of living in a city with plants brought in from all fifty states and from around the world. From Cross's conservatory, however, it seemed like a bright beginning.

His desk was a metal behemoth, and there were two black leather chairs in front of it. Against the far wall were a green velvet sofa and two plush armchairs pushed together around a cherry coffee table. I hated offices like this, which left the seating arrangement ambiguous. I also found it show-offy. There was no doubt that the man was in the majors. He wouldn't have a little room like mine.

I decided to sit across from his desk. I didn't want this meeting to devolve into obsequiousness or prattle. I wanted a deal.

And then, the man himself entered. "Kate," he said, reaching for my hand and kissing my cheek. "I've asked Donovan to join us. I hope you don't mind."

"Of course not," I said. It was the best possible turn of events, and I wondered if Donovan had insisted on it.

Cross pointed to the couch, but I said, "I really like this chair. Chippendale?" It was an attempt to hold my position through flattery, and it didn't work.

"My wife picked them out. I'll let her know you approve of her taste." Cross sat in one of the armchairs and motioned again to the couch. I lost Round One to him.

Donovan opened the door with a quick jerk. He raised his eyebrows at me and grinned. He was carrying a leather-bound notepad and a gold-rimmed pen. Cross urged him to the sofa as well.

"Hello, hello." Donovan asked, winking at me. "Trying to marry us off?"

"Whatever I can do to push you two kids along," Cross laughed genially.

I decided to get right to it, before I ruined everything by groaning. Cross was already primed. His fingertips rested together expectantly.

"I had a very interesting thing happen to me in Europe," I began. "I have a client there who has access to something you want, and you have access to something he wants."

I paused. Cross did not so much as flicker an eyelash.

"He has recently finalized an oil ... arrangement ... that should make him a lot of money. He's looking for investors."

"What kind of investors?" Cross asked.

"I would say the discreet kind that doesn't mind making roughly a hundred grand a day."

Cross allowed a small smile. "And you think I have access to that kind of person?"

"I think," I began slowly, "that *you* are that kind of person. And I think that you don't get involved in anything that doesn't make sense on several different levels."

"I'm glad to know you hold me in such high regard," Cross said. Under that layer of flint, he might have been pleased.

"He's not interested in keeping the controlling interest he holds—he's got his eye on something else. He wants the contract for the natural gas pipeline through Afghanistan." I shrugged. "Don't ask me why; I've explained all the risks, and he's well aware of them. He likes a challenge, I guess."

"The Defense Department plans to award that as a no-bid contract," Cross said, "probably to one of our companies."

"But it's not guaranteed return," I argued.

"Look at what's happened in Iraq," Donovan said.

"Then why does your client want the pipeline so badly?" Cross wanted to know.

"A promise he made to his dying parents. They were missionaries there until well into their eighties. My client grew up there for a time, and he feels a responsibility to the country."

"Come now, Kate, people don't go risking it all to build a pipeline out of the goodness of their hearts," Cross said.

"He's not risking it all. He wants the government contract. That's worth a lot of money. He also wants to do something he feels good about. That's worth more to him than money." I shrugged again. "I'm not asking you to understand him. *I* don't understand him. I think he's kind of crazy, if you want to know the truth. But he's a client, and I try to make my clients happy."

Cross looked at Donovan, who pursed his lips and cleared his throat and said, "If you don't mind me pointing out, I would gamble on oil, but not on anything running through Afghanistan. Too many variables and no loyalty—you can't even buy it. Kate's client—and pardon me for saying so, Kate—is a wee bit nutty for wanting the pipeline so badly."

"He's allowing his personal life to rule a business decision," Cross said.

"Indeed," Donovan agreed.

"Are you?" Cross was direct and quick with him. I sucked in a breath.

"Philip, I beg your pardon, but I think I have compiled a record here that speaks for itself," Donovan returned with infinite politeness.

Cross considered this. "Kate," he said, "are you going to tell us the name of this client of yours?"

"I haven't told my client your name, and I won't tell you his," I said.

"How very IRA of you." Cross tapped his fingertips together.

"Ask around," I said rashly. "I'm sure you'll hear all the right things."

A false report is always born out of the collective perceptions that pre-exist it. When I placed the glossy folder in his hands, I knew it was only as believable as whatever assumptions Cross had previously held.

"I'll take a look at your report," Cross said without opening the folder. "And I'll get back to you."

Donovan smiled encouragingly at me as I left the office. I promised myself that I would take him out for a nice dinner, and that I would figure out some way he could avoid getting burned by this.

There is nothing more excruciating than waiting for a deal to close. I tossed paper clips around my office and threw pencils at the door until my assistant suggested I leave. I couldn't go running. All I could do was hope that Donovan swung by Cross's office and chatted him up again. I refused, point-blank, to think, "What if this doesn't work?" Oh my God, imagine what Joe Joffre would do to me if he was out a million dollars for nothing—what he would do to my father! I then tried to drink wine, but found it made me sick. It was a bad day, indeed, when neither running nor drinking were viable options.

And then, Joffre called me. I was just about to leave the office for the evening when his voice came through the phone, loud as usual: "Your bastard boy Cross gave me a little call."

"About what?" Fear creeped up my neck.

"Wanted to know if I was the guy going through you to get my pipeline."

"Oh God." My heart dropped and my head felt hot, because I hadn't counted on that. I should have, but this crucial detail slipped,

"I didn't tell that sonofabitch anything," Joffre said. "I trust, though, that you've kept my name off the necessary papers and that you're a smart enough girl to know how to cover your tracks."

I opened my mouth and hoped my voice would be there. "Yes. Of course." But I was barely listening, my mind a news ticker. What if Cross had checked with Aramco, too? What if he was playing by the standard conventions? What if the curiosity of Aramco had been aroused by a phone call, or a dropped word or two? They could put a stop to everything right now, and— *oh God!*

"Get me that pipeline, and things will be just fine." Joffre was civil, but short.

And that was when I realized it was entirely possible that the worst had indeed happened. Either I was about to render Cross's reputation beyond repair, or he was about to destroy me. I had just handed him all the tools necessary.

19
The Resistance

If it hadn't been for Nina Scott Lee, I might have felt very sorry for myself. She called that afternoon, and being the sharp reporter that she was, she immediately noticed the edge of panic in my voice.

"Calm down," she said. "I think I've got a good idea who pulled the trigger. Still trying to figure out who delivered payment, but it's all narrowing. What's the problem?"

I wiped my eyes and steadied my voice. "I think I left a major hole in my grand plan."

"Nah." She exhaled a drag loudly. "You're betting on greed, and there's nothing safer."

"No, it's really serious." And I explained that I needed somehow, some way, to find someone to vouch for the oil deal, and fast.

Nina sent me an e-mail later. There wasn't much use hanging around the office, waiting interminably, so why didn't I come to Paris? Wait for Jack there, wrap up loose ends, continue to plan, and figure out the next move with the rest of "the resistance," as she nimbly called us.

"I'll even pick you up from the airport," Nina said when she called to follow up. "I've got something I want you to see, and I've got something else to tell you, and I sure as hell am not doing it over the phone or the Internet."

I had hoped never to see Paris again. The lacy bridges, the proper ladies, the yellow streetlights. To me, there was nothing romantic or appealing about Paris, where I did not have good karma. But there I was again, with a green canvas weekend bag slung over my shoulder, heading into a wine bar with Nina. Her hair was wilder than ever, and as soon as she saw me she asked, "When does your famous Jack show up?"

Nina insisted on having a few rounds before revealing whatever information she was harboring. We were in a neighborhood on the outskirts of Paris, and I did not notice at first the man sitting at the bar, hunched over a small glass of bright green liquid. It was only after he demanded, "What the hell are you doing here?" that I looked his way. Joe Morgan himself, a bit more stubbled around the chin and his face partially hidden by a frayed woolen hat, but the cheeks splotched red and white from climate swings and whiskey swigs were his, all the same.

"I might ask you the same question," I replied. Morgan held open his hands and shrugged, but said nothing. He was eyeing Nina, who had come up behind me, the ever-present cigarette dangling from her lips.

"How's business?" she asked. Trust her to successfully play spot-the-spy.

Morgan looked her up and down and turned to me. "Who the hell is this?"

"Nina Scott Lee." She glared right back at him.

"She killed a man in Peru," I told Morgan. Nina cocked an

eyebrow—I was only repeating what Lili had told me; I never had checked with her—but Morgan said smoothly, "So have I."

"Oh, swell." What a pair. I pulled a chair toward Morgan and planted myself. Nina remained standing.

"How long have you been here?" I asked him.

Morgan coughed a laugh. "Kate, you know better than to ask that."

"If that's absinthe, you should be careful," Nina said to him, tossing her long curly hair over her shoulder, a gesture I had never seen her do.

"Thanks," Morgan said dryly. "I know how to handle a drink, even a banned one."

Nina opened her mouth to begin again. So that I might stave off another round, I leaned on one arm across the bar and grinned at Morgan, who looked increasingly miserable, and asked, "So, Joe, what do you think of oil?"

"If you're going to make money, it's the way to go," he said, sliding me an indecipherable glance.

"I did a story on oil once," Nina said. "In the Congo." She tapped a cigarette on the bar before lighting it and waited for Morgan to respond.

"Like I said, Katie, it's the new world order." He spoke to me but he looked at her. "You watch: In twenty years, we're not going to talk about ideology. A lot of people are going to have to rethink their careers when that happens, but it *will* happen. It'll be about economic competition, some regional struggles, an ethnic rivalry or two, but it won't be about ideology. And all this can be yours, with the proliferation of modern weapons thrown in, to boot."

Well, there you go. Smart Morgan. No wonder he was giving

me a head start on this one. By hooking me up with a Chinese bank manager, he was putting both of us in his debt. He was gambling on his financial future. I had to admire guts like that. He finished his drink and waved for another.

"You gotta get out, man," Nina observed.

Morgan stared at her wordlessly, and then he turned to me again. "Good luck with what you're trying to pull off. I hope you can do it. Understand, though, you're going to be in real trouble if you don't pull it off real fast. And these guys—*all* of them—when they're fucked around with, they don't mess around in return."

He rapidly threw back the tiny glass the bartender had refreshed, adjusted his hat, and walked out. Nina stared after him and shook her head.

"How do you know him?" she asked.

"I've known Joe forever," I said. Suddenly Nina appeared to regard me a bit more highly. Still, the slightest shiver tingled the back of my neck. I firmly decided to chalk it up to the unseasonably damp chill in the night air, even if the bar crackled with electric heat.

Nina showed me the photograph then. She opened a thick folder, pulling out her jotted and blotched notes and maps. "And there's this, now." She handed me a picture of Jaures's body, was taken just after he had been pulled from the Seine. He was in the charcoal suit he'd had made in China, and his heavy black shoes; twine was tied three times around his ankles, which splayed out on the ground. His hands, clenched in rigor mortis, were stained with mud from the river and were also bound tightly with twine. His mouth had fallen open in an expression of angry surprise. His eyes were covered with a piece of cloth. "The police put that over him," Nina said.

I could only put my hand over my mouth. He *did* see the bullet coming. Jaures, Jaures, Jaures, my lovely amazing friend, so brave and reckless.

"Don't cry," Nina said, "don't cry. I haven't cried since 1979."

I looked at the photograph again, and I remembered why it was worth gambling everything.

Lili opened the creaking door to her apartment; she had insisted the best place for me to stay would be hers. The apartment was delicately fragrant with lavender, and the yellowing shades on milk-glass lamps made the room glow warmly. It was almost soothing. She had good cheese waiting on a flowered plate she had rescued from a flea market and lip-smacking dry white wine in the refrigerator. "I broke up with Laurent again," she said as she leaned against her sink, rinsing two glasses. "He's a communist."

Nina lit another cigarette and laughed. I pointed out to Lili that she didn't usually care about a lover's politics.

"No, but in the true spirit of communism, he shares everything. In Reims, when we went champagne tasting, he was visited by the different mothers of two of his children, and neither woman seemed thrilled to meet me. Anyway, he is the devil."

She looked at us. "Tell me, what's the plan?"

I almost laughed, because there wasn't so much a *plan* at this moment as a reliance on hope and fate. What a position to be in! How many times could I throw salt over my shoulder, rap my knuckles on wooden tabletops, or steadfastly avoid walking under ladders? That was what I had been reduced to—along with murmuring prayerful things to the divinity that I wasn't quite sure was there, but I sure as hell wasn't taking any chances.

"We've got a small problem," Nina told her, "but we should wait for this Jack to show up."

Nina fixed an eye on me, and leaned back in the frail caned chair that Lili had plucked from the maze of the Marché aux Puces de Montreuil. It cracked ominously. "You know," she began, "I never killed a man in Peru."

Lili stopped her pour in midair and looked over at me. I felt hot; I was not up to this today, I thought. But Nina went on: "I didn't kill a man, but I *could* have. He was wicked, nasty. I meant to kill him. I would have liked to do it. Someone else did it before I got the chance."

"You went to jail, though," I murmured.

Nina shrugged. "Briefly. I got out. And, look, he's still dead. One less evil person polluting the world."

"You're cavalier about a Peruvian jail," Lili observed.

"It *was* cold," Nina admitted. "But one good thing did come out of it: Everyone hears this story about me, and very few people mess with me after that."

Lili pushed her way to the table with the glasses. And I thought, cruelty cannot be finessed; war cannot be civilized; and sometimes, evil demands retribution if we are to retain our sense of what it means to be human. That set of convictions was sealed by the fact that my friend was dead, and my belief that the man responsible for it deserved to be punished. It wasn't as if I was wracked with guilt over what I was about to do to Cross, the man I was about to sucker-punch. What I was doing, in many ways, was so much less than what I *could* do.

Jack showed up an hour later, wearing a wild purple tie and carrying a bag full of Iranian caviar. He hugged and kissed Lili enthusiastically. To Nina Scott Lee, he gave a full-blown smooch on the lips. "Hel-lo, mama!" he cried out. Evidently, the time with the prince had affected him profoundly.

Then he saw me. He drew me close, but he could tell something was wrong. I told him about our new snag, and suddenly he looked very, very tired. He sagged in an armchair by the shuttered window, his face drawn and splotchy, and I felt the urge to wrap my arms around him again.

"Oh, come on, guys," Nina said, lighting another cigarette, "don't be so pathetic. You're talking to Ida Tarbell here. There's always a way."

I jerked my head. "*You're* Ida Tarbell?"

Nina grinned. "How do you think I get the truth out?"

A general once told me that there is no truth in war; there are only versions of reality. This same general thought that laying one's life on the line for an idea was "an awfully high price to pay for conjecture." I always wondered how he bumped up through the ranks, with theories like those.

Nina's moonlighting job as a blogger made her privy to the varying degrees of truth that we were up against. She had lists of reporters and news organizations that had been paid bribes not only by the Essex Group but by other multinationals. A few of them, incredibly, were even listed on Essex's official payroll. She knew about "fake" bloggers, frontmen (and women) for corporate and ideological interests. I decided that I would never again believe outright anything I read—even in respected publications. I should have always held that opinion; how many times had I planted a story or a spin on a story myself? I was very good at it, too.

Nina had once dished out a flashy line, about when she was out on maneuvers with Hezbollah. I decided now to call her on it. "If you really know people with Hezbollah," I said, "then go through them and get me someone to connect with."

"I don't think you understand what you're—" she started to say, though unusually hesitant.

"I need someone," I boldly interrupted, "who is respected and who can vouch for the deal. Someone who can spread the word, very carefully, in the right circles."

"Without the Saudis finding out." Nina was flat in her disbelief. "This is how people get killed, you know."

"So figure out who you can make it work with. Someone who you trust."

Nina fairly snorted. "Trust!"

In the end, she did serve someone up. She thought he might be an arms dealer, "but there's really no solid way to know," a turn of phrase that left Jack shuddering. He was a man in the import business, whom Nina heard had worked the Beirut-Milan and the Beirut-Brussels routes for years with the quiet approval of most of the powers-that-be. "He's got a real knack for paying off the right person, whatever he's involved in, because he's plenty wealthy," Nina said. "And you've got something he wants."

"Forget it," Jack cut her off. "No way Kate does that."

"He wants to meet with U.S. operatives to do a little business," Nina explained. "He's willing to meet with you to discuss it all, Kate, if you can make an introduction to Joe Morgan for him."

"Morgan will do it," I said quickly, because, I figured, why wouldn't he? Didn't everyone in his line of work want to know an arms dealer or two?

I overestimated his eagerness to expand. When I tracked him down on his cell, Morgan was decidedly not interested.

"I am not a worm," he said. "I will not be held out as bait."

But he did a little checking around, found out Nina's contact was actually quite a player in international business and intrigue, and changed his mind. He even promised to meet me in Beirut if that was what it took, although I wasn't exactly banking on it. He was supposed to meet me in Brussels, too.

Jack and I flew back to Washington, where we would wait for Nina to arrange everything. There was still no word from Cross, although I did have a message from Donovan: "Patience, love, patience." Jack got to grapple in the office kitchen with a falsely teary, manipulative Mandy, seductive in a lacy blouse and a lemon-colored skirt, as she cuddled him in a desperate way. The prince had checked in several times to find out where the deal stood, and I had two messages from my father, three from my mother, and one from Joe Joffre.

"We might need a lot of Valium before the end of all this," Jack grumbled. "This is far worse than any Election Night I've been through."

But trust the girl moonlighting as Ida Tarbell. Nina came through within twenty-four hours. She messaged me: "He wants to talk to you." Seven-and-a-half-hour time difference or not, I rang up Nina's contact in Lebanon.

The conversation was short. The man had a gruff voice and spoke English with a French accent, and he asked me to come to him. Jack and I weren't sure this was the wisest course of action, but what other alternative did we have?

* * *

I had been to the Middle East once before, on a cruise in the eastern Mediterranean with my parents (and probably the only thirteen-year-old American in Israel who wasn't Jewish), and it was not an area of the world I longed to visit again. Morgan swore on all that he held holy he would, absolutely, meet up with me. And Jack—well, Jack took up smoking, an activity that was not going to go over well with his yoga instructor, and as he lit up his third cigarette in thirty minutes while driving me to the airport, he turned to me and said, "I sure as hell wish you knew how to shoot something other than skeet."

20

The Wild, Wild East

So that was how I ended up in Beirut, in the mountains, in the house of an alleged arms dealer, with a bottle of good tequila.

He was quite appreciative of it, as he was having a dinner party that night, and he poured some for each guest. I demurred, having had a very bad experience with tequila in college. The man then turned to me and asked if I would like to see his olive trees.

It was dark, of course, but checking out trees wasn't really the point. While the other guests retired to the drawing room, swilling tequila and arguing about corruption in the Lebanese parliament, I followed my host through an antique-lined hallway and out stained-glass doors to a terrace.

The view was lovely. I could see the twinkling lights of Beirut below, and a breeze ruffled through the leaves of the olive trees. But the full effect was lost—it was very black in the mountains, and quiet. I could hear the man strike a match as he lit a cigar.

"I won't ask how old you are," he began, "but did you know

that every seven years, your cells have entirely regenerated themselves?"

"No-o," I answered slowly.

"Depending on your age, you could be about to become a whole new person."

"I am turning thirty-five in a few months," I admitted, and I thought, what an odd subject to discuss.

The man raised his glass of tequila—I caught the barest glimmer of it in the moonlight—and said, "To the new you."

I laughed and raised my champagne. The new me. Well, I was declaring myself rather loudly, considering my current course of action. I might have continued pondering this, except that the man leaned in toward my ear, placing a heavy palm on the left side of my face, and said very softly, "You certainly are daring." He reached over and patted my leg. "Or else, you're trouble."

"I'm just a political consultant," I replied.

I could see the end of the cigar glowing, and the outline of the man's jaw. He was smiling.

"Perhaps I should go in for politics, then," he said, but he made no further move toward me. "Now, princess, what can we do together that makes sense?"

I took another swallow of champagne to bolster my confidence, and launched into an explanation of what I needed. The man listened intently, the cigar burning orange then red as he sucked and puffed through a quarter of it.

"The Gulf Arabs often come here," he said. "I know many of them." He tapped the ashes onto the terrace. "I also know a few people at the U.S. embassy."

"Really?" I couldn't hold back my surprise.

"This is a very small town," he explained. "Find out who

your Essex man knows at the embassy, and I'll get word to that person that your deal is authentic."

"And what happens to you when they find out it's not?"

"'They'?" he repeated. "The Saudis or the Americans?"

"Both."

"The Saudis will never know, and the Americans will think this is simply business as usual in Lebanon." The man might have shrugged in the darkness. "Now, what's in it for me?"

I told him that Joe Morgan was on his way to Beirut, ready to meet with him tomorrow at a certain beachside café. The man seemed pleased by this—he enjoyed the coffee there very much. He put his arm around me as he finished his cigar, and said in his gravelly voice, "This is the start of a much longer conversation."

To the end, he was quite the gentleman. He escorted me to the front door, his dog padding after us, and gave me a bottle of olive oil—"from my trees," he pointed out—and two bottles of Lebanese wine. And as the door closed behind me, I heard laughter ripple out from the drawing room as one guest exclaimed, "Guns make it all so confusing."

I took care of business in the Beirut airport. Snag a couple of scarves for Lili and Nina, check in with Jack to find out who Cross might know at the American embassy. In the insular world Cross moved in, it turned out he knew the ambassador's deputy. I sent a text message to the man and headed for Paris.

It was as I was running through Charles de Gaulle airport to catch my connecting flight to Washington that I heard my name being shouted. When I turned, there was Roberto, looking at me with astonishment.

"What are you doing here?" he asked. A tall woman stood

next to him, with long, wavy chestnut hair and large brown eyes. She was gorgeous.

"I'm on my way back from Beirut," I replied. His jaw—and her's—dropped. "What about you?"

"We're—we're on our way back home," he replied.

"In that case, *au revoir*, Roberto, and *merci!*" Waving, I dashed to catch the shuttle bus to the next terminal.

Jack did his best not to interrogate me too much. Besides, I brought him a bag of the Lebanese cardamom-infused coffee, duty free. He couldn't help asking what the man was like. "Oddly handsome, an excellent host, very witty," I said while Jack dumped several scoops of coffee into our fancy espresso machine.

"A lot happens in Beirut," I said absent-mindedly. "A lot of politics. Maybe we should open a satellite office there."

Jack glanced at me sideways. "That's like opening an office on a pirate ship. Check with Bluebeard to find out when pillaging is scheduled, on your way to get your morning newspaper."

"Lebanon wasn't anything like that," I retorted. "It wasn't anything like what we've read about."

"What is?" Jack sighed.

We hadn't heard yet from Cross. We had our own ways of dealing with the anxiety of waiting. Jack re-reorganized his cupboards, trying to put back what Mandy had altered. I went running and then suddenly started painting everything in sight. I painted my bedroom blue with brown spots, like an eggshell. I had to be desperate to do this—I don't like birds all that much. I even planted flowers in terracotta pots on my terrace, which hadn't seen this much attention since last Fourth of July, when I hosted a margarita party in between campaign gigs.

A week passed. I dragged myself into the office, past the brimming face of Mandy—"Jack, do you want me to pick up more bagels for you?" she cooed—and fell in a heap in my desk chair. I glared at the phone. My assistant, worried, brought me coffee, a first, as I abhorred having her paycheck go toward that service. The smell was comforting, though. We were still running through the stock I had brought from Beirut, and I thought of the man and wondered if he was at the seaside café now with Morgan.

The phone rang. I refused to look at it. For all I knew, it was my father calling to disown me, which he had every right to do. But presently I heard the vinegary sweet words: "Philip Cross for you, Kate!"

Jack came into my office as I picked up the phone, his face dry and cold and the color of bone. "Mr. Cross," I said.

"Kate," he said, and he hurtled straight into business. "I read through your proposal. A nice offer."

Oh, no, I thought, my heart stopping, there is a 'but' coming. Jack's eyes widened because he recognized the panic flitting across my face.

"But it appears there is something missing."

Here it was. I braced myself.

"I don't see any mention of Saudi Aramco."

"No, you don't," I said. Walk the walk, I bolstered myself; wouldn't Nina Scott Lee bluster *her* way through this? And in a voice much stronger than I felt, I added, "I think you know what I mean."

If I had learned anything during the past few months, I

should have been more careful about what I said over a telephone. What if Cross was taping this? What if he had someone listening in? But I was banking on the power of avarice—and the compelling need of every man to be The Big Man.

"What do you say," Cross began slowly, "a cent for every gallon?"

My hand wrapped tighter around the phone; I scarcely believed the words, because Nina Scott Lee was *right*, bless her. A payoff! He wanted a payoff, and this on top of what he was likely to get as a commission (if Essex did things that way, and why not, in a multimillion-dollar deal) as well as credit at his firm. But I should have understood that the lure of becoming a millionaire several times over was doubly tempting when one regarded his own smarts so highly. Why wouldn't Cross think he could outthink the Saudis *and* the Essex Group?

"I can't do that," I said. "But I am authorized to offer you a half-cent for every gallon." I knew nothing about the secret oil-grafting world, but somewhere in the furrows of my brain that figure popped up, a vague memory of what Jack had offered the public relations man in Paris. My partner, holding his breath, nodded enthusiastically.

"That sounds agreeable," Cross said. "I'll take the deal in here, and I will make sure your client gets his pipeline."

"How soon will we know?" I asked. "Before any paperwork makes its way over to you, I need to show him that the pipeline contract is under way."

"Kate, are you with us? Are you really *with* us?"

The question was so unexpected that I had to try hard not to stammer. "Yes."

"Very good. If you're our girl in Washington, then, what do you think?"

"I think you'll get this done in record time," I said, and I added a chuckle just to show we were chums.

Jack finally exhaled when I hung up. "Well?"

"We're in," I said.

Before I could scream with relief, Jack held up a finger and warned, "Not until the papers are signed. And when they are, I'm taking my Ferrari out for a spin, right past Donovan's house."

In a marvelous display of How Things Work, Joffre, who set up a separate and relatively untraceable company specifically for this deal, got his pipeline by the close of the business day. I was in awe. Here is what happened: Cross called the secretary of defense, a man who recently was appointed to the post and who had been with the Essex Group for the previous five years. The secretary called the undersecretary in charge, and just like that, with no fanfare or press attention and right under the noses of the poor sods on Capitol Hill, the eight-billion-dollar pipeline contract was awarded to Hephaestus Enterprises (a nod to my ankle injury, Joffre had said). Joffre's office got the call by five-thirty. I had just witnessed a most valuable—and expensive—lesson in how to do big-time political business.

I called my father at five forty-five. "Dad, I—"

"Two weeks, Kate? You took two weeks to come up with an explanation?"

Two weeks! Two weeks was nothing! If only he knew I had been to Paris and back, and to Beirut and back! Two weeks?

"Call Joe Joffre now," I said, and I hung up on my father, the first time I'd ever done so. I did not know what else to do.

Whatever his reservations, my father must have telephoned Joffre, because he very quickly called me back. He was a little unsure of how to proceed. Ultimately he could only say, "Kate, I am not sure what you think you are trying to pull."

I decided to ignore this lack of faith. "I need some work done, and very fast. By tomorrow morning. Can you do it?"

"I don't know . . ."

"I'll fax everything to you. Just turn it into legalese and get it back to me by seven tomorrow. And make sure it's not on your stationary. Plain paper, okay?"

"Well, all right, I think . . ."

My father was still confused, but I had no time to enlighten him. I shouted for my assistant, and I sent Morgan a text message: Get out of Beirut now.

21
Terrible Angels

Donovan swung by the office to both properly appreciate Jack's Ferrari and to take me out to celebrate the deal. "My girl, my girl, my girl!" he shouted, smiling broadly at me. He came equipped with a bottle of champagne for us and a pair of racing gloves for Jack.

"To drive your new baby in style," Donovan said, and Jack was very pleased. I watched the two of them on the sidewalk at twilight, the time of day when Washington is most beautiful. My partner was accepting gloves to go with a car he could not ethically keep from a decent young man whose career we might have surreptitiously ruined.

Donovan was so kind and so thrilled—we had pulled off a deal together, and it was enough to make Celerie Worth seethe!—that I looked at him across the table at the little bistro on the edge of Old Towne Alexandria and cringed inwardly.

"Maybe we shouldn't be so tough on Celerie," I murmured.

Donovan cocked an eyebrow. "You're not losing your sense of humor now that you're a player, are you?"

I leaned toward him and whispered fiercely, "No one can know I had anything to do with this, understand? No one."

He stirred his martini with a plastic sword—I wondered when he started with martinis—and then murmured in a peculiar voice, "No one can know any of us had anything to do with it. It is highly illegal, on many fronts. Celerie knows nothing. She only knows Cross has been paying more attention to you lately."

I brushed my fingers across the lightly raised line on my forehead. Donovan reached out for my other hand.

"You have not betrayed your friend," he said.

"What friend?" I looked at him incredulously.

"The journalist. The one who was killed." He stroked my palm. "It must have been very hard to go on television and defend us like you did, and even more difficult not to suspect the company. But you have *not* betrayed Jaures. His was—" Donovan searched for the right word "—an unfortunate death. Part of the risk of doing his job."

I nodded numbly, and the photograph of the bound and shot Jaures flashed through my mind.

"You stuck with us, and look what you've accomplished." Donovan smiled. "Cross won't forget this. You're as good as made. You're going to be rich, you're going to be powerful, and you're going to be right with me." He squeezed my hand, and I realized then that this was enough for most people, more than they dared expect, actually. And it left me feeling horribly cold.

I carefully edited the Jaures notes into an "acceptable" narrative, something Crispin Mulch would find jived with the crap churned out by the State Department lackeys and other officials. Therefore, instead of Philip Cross financing a dodgy meeting at a château in France with congressional staffers who were offered bribes of jobs, he sponsored a "research" weekend that included seminars to educate staffers on the business options available through the former Soviet Union. In this version, he was, in effect, trying to demonstrate responsibility with government money. Instead of deals and bribes with shady Uzbekis, it was partisan sniping to snag up a good, hard-working, God-fearing citizen. In fact, it was sad, really, that Jaures was dead, because he had evidently been working such a lost cause. Such was the curse of investigative journalism, though.

I was almost embarrassed for Jaures, to hand over the altered notes to Mulch, and I said as much to him when we met at the Ritz-Carlton for drinks. I watched Mulch sift through the file. Finally, I asked, "You won't be too hard on him, right?"

"Of course not, my dear." Mulch was fairly licking his chops. "You did a good thing, bringing this to me. I'll be very careful."

If you want to galvanize the press, you must have an ally. I needed someone who wasn't on the Mulch Committee and who still had status. Good luck, I thought to myself. I was waiting for Jack to join me at the 116 Club, a lunch club on the Senate side of the Hill that had all the ambiance and charm of a fifties-era rec room. Jack was a member; he said it was useful for meeting with congressmen and their staffers, even if there was no decent menu and the specialty was chicken and dumplings, a dish Jack had steadfastly avoided since a bad road-food experience during a southern Florida campaign.

Despite the humble surroundings, the 116 Club was a place

to be. I noticed the woman sitting at the table next to mine—but then, it was hard not to, as she was wearing a beautifully tailored gold dress that probably cost more than my yearly salary, her strawberry-blond hair falling coyly into her eyes as she earnestly addressed the thin, elegant man next to her. He looked like the president's nominee for ambassador to the Vatican. I shook my head. I was really, truly, hopelessly an insider if I could recognize *that* guy.

I seized the glass of sparkling water on my table, my mouth twisted in an amused grimace. Scanning the room, I almost missed spotting the slight shoulders of the ferret of a man who anchored the "thoughtful" evening news program on one of the networks. I was surprised to see him; he was known to prefer the golf course to schmoozing potential sources.

I knew him a little. He had chain-smoked his way through one of the most trying days in modern American history and when, a few weeks later, I had run into him on a flight between New York and Washington and had offered my compliments for his job that day, he had replied, "Yeah. I needed something like that to happen for me." He believed himself to be the savior of his network. I tapped my fingers on the water glass and realized he was just the man I was looking for.

I sidled up to him and reintroduced myself. The anchor gave me that vague look of recognition that a dog occasionally grants his owner. I complimented him on his recent book, which was a memoir of his adventures committing journalism.

"You've been so many places!" I gushed. "Japan, China, the former Soviet Union."

"That one was scary," the anchorman said, his voice swelling. "I remember talking with the president of Georgia once, and being told how he wanted the head of Ukraine assassinated 'for the good of the people,' and not two days later, I had the same conversation with the Ukrainian president about the Georgian, again 'for the good of the people'!"

"Were you ever in Uzbekistan?" I asked.

"Certainly. We've all been in and out of those places. I remember—"

"Azerbaijan?"

"Naturally." The anchorman straightened his tie. "I've had to ask the State Department for additional pages to my passport at this point."

Although they are shown sitting behind a desk, all anchors consider themselves to be hard-nosed reporters, sort of like the way some Pentagon civilians consider themselves actual soldiers. With that in mind, I suggested to the anchor that I might have an interesting tip for him, and very soon.

"It's just a little dicey," I explained. "A lot of odd motives, if you know what I mean."

"I certainly do!" the anchorman exclaimed. And then he launched into a long, tired speech about greed, the human condition, the art of the teleprompter, and taxes. The anchorman only wound down when the waitress approached with his salad. "Let's continue this conversation later," he said.

"Oh, definitely!" I was a bit disgusted with myself, but not as much as I was with him. He was the voice of reason for millions of people, when in fact he was just an old windbag.

My father was not, by nature, the trusting sort. Decades of dancing through the legal system had stained any possibility of trust, the mumbly-mouthed characters he partnered with having honed duplicity to an art. I know he liked to make money, although he suffered for it. He had wandered through our townhouse existence in Lincoln Park with the numbness of a sleepwalker; things were simply there; and then, one day, when I was sixteen, I found him sitting in the living room in a velvet armchair, a tumbler of scotch in his hand, staring at a clear bowl of Venetian glass candies. The stripes and bright colors were cheerfully decadent. Without lifting his head my way, my father said, "I work seventeen hours a day, pushing papers for bastard clients, in order to buy expensive, *fake* candy." He never said anything about this to my mother, as far as I knew, but overnight his face became long and lined in the way that people age when they've tired of their lives.

Why he prepared the necessary papers for me, I am not sure. I guessed, when I held the copies in my hands, that maybe somewhere in those folds of disappointment, my father had one gamble left in him. He knew that we needed financial documents and letters of intent to give to Cross. An illicit deal still requires the appearance of delivery.

Cross received the papers the following morning. I knew they were sitting on his desk, awaiting the scratch of his pen. Again, the wait, the endless stretch of beige, curdling with each passing quarter hour. I tried to think about my yoga lessons and breathing techniques, but as I had been a sporadic student at best, I remembered nothing. I had no Zen to fall back on, and no one to call up, because Lili could not bear to hear my anxiety pouring forth yet again. It would have only frightened her. Jack was still being tortured by Mandy, who wanted to talk wedding dates (how long could a wine angel take off from work, anyway?). My assistant cowered at her desk, nervous, without realizing why, exactly.

The deal was not a deal without those papers signed. I reviewed the process step by step: Cross and I had talked; we covered the points; he asked me for a bribe, I gave it to him. If that was not a deal in principle, then I didn't know what one was. But it wasn't nailed yet.

I thought about where I could run to—but the only place that appealed to me was my bed, with all the blankets and the duvet pulled over my head and around my body. I glanced at the clock. Cross would have had the papers for three hours. I thought about a new career: I could become a human rights advocate, or maybe a clerk in a pretty clothing boutique. Three and a half hours. I could go to Chile and pick grapes at a winery. Four hours. There was always law school. And then my assistant, her face beaming, brought in a package from a messenger: the papers, autographed with Cross's tight signature.

I didn't even have time to feel relieved; a headache was ripping across my forehead, the stress releasing itself. What was a bit of temporary pain, though? We were in business at last.

Whiz Kids—from the transitory desk of Ida Tarbell
    The unleavened lumps that call themselves the Mulch Committee have yanked their French investigator from the noble cause of figuring out who killed reporter John Jaures. Remember him, boys and girls? You could be forgiven if you don't, as the unleavened lumps would prefer it that way. So, wha' happened? Frenchie was getting the same evidence yours truly has received. Ain't no 'terrorist murder' evidence turning up, so it ain't a clean, easy ending to this case.

I called Nina Scott Lee on this. She said it was worse than she dared to put in the blog. "I found out how Cross and John had their meeting. They were in the same hotel—there's only one hotel in Baghdad that has really good security—and I was told that one night Cross sent him a bottle of very old Bordeaux. You know how hard that is to get in Baghdad? And very, very expensive."

I remembered the dinner at Comme Chez Soi. This cabal did have an interesting style.

"They were letting him know that they knew what he was up to," Nina explained. "Only the powerful, with a ton of money at their disposal, could come up with a bottle of *that* wine *there*."

Nina inhaled so deeply I thought she might suck down her phone, too. "Bleed the greed, Kate," she said. "That's the only way to deal with these guys, because that's sure as hell the game they're playing."

Four French Arabs were plucked from the slums of Paris, the housing projects that seethed with unemployment and unrest, and labeled the alleged killers of John Jaures. A lot of fanfare accompanied the arrests—flashing cameras, microphones shoved in the tough young faces.

One of the foursome swore—and produced witnesses that swore, too—that he was hundreds of kilometers from Paris at the time of Jaures's death. Another, who published a radical, anti-government newspaper, was in his makeshift office at the time investigators said Jaures was dumped into the river. The other two were frequent participants in protests against the French police.

Crispin Mulch immediately hit the talk-show circuit, endorsing the assertion of the French Sécurité, and firmly stating that justice had been served. He even promised to reveal more

in his column the following day—"I have been given information that leads me to conclude this is a sad end to a terrible
story," he entoned. Even Jaures's old network backed the
French solution. There was a dangerous lack of skepticism, but
then, it didn't serve Mulch or his colleagues to question the
"truth." It was much more important to stay in the good graces
of establishment friends who found Mulch a convenient conduit
for spreading their views

I knew what kind of a man Mulch was—and I was working
him, too. But that did not prevent me from watching his performance with a sick, heavy heart. Jack closed his eyes and
rubbed his temples with his fingers while the television in my
office continued to spew out factoids and outright lies.

"That was really nice of your dad, to do all the paperwork
for us," Jack said. His face looked gray and more tired than
usual.

"Yes." I wished I had a beer to give him, always a surefire
route to salvation.

"My dad wouldn't have done it," Jack said.

"Your dad isn't a lawyer."

"You know what I mean," Jack said. "Not that he wouldn't
have appreciated the intentions. He's more of a bottom-line
kind of guy. I hope Nina Scott Lee is ready to refute all this,"
he said.

With that, I flipped open a notebook with my list of phone
calls to work through.

22
The Great Communicator

There was no real way to know exactly when Saudi Aramco would become aware of the scheme, other than when and if the prince called Jack—my partner thought they would surely go to him first to begin breaking the deal. We had to wait to make the next crucial moves, and we had to be patient.

Patience, however, was not my specialty. So I called the man in Beirut.

"Hel*lo*, princess!" he exclaimed. "Have you tried the wine yet?"

"I'm saving it for a special occasion," I told him. "Is this a bad time?"

"No." He was emphatic, but I could hear the sound of metal smacking against metal behind him. It sounded as if he was at a fencing camp.

"How was your meeting?"

"Good, good. Now what can I do for you?"

I admired his ability to get straight to the point. "All those Gulf Arabs you know, are any of them with Saudi Aramco?"

There was a pause. "Perhaps."

"How do you feel about giving one of them a little call?"

Another pause, and the man laughed. "I would be delighted."

And I would probably owe him. This was a risk I was willing to take, though, considering we had exhausted our million-dollar kitty and needed to push this situation to the next stage.

"I love that guy," I told Jack, who was only half-jokingly looking into Brazilian visas for us. ("In case this all goes horribly wrong," as he had put it.)

"You may find him intriguing, but this cannot have a happy ending," Jack said, shaking his head. "This is going to end in a huge fiery ball of molten lava."

Our assistant stuck her head in the doorway. "Donovan's on the phone for you," she said, and Jack gave me a significant glance.

"See what I mean?" And then he went back to checking about Brazil.

The right message delivered by the right person can work wonders. That, and the threat of endangered profits. Jack got the call at three the next morning. He told me he was buried under blankets and almost didn't hear the cell phone ring. Bleating from the sands of Dubai was none other than the rogue prince himself, irate and panicked. Somehow, the officials at Saudi Aramco had heard about the deal! Did Jack realize what that meant? Did he?

The prince, Jack reported, was not in full-blown hysterics, but then again, he would not suffer too much; what could one do to a member of the Saudi royal family? But the enraged House of Saud could inflict a lot of damage in other places. The prince announced that the oil agreement with the Essex Group was effectively dead, and would Jack be so kind as to tell the sons-of-bitches they were screwed? Jack politely acquiesced. The prince added that Jack was not to contact him again, unless he happened to run across a couple of stinger missiles; in that case, the prince would be happy to entertain him again.

Jack then called me. We had only a few hours to run the system.

Mathilde was having breakfast in Canegrate. My neck ached and my tongue felt thick. (I am not a morning person; I am really not equipped to function before the break of day.) I ticked through the necessary elements and asked her to help.

I let the words hang, suspended in dreadful silence. Finally, Mathilde said, "I believe in civilization, and I am willing to fight for the concept of what it means to be human. Do not think, then, that this is because I wholeheartedly believe you or in your passing judgment on others. I am not a backer of individual justice. Do you understand this?"

"Yes," I said.

"I will call a few friends here. They are in media. They are always happy to get a story about American greed," she said.

The television network anchorman, despite being roused at an ungodly hour, was delighted to hear from me, especially when I told him that I had recently been working for the Essex Group. Just uttering the name made him audibly perk with interest, and when I added that I had, unfortunately, become privy to a terrible turn of events, he nearly began to pant.

"There's this big deal that they did on the side," I told him. "An oil deal. It's all gone wrong, and I've got to bail them out now, and, I have to tell you, it might be beyond me."

"Well, what happened?" He was straining despite his attempt to sound relaxed. I took a deep breath and began to spin the tale of Philip Cross, a man betrayed by his own avarice, and how the Mulch Committee had been complicit in papering over the death of John Jaures. The anchor did not care why I was telling him this story—he reacted to a twenty-four-hour news cycle. All that mattered, I knew, was the story. The Washington media have always had a fierce rivalry with the New York media, and the television anchor had just been given a way to prove his superiority. He could hardly get off the phone fast enough.

Nina posted immediately on the Ida Tarbell blog: "Here's a slab of meat: that a major, secret oil deal cut by the overreaching Essex Group had just been canceled—what else is Aramco going to do to the company?" Her blog was linked to a half-dozen others, and as bloggers do not sleep, online discussion threads fired up and quips and investigations were launched.

Jack touched base with the public relations man in Paris, the one who had introduced him to the rogue prince to begin with. He patched me in for a three-way call because, as Jack said, this was going to be quite amusing.

The public relations man was quite happy to hear from his "buddy."

"Jack! You should be here tonight! These Russians, they said, 'Jean-Claude, you are the best at what you do—give us a party, a beautiful party, as much money as you want.' So tonight, the best champagne, the best caviar, the best women."

"I'm sorry to miss it," Jack said.

"Eh, they are whores," the p.r. man replied nonchalantly. "They come to Paris, waving around bags of euros; they drink Cristal because they have no imagination and no taste. And then they return to their countries, to their oil, their gangs, their crimes. Me, I do not care. They act like pigs, but many people act like pigs. I am a pig! Yes! And you—you are a pig! Yes! Because what do we do? We make people such as them palatable—we shine them up, we give them a phrase, and we present them to the world. *I* do not care."

I wondered if Jack took exception to being called a pig. "Speaking of making people palatable," my partner said, and he related the sudden turn of events. There was an immediate reaction across the Atlantic. Howling like a banshee, the p.r. man screamed, *"No!"*

"Yes!" Jack cried back.

"What is my name on?" he demanded.

"Your part of the deal was not specifically spelled out," Jack assured him, and his breathing instantly became less ragged.

"Your Essex must be abandoned!" he exclaimed. "You must give them up!"

Gallant cowardice. Admirable.

"But I can't," Jack said. "They're my client."

"They will be half a client after the Saudis are through with them," he spat. "I have a friend with Agence France-Presse," he said. "I will tell him now. Maybe he will write a story to help you. Maybe he won't. He is a pig. He feasts on the remains of American capitalism."

"It's worth a try," Jack said, and as I listened in on the conversation, I knew that if we had been in the same room, we would have been stuffing our fists into our mouths to stop from laughing.

I drove through the city, on my way to the office, my brown leather satchel tossed in to the trunk and my hair pulled back in a ponytail. The one big hit by Charles Péguy's band poured out of the radio as I crossed the river, away from the crowded recruiting offices and the yellow stone of the Pentagon, whipping past the brick rows of Georgetown where those wealthier than I ever would be—including Philip Cross—happened to reside, and approached the concrete and marble canyon of office buildings where my kind plied their trade. I checked my watch to estimate how long it would take for the story to spread out of the hot zone and into the general population, because there is nothing more contagious than a potential scandal.

My assistant barely looked up as I walked in, abrupt comings and goings being the usual around here. She was waiting with a stack of pink message slips and a hard copy of a story moving across the wire: U.S. FIRM IN HOT WATER OVER ILLEGAL OIL DEAL. There it was. The press should be staking out the Essex offices by midafternoon, I thought. I would be expected to be part of the crisis management team. I would have to speak to Cross. I wasn't nervous. I was unnaturally calm.

My e-mail was overflowing: Crispin Mulch, asking what the hell was going on; a dozen messages from Celerie, written in varying degrees of hysteria; and Donovan. He sent only one, and it was the briefest of all: It consisted of only a question mark. I felt a slight pang, but that was all I could allow myself. I was all head, not heart. Take care of business now, Donovan later. I went immediately to Ida Tarbell's blog, which was now running with the real Jaures notes:

Was John Jaures about to ruin uber-businessman Philip Cross? The sycophantic grovellers at the Mulch Committee would indicate Jaures was a "sad" hack. But everyone has a different take on the notes. Here they are, boys and girls: I post, you decide.

"Philip Cross's office is on the phone," my assistant called out, and I pushed back from my desk. I had been summoned at last.

I did not see Donovan or Celerie as I rushed through the Essex offices, the embodiment of the media strategist. I had my folders organized, every hair in place, my lips faintly tinted pink and my skirt falling at the knee, the "serious" length. The press gathered outside had crowded around me: Kate Boothe was arriving, and that meant business.

Cross, as I saw at once, was hardly the picture of the defeated man. He sat behind his shiny, tidy desk, pressing his fingertips together as I entered the room, his jaw set firm and his eyes glowering. My step nearly faltered at first, but flinching would not do *now*. It was too late for that.

"So," Cross began in a tone pruned of emotion, "Saudi Aramco is not very happy."

"They're not," I agreed. Cross made no motion for me to sit; I remained on my feet. All the better to make a mad dash out of the room, I thought. But it was a pointed trick: stand, because you are being granted an audience, not a meeting.

"We have other agreements with the Saudis. *Official* agreements. These are now in jeopardy." Cross did not even blink.

"Yes," I said, because I had to insert something into the silence.

Men who regard themselves as inviolate give off an air to suggest that they view the world as ghosts might, from an all-knowing, impenetrable position utterly detached from life. There was no fear, concern, anger, or hatred passing over Cross's countenance. He was waxy; he was untouchable. I shifted my weight from foot to foot and wondered if he was even quite real. My heart began to pat a bit faster. *Jaures, Jaures, Jaures*, I chanted in my head, steeling myself.

"What I am eager to learn, Kate, is what you plan to do about it," Cross said.

"Me?" My eyes widened, because for a horrible, bottomless moment, I wondered how much Cross actually knew.

"You are the one who brought this deal to me. You are also the expert in crisis management. This, I would say, is a crisis, and one of your making."

He said this without irony, and he gestured for me to sit, which I did. Evidently my blushes and fidgets were interpreted as a young sparrow's attempt to show contrition. In the strange political code, being asked to take a chair meant that I was now in for a consoling lecture.

"Kate, I told you a couple of months ago that you could go further than you ever dreamed," Cross began. "You never told me what you thought of that."

"I think that is quite an offer," I said, and meant it.

"But it's not quite enough, is it?" Cross had gone cold. "You felt the need to go out on your own. Now, Kate, what kind of man do you take me for?"

"I think you are the smartest and most powerful man that no one reads about or sees on TV."

Cross smiled. "I'd like to keep it that way."

"I understand." If I was truly his lackey, this would mean that I was about to throw myself on the proverbial sword, the serf sacrificing himself for his liege. And suddenly, as I sat across from him, I wondered if this had been his plan all the while: to maneuver me into a submissive position.

"I have forced the French to get a trial going," Cross continued with significance. "Do you know what true power is? I outmaneuvered them all. I beat them. I gave them someone they could hang it on. They'll have their man who killed John Jaures." His eyes flashed, but his face remained implacable.

I stared—I couldn't help myself—and the back of my head prickled. Who the hell thought this way? Cross was not confessing, exactly, but it was enough. And he believed what he did was fine. All that talk about a higher purpose and God, it was a sacred seal of approval on some of his worst fantasies about other people and himself. Every bit of control that I have learned over ten years of running marathons and a few months of yoga were summoned in that moment. Otherwise, I would have leaped across Cross's desk and strangled him.

He was through with me now, though. He dismissed me from his presence by saying, "Let me see what you can do now."

I felt numb as I stumbled out of his office. I wasn't at a loss for words, but one did not argue with the living dead. Once, I attended a christening of my cousin Gatty's son. Gatty had married a Catholic, and as part of the ceremony the priest asked us, "Do you reject Satan and his empty promises?" A leading question if I had ever heard one. If you knew it was the devil, would you take his word for anything?

23

Christ Stopped at the Mason-Dixon Line

I didn't speak to Donovan at all that week. I didn't have time. The international wire services, worked hard by the Parisian public relations man, began tapping out the story first, confirming details of an oil deal developed for the Essex Group by none other than the well-connected Philip Cross, who, it was assumed, still had many ties to the American president, whose family had invested in the Essex Group.

This was slapped onto the Internet. Those squeaking voices of democracy known as bloggers began posting their opinions almost immediately, and they were *most* upset about *Yellow Belly*. The lack of support for the listees by more powerful members of the media, the connection with the Essex Group, the perceived coziness among the elites rolled and rolled until a very astonished Crispin Mulch found himself the target of a blogging investigation. HOW MULCH BETRAYED JOURNALISM was one headline.

Jack and I had our own concerns to deal with. The Saudis aren't exactly the golden boys of public perception, what with the choking bubbles of hatred and death coughed up from the same pumps and drills that give us dear things like gasoline and plastics. Slamming the Essex Group for cheating the Saudis out of money ran the risk of creating folk heroes out of Cross and company. The trick was to portray the Essex Group as a bunch of greedy bastards in bed with other greedy bastards—and where was the loyalty in *that*?

I thought about mentioning this to Nina, but I needed someone more mainstream than her. The sun squeezed through the slats on my windows; it wouldn't be long before it went down. Who had the self-possession to declare right and wrong, to judge the mood of the nation and to cultivate and change it? One man, whom I had intentionally avoided for years.

There was a time when the bilious radio host and I worked together, when we served each other's purposes nicely. Then came the sea change of the Gold affair. I squared my shoulders and thought, no sense in bearing a grudge too long. I didn't have to *like* him to work him, after all.

I decided that the best approach was not through a phone call but the less on-the-spot medium of e-mail. I also wanted a written record. A certain swath of movers and shakers had to know that Vanzetti/Boothe did not condone the practices of Philip Cross and his colleagues, and that we were not idly standing by. The third way: our way.

You have stated so elegantly the need for loyalty in these trying times, how we are regarded by our level of self-sacrifice. This has resonated with me. I have been thinking nonstop about it. For the last few months, Vanzetti/Boothe has worked with a company called the Essex Group, a company that, it has come to our attention, has happily and profitably consorted with avowed enemies of our state, shady figures in oil and arms. I am shocked that money trumps patriotism, but I am told by others that this is "the way things have always been." I know you don't believe that; I know that I refuse to believe that. We may not be able to "change things," but we don't have to leave situations worse than when we found them.

The radio host called me immediately. "Are you on the record with this?" he asked me.

"Use it as much as you want," I said. "But don't put my name publicly anywhere near it."

As the sky turned velvet black, the anchorman, who had dyed his ferret-colored hair a deeper brown, looked significantly into the camera and promised viewers that "there is much more to come." He was devoting his entire hour-long show that night to the Essex scandal.

"It's cracking," Jack said, watching this in our reception area with his arms crossed. "It's time to fax in our resignation."

"Cross will fight back," I murmured.

"I don't think he'll get a chance to," Jack replied.

The strange onslaught continued. The following morning, I awoke to the morning television shows blasting the news between cooking and lifestyle segments: COMPANY PROFITS FROM DEATH; HOW ESSEX GROUP MAKES MONEY FROM WAR ON TERROR. By the time I reached the office, I had received sixty phone calls from various news outlets, asking for comment from Essex and, specifically, Cross.

"I'll call you back," I said for the sixtieth time, as Jack informed me that we had just gotten a call from the *New York Times*."

"The Saudis are canceling all contracts with Essex holdings," he said. "That's a few billion to you and me. They won't even take a payoff. They're that pissed about it."

"What does that mean?" I asked.

"That—" and before Jack continued, he looked over at Mandy, who was lingering kittenishly nearby. "I, uh, need to speak with Kate alone." He glanced at his shoes, then back at the face of his beloved. Mandy was no pushover. She squared her shoulders, pursed her mouth, and shrugged.

"I get it," she said, and left.

I gave Jack a moment to compose himself.

"The sharks begin circling," Jack said to me. "The Saudis have other arrangements with Essex. There's an order for F–15s through one of their defense companies, there are some tanks and helicopters. All of that, gone."

He held up our resignation letter. I smiled grimly and signed it.

"I think I should keep my Ferrari, though," he said.

The radio host read my e-mail verbatim on the air. He omitted my name and the Essex Group specifically, but to his audience of millions, he opined, "You don't need to know the names, just the sentiment. *This* is the essence of the nation, ladies and gentlemen!"

Economic stories, even those with a distinct villain, are never as catchy to the mainstream media as, say, a sex scandal. I knew ours would, at best, be good for a steady growl. I did not expect the general public to stomp its feet and scowl about it. I was banking on outrage among Cross's peers. Far, far worse for Cross to be judged poorly by the lesser princes and princesses he consorted with than by the populace.

There was nothing much for me to do but to sit at my desk and watch the blocks stack up in news bulletins. All Gulf contracts with Essex and its major holdings had been canceled; a significant amount of money that Saudis had invested with Essex had been withdrawn (although who was to say if it would remain that way; there are always loopholes after a decent waiting interval); defense contracts with Essex companies had been broken. I am not sure how much this cost the Essex Group. I am not sure I can even count that high.

It was a long, bad stretch for them, all right. And by the time the carnage stopped, the company had taken a significant hit, enough to warrant an emergency meeting (according to Nina Scott Lee, who had a contact serving as outside monitor). The wound was salved rather quickly: Philip Cross issued a statement of resignation. Cross, for now, was out.

But that did not mean he was finished. I saw the video of the man leaving the offices, his expensive briefcase in one hand and a hat in the other. He looked straight into the television cameras that clustered around him and the photographers who snapped and flashed with the frenzy of a level-five hurricane, and he *smiled*.

24
Fair Is Far

I decided I owed it to my parents to tell them everything, and in person. This was something new for me—usually I operated on a need-to-know basis with them. But considering how my father had trusted me blindly, and also because I wanted my mother to still believe her daughter had broken through the old boys' network, I showed up unexpectedly at their house in the Chicago suburbs.

This was not the home I had grown up in. It was the place they felt they should live in at their age: one level, with a vast lawn and a sprinkling of flowerbeds—a dull place that I still hoped they would outgrow. They had given up the townhouse in Lincoln Park for this? I shuddered when I stepped out of the taxi.

Truth be told, they were a bit puzzled to see me. My mother looked slightly put out as I closed the front door behind me and asked them to sit down. They exchanged an indecipherable glance, and then both of them sighed simultaneously. Although I had never been arrested, hadn't used (many) drugs, and paid my taxes on time, they were assuming the look of long-suffering parents before I said even one word.

But as I plunged in, spilling out what I knew about the murder of Jaures, the plundering deals and Faustian bargains made by Cross, and the oil scam, my father's chin dropped lower and lower, and my mother blinked repeatedly.

"I don't know quite what to say." She turned to my father. "And Joffre? Is his part . . . all right?"

"He's got the pipeline deal, and he's extremely happy," my father told her.

My mother tucked her graying bob behind her ears and digested this. "Does this mean you're a corporate consultant now?" she asked me.

"I suppose this means she's doing a little of both," my father tried to be helpful. "Some politics, some corporate."

"Actually, I'm not sure how much of a difference there is," I told them.

Last year, I met a diplomat from India, and I asked him what the most pressing problem in his country was. I expected him to say it was poverty or disease or even the threat of nuclear war with Pakistan. Instead, he replied, "God-men. We have too many men running around who say that they are gods." That was our problem, too, here in the U.S., although it took a bit more effort to see it.

The god-men of Washington were not just the Crosses but the Mulches, too. I held Mulch and his esteemed committee as responsible for the death of John Jaures as I did Philip Cross. Mulch and company never wanted to know who killed Jaures. His death was incidental in the larger pursuit of geopolitics, fortune, and fame.

So it wasn't surprising, then, that the Jaures story, as it was, vanished within a few days. The public—the people beyond our stifled circle—didn't give a flying fig. Maybe Mulch had taken a hit to his credibility, but he was still a syndicated columnist with awards to his name, and that could not be wiped out because of one lousy committee. He was still regarded with fondness at the press club, and he would undoubtedly do skits at the Gridiron, play a round of golf with the White House chief of staff, and perhaps offer up a "Lunch with Crispin" to the highest bidder at his son's private school's annual auction.

When he did call me in late May, his voice had a jolly ring. "No hard feelings, my dear, although you didn't quite play fair," he said.

I thought about what I would say in reply: "Would 'fair' describe the hack you hired to do a sham investigation?" or, even "Were the bribes you allowed the Essex Group to give you fair?" (Nina Scott Lee had yet to post that little tidbit on her blog.) But I thought better of an easy shot. Mulch knew who he was and what he had done. He also knew the part I had played—his interpretation of the Jaures papers had been roundly ridiculed by the alternative media, which meant his hipster quotient had plummeted, and he wasn't likely to take me lightly again.

"Well, Crispin, maybe I can buy you a drink sometime to make up for it," I said. Mulch chuckled and agreed. Neither of us were kidding ourselves; we'd never have that drink together.

I had been naive, of course—and in hindsight I know Jaures certainly had been, too. My friend had stepped into an arena where the government, and the men behind the government, are spending maybe ten billion, and earning back several times that sum. And if some guy wanders in and starts filing stories that are contrary to their interests, they're not going to change their policy for a two-thousand-dollar-a-week employee.

But that did not mean that the men responsible could not be made to suffer. They live in an exalted world, where they believe they are untouchable by media or the populace. And there lies their fallibility. Loyalty to them most certainly is *not* the same as loyalty to country—and what a shock it is to them when they realize that.

And then, there is a different sort of loyalty. Donovan was waiting in the parking lot of my apartment building when I returned from visiting my parents in Chicago. His lanky frame leaned against his beloved vintage car. The edges of his eyes were cold and crinkled with fatigue.

"I thought you might have called by now," he said. I looked at my feet. I had been avoiding him, because what in the world was I going to tell him? That I willingly sacrificed him to the memory of another?

"I'm sorry," I said softly. This was quite true. But Donovan coughed incredulously.

"You're a mature young woman. Why'd you have to lie to me, of all people?"

"Would you have understood?" I asked. "Would you have done it if I had told you the truth?"

"Would I have fucked over my loyal employer of more than a decade because I thought you were pretty? Or do you mean, would I have fucked over my boss because you were seeking revenge for some crime you perceived as having been committed?"

"Perceived?" I repeated. "My God, Donovan, your boss had *everything* to do with Jaures's murder. Just because Essex has paid off every big-time journalist between Washington and Kiev to avoid a mainstream exposé doesn't mean you're not the bad guys."

"Do you think I am a bad guy?" Donovan demanded.

"Not you specifically." I stared at my feet again.

Donovan leaned against the car door and looked away from me. "I believe in having faith in people. You lied to me. You used me. I do not have faith in you, not anymore."

I cleared my throat. "Did you get fired?"

He shook his head. "My division has been destroyed. They've simply moved me to another." He paused, and then, in a hollow voice, he asked, "Why'd you do it, Kate?"

"It was the right thing—"

He cut me off. "There are no 'right things' in this world. We can only do our best."

"That's what I did," I said.

"You didn't do it *kindly*." Donovan, stiff and unforgiving, opened the car door and, without glancing back, drove away.

I realized that, in the pursuit of a new way to do business, I had hurt people without wanting to, or even trying. I rattled through the justifications for doing so the rest of the day. I was upset enough to allow Jack to drag me to yoga. And it was when, with the rest of the class, we lay spread out in deep relaxation, while the instructor intoned a spiritual reading about why we lie, and how our soul is affected when we do, that I grasped that I had done to Donovan what Cross had done to Jaures, just with a less final and brutal outcome. As I squeezed my eyes shut and hoped for forgiveness—if not now, later, in the lengthy ways of Washingtonian absolution—Jack reached across his mat for my hand. He always knew.

My father maintains that a regretful life is a good sign, because it means you took chances, you truly lived. On the other hand, my father also has spoken of missed moments, like how he wished he had not been so frightened by a tempest off the Mexican coast and could have finished sailing around the world, or how much happier he might have been had he turned down an unsavory client or two, the ones he simply could not refuse because he had "responsibilities" to his family.

We talked often now, my father and I. He said the oddest thing to me one night: "Sometimes, I think you are living the life that was meant for me." I did not know how to respond; I did not know even what to think, because among his host of regrets not one had been anything I had actually done. I never sailed around the world, and I didn't exactly turn down Essex.

My father then added, "You did a fine job."

I was forgiven by some, for now.

I expected that Cross would be, too, someday soon. The people he associated with would protect their own. They believe that in the entire world they alone are preserving mankind from extinction. They feel they are benefiting the world, even if they are committing random killings or doing dirty deals. Cross would survive, in some shape. For now, he seemed to have slipped into the hedges of suburban Washington, probably counting his money and his contacts, licking his wounds.

In the weeks after the oil deal blew, I did not hear anything from Cross, nor, in fact, from the Essex Group itself. Jack received a single piece of correspondence, an oppressively polite note from Harcourt, the CEO, conveying the sentiment that he "regretted" losing us. It couldn't have hurt too much. The Essex Group was cleaning up on contracts for homeland defense money for its high-tech clients.

There would be a treatise on Jaures, of course. Nina Scott

Lee was writing it, and not as "Ida Tarbell." This time, she had sold it to Jaures's old stomping ground, *USA Today*. The editors there expressed a profound wish to receive the piece in a timely fashion, but Nina curtly informed them (and me) that it was not quite ready yet. "This is going to be the most important thing I've ever written," she said. "I think I can take as long as I want."

Nina added, almost offhandedly, "Oh, hey, I should tell you—you know when your friend Joe Morgan comes back to Washington?"

"Is he coming back?" I asked.

"Yeah. Not sure when. But thought I'd let you know, I'll probably be with him." She said this gruffly, so there was no pressing her for details. In a way, it figured. Who else was more appropriate for Nina other than a much older intelligence operative with a few dozen kills to his name, three ex-wives, four children, and a couple of restraining orders? Joe Morgan and I went back a ways, and I had to concede, who else was more appropriate for *him*?

Jack couldn't stop laughing about it all. But then, he was rather insufferable in the immediate aftermath, bragging to his pals at the Cosmos Club about his Ferrari, which he tooled around town in for two days. He had also developed a taste for caviar, which he previously found too salty, but after having addled his palate with Iranian caviar during his travels with the prince, he announced he was a changed man.

He must have been changed, the way he broke off with Mandy. The usual method Jack employed for ridding himself of women was to toss out an all-purpose "I'm not the man for you" and follow with a bouquet of daisies. Jack dispatched Mandy back to Vegas, but he did it with style. He actually gave her the Ferrari. I saw her screeching down K Street in it, a bright red flame headed for the Interstate.

"What else was I going to do with it?" he shrugged when I found him in his office. "I couldn't keep it. I didn't want to sell it." He shrugged again. "Seems like a fair trade: She doesn't get me, but she gets a hell of a car." And a Ferrari would look better in Vegas than in Washington, that was for sure.

Some time later during one of the lightning storms that break across the mid-Atlantic states in late spring, knocking out power lines and generally scaring the bejeezus out of small children, it happened. Jack tracked me down one morning as I was struggling with my umbrella on my way out of my apartment building. "Have you seen the paper?" he asked. "Get ready for this." Nina's story, finally. I read it in the office, and Jack came around my desk to look over my shoulder at words he had already tried to process once.

THE DEATH OF JAURES:
How an Albanian Assassin Brought Down the Best Reporter of His Generation

By Nina Scott Lee
Special to USA Today

Mhill Durda did not know the man he was about to kill. He did not care. He was 20 years old, a neglected remnant of Albania's communist rule, shunted from orphanages to prisons. His allegiance was to his gang, the men who paid him, and they said he must kill John Jaures.

Less than six months later, Durda would be dead himself.

My mouth went dry when I read the story. Nina had found the killer, and he was no longer alive to tell her who had paid for the bullet. How handy. Even the investigator hired by the Mulch Committee told Nina, on the record, that the car wrapped around a lamppost on a well-maintained street in the south of France seemed an unlikely turn of events, especially as Durda had no trace of alcohol or drugs in his body.

> Durda inhabited a world where anything can be bought, and the higher the price, the fewer questions are asked. In a way, it is a job, like any other. Who ever sees the man who signs his paycheck?

I am not sure how one is expected to react to such a story. With incredulity? I was not a conspiracy theorist, but now I firmly believed in the existence of those who had no inner dialogue with themselves about basic decency, or who were able, at least, to excuse a lot of bad behavior. It was a filthy way for Jaures to go, at the hands of a hard, hired man. Nina had not been entirely successful in tracing all the checks—although circumstantial evidence might lead one in the particular direction of a certain former Essex Group partner. But, as Jack reminded me, Jaures might get his revenge after all: Nina's article was optioned by a famous movie producer, and there was nothing like central casting taking a whack at a story to dramatically improve the odds of comeuppance in the court of public opinion.

I sent copies of Nina's article to everyone who had been part of our "resistance." Mathilde appreciated it. I don't know for sure if Roberto read it, though. I never followed up with a phone call. I remembered my manners, however, and sent him a brief note of thanks, a gesture that Jack regarded as lame. But what was I supposed to do? Call him up and invite him to dinner the next time he swung into Washington with his wife? Roberto and I were even now. It was best just to leave it.

And then, there was the man in Beirut. He rang me up out of the blue and boomed, "Hello, princess!" His voice was loud enough for Jack to hear, walking next to me across Capitol Hill. "Intriguing little article. Assuming you are on to new business? Now: I've almost finished the tequila. When are you coming back to Beirut? We have a conversation to continue."

After we hung up, Jack pushed his sunglasses back over his head and looked me in the eye, "For God's sake, Kate, *stop* with all the guys with the accents."

It had been a while since any effort by Jack and me reaped a reward. Although we might not be dabbling in the energy field again for a very long time, our names had been circulated by none other than Joe Joffre as owners of a fine firm for corporate consulting needs. "Do you have any interest in opening a New York office?" Jack asked. I did not, especially when there were abundant flights and trains between the two cities. But Jack felt that as we were fielding several inquiries a day from New York companies about our services, it warranted a quick trip north to take a few meetings. Besides, he reminded me, we would certainly eat well. Lili was back in town, and would meet up with us in New York.

Having had her fill of the magic land of Paris, Lili planned to search for a job in Washington or in New York City. Her work at the Bristol had paid just fine, but she'd had enough of tourists. On one occasion, she had quite accurately translated *ris de veau* as "sweetbreads," but this had been loudly and disastrously declared misleading by a white-haired WWII veteran, who had his brood of grandchildren in tow to see the Normandy beaches, and who was mighty surprised when chewy thymus glands, not muffins, arrived at his table.

Being a Chicago girl, I appreciate the Manhattan crunch and grunt, but I don't particularly like it. The faces of the women are very hard, perhaps the result of too many chemical peels or too much stress. And the men are loud and wear pinky rings. The corporate men we met with were barreling bullies, but they did seem like they might pay their bills fully and on time, a clientele we certainly needed to develop.

And they had an interesting flair for meeting locations. Our first night in New York, we had drinks with one multinational maven, who brought along a pal. I immediately recognized the man, who had tufts of wiry white hair growing out of his ears. He was often on the Sunday-morning talk shows because he was an advisor to the president on matters relating to the Persian Gulf. These two men, who between them were wealthier than many small nations and one of whom decided foreign policy for ours, suggested moving the meeting to a new location. A strip club. And so it was in one of New York's finest that I found myself discussing matters of national security. I decided that my only escape would be through drink, which led, the following morning, to my first migraine headache—penance, probably, for Donovan.

Jack Vanzetti, nursemaid, even put a cool cloth on my head. He left my side only to answer his cell phone in the other room. I thought I might be delirious, because I could have sworn I heard the words "Nina" and "married." And after I heard a shout and a *"no way!"*, Jack returned and said, "You really are not going to believe this."

It was true. Joe Morgan and Nina Scott Lee had done a most extraordinary thing. They met each other in Ramallah— I didn't ask for the details—and, four days later, ran into each other again in Cairo, and of all the nutty twists and turns, they got married.

"*I* didn't even get married, and I was actually engaged!" Jack exclaimed.

Two determined people, having arrived at a decision, are not easily dissuaded or even very patient. The official routes, embassy to church to consulate, required daunting paperwork and a wait of days, if not weeks. But it was suggested by their taxi driver that they try a mosque. He assured them that this was the quickest and easiest way to get married in Cairo. Off they went to a willing imam, who uttered words of conversion (Morgan, at least, understood them) and then announced, "You are now Ali, and you are now Fatima," and so they were married. Ali and Fatima, the spy and the journalist.

"Now *that*," Jack said, "is cover."

Even with my headache, I had to laugh.

The following night, I met up with Lili at the sleek New York wine bar she loved. Jack was handling a final meeting himself, and Lili greeted me as if she hadn't just seen me a few weeks before. I could allow us a small celebration, I supposed.

The place was crowded and glamorous in a slick-magazine kind of way, and most of the glittering patrons were eagerly poring over the extensive wine list (which the restaurant actually sold as a souvenir for a cool sixty-five dollars). The bartender immediately recognized Lili and, as we squeezed into two seats in the corner, near an array of Calvados bottles, she handed us two glasses of champagne.

"Haven't seen you in a while," the bartender said to Lili.

"I've been in Paris," Lili told her, but the bartender had to rush to the other end of the counter.

"Sorry—we have a high roller here," she hurriedly whispered.

We looked down the bar at the steady line of variously filled wineglasses, a newly opened bottle between them, but there was no one to be seen who looked like he fit the bill. Well, high rollers probably saw value in remaining incognito.

"I think we're drinking an '88 Premier Cru," Lili said under her breath.

"Oh, now, what do we need with a six-hundred-dollar bottle of wine?" I asked. "In bubbles, there are no troubles!"

Still, luckily for us, the bartender was working on our side. She came back to us with a tasting of the red.

"From him," she said, jerking her head toward the end of the bar, where there was nothing except empty space. The invisible man.

The wine was all right. I found it watery. Lili ordered another round of champagne and a cheese plate. And then, our mysterious benefactor sent over another tasting of another red, this one a Bordeaux. And then another Bordeaux. And then another. He must have been spending thousands and thousands. I shook my head. Well, why not—live for today.

Then the bartender returned, bearing a new glass with reverence. "This," she said softly, "is an 1870 Latour."

Both Lili and I stared at it. Jack walked into the restaurant just in time. He sauntered over with the air of a man who has enjoyed a good business day, and when he checked the wine, I warned, "*This* one will not be doused with mineral water."

I tasted it, and I thought of a time, just before Jaures left for his overseas assignment, when he, Jack, and I had gone hiking near Harper's Ferry. There had been a light rain, and the smell of damp wood quietly washed over us. That was what this wine reminded me of, and when I glanced over at Jack, I knew he was thinking the same thing.

I felt obligated to express my thanks personally to our benefactor. Some aficionados can get crochety about this—they prefer to send along their little drippings of heaven as anonymous donors, and the bartender only shook her head when I asked about him. Lili agreed. "It's a random act of kindness," she said, cradling her glass. "Let's just appreciate it."

With such extraordinary wine, it seemed fitting to toast to John Jaures, who surely would have delighted in us "getting those bastards," as he put it back in Paris and over a different drink, and to Joe Morgan, the newlywed, with his busted knee and jaded liver, who was no doubt plundering a bottle of something tough and awful that very moment with wonderful Nina, who deserved a raised glass of her own. On and on we went, and we weren't particularly quiet about it. We shared the last few drops of that excellent wine, and just as we were about to finish it off, I caught a man's visage in the corner of my eye. Standing at the door, his coat already thrown around his shoulders was Philip Cross.

He nodded at me and said, "Glad you liked the wine, Kate."

We got the bastards, and then the bastards bought us wine. I knew what that meant. Jack placed a hand protectively on my shoulder, and Lili froze, her glass in midair. But I smiled right back at Cross. I had wondered what I might do if Cross ever found my fingerprints on his throat.

But men like Cross feed upon fear. If he could not detect any fear, he had nothing to wield over me. I leaned against the bar with my elbow, and I cocked my lips in a half grin. "Well, Mr. Cross," I said, "it's not as if I expect to live forever."

Without another word, Cross turned his back and slipped out into the buzzing street.

Acknowledgments

Many thanks to:

Trena Keating, Emily Haynes, and Sarah Burnes for their hard work.

Jef Pollock and the gang at Global Strategy Group for letting me research their research and giving me a place to do it.

Jim Duffy, Pete Kant, Pete Rose, Patricia Sabga, Ahmed Husseini, Andrew Komis, and Kirk Harrington for feeding my inspiration.

James Danos, Massimo Crippa, Chris Matthews (the one in Rome), Marcella Valentini, Massimiliano Quintana, Bernard Ros, Dave Pasternak, Francis Boulard, and the mean bartender at Taverne Henry IV for feeding *me* in the name of research and inspiration.

Nick and Barbara Taylor, Lynn Pleshette, Michael Cendejas, Michael Costigan, Wendy McCallum, Barbara Messick, Maxine Albert, Clarence Page, Suzanne Quinlan, and Audrey Kurlin-Marcy—one fine collection of smarty-pants people—for their support.

My parents and sister Sonya, for their patience.

About the Author

Michele Mitchell is the author of *The Latest Bombshell* and correspondent for *NOW* on PBS. She was the political anchor on *CNN Headline News* and began her career on Capitol Hill. She lives in Brooklyn.

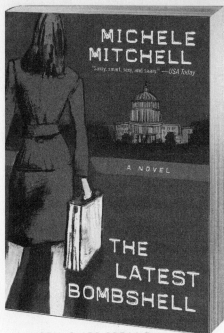